BLEEDING HEART

JODY KAYE

Special Edition Paperback
First Print: January 2024
www.JodyKaye.com

Falling in love doesn't make

a difference when I already know

forever isn't guaranteed.

For Kate

Chapter One

Paisley

"Paisley, will you have Gavin as your lawfully wedded husband, to live together in the covenant of matrimony? Will you love him, comfort him, honor and keep him, in sickness and in health, and forsaking all others, keep you only unto him, for the rest of your life?"

The end of the minister's sentence fades, overcome by the loud whooshing in my ears. Sweat that has already dampened the satin at my armpits and down the back of my gown, making the soft fabric itchy and uncomfortable, now trickles between my breasts. My breaths come in short pants. My heart, searching for escape, is threatening to beat outside of my chest. Not literally, though once a man like Gavin held it cradled in their hands as gently as my husband-to-be is holding my hands.

My tongue darts to wet my parched lip. The underside gets caught on the smudge-proof lipstick the makeup artist applied. We've spared no expense for this wedding. I'd seen candelabras. Gavin suggested the ceremony be at night. And the chapel is lit by candlelight! We are what everyone deems perfect for one another.

Gavin loves me. I love him. How could I not? He's a good man.

But do I not honor Gavin and devalue our relationship by continuing with this wedding? Or do I love him enough to be the "anyone who knows a reason" why we shouldn't marry one another?

keep you only unto him

for the rest of your life

I'd abide by those words if somewhere deep in my gut my shriveling soul was interpreting them the same way that Gavin is.

That's what I have.

A black soul for playing along with a lie until it was too late and embarrassing Gavin in public.

We're in a church, for Christ's sake!

Oh, crap. If I weren't spinning the wheel trying to decide which path to hell the arrow will point me in, then taking Lord's name in vain has added a short, direct route.

Lightheaded, I wrap my left hand over my stomach and bend at the waist. Gavin's thumb presses into the top of my left hand. His fingers pinch into my palm.

"Paisley, are you okay?" His voice filled with concern, Gavin shifts his stance so that he's shielding me from the pews occupied by our family and Gavin's friends and colleagues from the hospital.

"Just, *ah*, give me a sec." The sheer fabric of my veil flops over my shoulder, covering my watery eyes. I try some deep breathing exercises. My chest aches. My fingertips are cold and tingling. Perspiration drenches my scalp.

My mother's compliment from before she escorted me down the aisle rushes at me like a tidal wave. *You're going to have the most beautiful marriage, Paisley. I'm so happy you found a man that loves you unconditionally and that you have a bright beginning, similar to what your father and I had.*

I wanted to tell my mom that Gavin's love comes with strings attached. That he couldn't keep me only unto him, no matter how short our life together winds up being. Gavin needs more.

I can't live trapped in the cage of domestic bliss. I don't want him to kiss me goodbye in the morning and drive away in his BMW, pretending I'm the woman he still wants.

Both of us can't lie.

I can't marry Gavin.

And now that I've made up my mind, I'm in a huge pickle, aren't I?

"Oh, gosh!" I whip my head back, standing ramrod straight. I brush away the layers of tulle resting on my head to get them out of my face. When that doesn't work, I grip the tiny pearl and silver tiara from Sterlings that the veil is attached to and rip it entirely out of my hair. Giving Gavin a wide-eyed and wily smile, I'm positive he's ready to have me committed to the psychiatric wing.

"Sweetheart?" Gavin's gaze is wrought with concern.

"You are going to make an amazing husband." I pat underneath the knot in his silk cravat. "But you shouldn't waste the happiness the world has to offer you on me."

I turn toward the chancel and bolt. My skirt swishes past the altar and I duck out the door in front of the minister's vestry. The corridor leads to the stairs, to the lower floor where I waited to march down the aisle, and outside to the parking lot.

"Paisley!" Gavin yells.

I doubt he'll stay put. I mean, would any groom if they were questioning why their bride left them at the altar? But I don't have an answer Gavin will accept. He'll coerce me back inside and I'll give in so as not to disappoint anyone.

The streetlights above light up the sky the moment I step outside. It casts a glow over the rows of parked cars, highlighting that none are of any use without a set of keys. The limo driver, charged with whisking the new Dr. and Mrs. Gavin Laughton to the reception, is waiting at the entrance of the church. Quickly, I realize I've skipped from one problem to the next. I need to find my way out of here.

"This is why robbers don't wait until the last minute to figure out their getaway plan, Paisley!" I chastise myself aloud.

I lift my gown off the blacktop, ball it in my fists, and start running. My high heels pinch my toes when my feet land on the pavement, making my lips twist. *Shoot!* I was sorely mistaken thinking the blisters I'd have by the end of tonight would be from dancing the night away.

I stop, hop up and down, remove my shoes, and let them clop to the ground. A twinge of guilt hits me. They were such nice shoes. It's followed by a second pang of regret. How can I be sad about ditching Jimmy Choos when I just left the man I was supposed to marry in the most compromising position anyone could find themselves in?

Well, maybe it's not *the* most. But getting ditched ranks up there for embarrassment. Poor Gavin. And my poor mother... *Eeeh.* My mother. I'll find a way to live this fiasco down, but can they?

"Paisley? Where are you?"

"Oh shit, he's still after me!" I squeak.

Skittering onto the cold and damp sidewalk, I pick up the pace. Within the next few blocks, I'm going to go from Historic Brighton to Downtown Brighton to the back alleyways that investment firms thought twice about revitalizing.

Beyond a chain link fence, flashing pink letters on a neon sign catch my attention. Almost out of breath from the heavy layers I'm carrying, I have two choices. I can keep running and risk the possibility of getting hepatitis when I step on a needle. Or I can duck inside and pray that Sweet Caroline's is the last place on earth anyone—especially a well-respected heart surgeon—will come looking for me.

There's a single car in the lot, so I take my chances that the customers won't think I'm part of the stage show. I scoot under an awning, ignoring the marquee advertising the scantily clad headline acts, and pull on a door handle.

"No, no. Don't be locked. Don't be locked!" I dare to glance over my shoulder, reaching for the other door.

Not as heavy as I expect, it swings open, nearly toppling me over. I step into the dark strip club, pulling my dress inside before I can't see anything anymore, and risk it catching between the doors. My practically bare feet can feel the holes in my stockings and the short pile of the rug.

"We're closed," booms a voice from down a dark hall.

"I need to use the phone. Make a call." I arch my spine six ways from Sunday, trying to see in the shadows.

I'm also wondering who exactly am I calling? And how am I paying for the lift because my purse, with my phone and my credit cards, are in the church's undercroft.

Thank fuck I own a boutique because not making off with the money would make bank robbery an exceptionally poor career choice.

A tall silhouette emerges, back lit by the hallway. He uses the top of a liquor bottle to flip a switch, washing the entire theater in harsh light. I cover my eyes for them to adjust.

"Don't you have a cell?" The man demands, accusing me of being an idiot.

A whole congregation agrees you're not far off, dude.

"I lost it." Along with my sanity.

I blink, and the man across the room is staring at me in shock.

Can't say I blame him. I'm sort of shocked about how my night is going, too. Although, I'm the slightest bit more prepared for this encounter than Sweet Caroline's proprietor is.

From the looks of the desolate parking lot, I thought there would be a bartender in here. A bouncer. A regular watching a dancer spin around a pole, too enamored by the woman taking her clothes off on stage to become involved in my little circus act. After humiliating myself in front of two hundred people who I know, what difference would half a dozen who I don't make?

However, I hadn't factored Jake Ballentine into the mix.

No downtown business owner has to have met him to know him. Jake is a man whose reputation precedes him. His omnipotent presence in this small town is as much an institution as the gentleman's club he owns.

More than Jake's questionable dealings tower above. From across the room, he looms gigantic. Long and lean, Jake is dressed in crisp black trousers. His unbuckled belt jangles at his hips. Several buttons on his shirt are undone at the collar. The power in his neck and broad shoulders is similar to a competitive swimmer. His tie hangs loose. His blond hair is disheveled like he's gripped it at the root, but it appears he's also tried to mat it down and back into place.

I'm uncertain if the attempt to make himself look presentable is for my benefit. I would have buckled the belt first, but that's just me, and I'm a girl.

Jake strides over the carpeting with the bottle of amber liquid in his grip. He sets it on a small round table as he passes.

"I thought the princess lost a shoe leaving the ball?"

I crane my neck to reply. "Oh, I did that bitch one better." I lift the tattered hem of my soiled gown and wiggle my toes.

His cantankerous laughter bounces off the walls. "Come on, which one of the guys set me up?" He shakes his head, unbelieving. "I could have sworn Trig and Carver were having too much fun with their respective wives to notice I left."

I shake my head in response. "No clue what you are talking about. Didn't know you were closed. Didn't remember my cell."

Jake plays with the cleft in his square chin. His pupils are wide and black with an icy blue halo. He stares, daring me to hide the truth from him. "It can't be that simple."

"Uh, yeah. It can," I say sarcastically. It is the truth and I'm coming down from the adrenaline high of hot-footing it out of a church during my wedding. "So can I—"

The door flings open interrupting me.

"I need to use your phone. Please! I left mine at the church a few blocks away and I need to tell my fiancée's mother... Paisley?"

Oh, fuckkity, fuck, fuck.

My shoulders hit my ears. I'm caught in Jake's blue-eyed tractor beam, unable to turn and look at Gavin.

"Just go with it," I whisper under my breath.

I jump before even realizing what I'm doing. Wrapping my arms around his neck, the Norse God's palms encase my ass, and our bodies press flush together. Jake plays along, kissing me as if runaway brides barrel into his establishment every single day, searching for sanctuary.

And while this kiss isn't the one I anticipated ending my wedding day with, I have to admit Jake Ballentine is an amazing kisser.

Chapter Two

Jake

"Paisley?"

The guy in the tux has repeated himself a bunch of times. But I'm languishing in the lady in white who has my full frontal attention. She didn't think twice about opening for me when I licked the seam of her soft lips. She faintly smells like a spring morning, but she tastes like adventure and the night. Darker. Spicy. Chaotic. Her velvety tongue strokes against mine and I cradle the back of her neck in my palm and twist her face so that I can dive in deeper.

I give into kissing this woman because… Well, the fuck reason do I have not to?

Whatever we're doing is a good show. And being the owner of a semi-classy strip joint, I'm the master at putting on a damn good show. Neither of us are coming up for breath and the chemistry we've got going is combustible. For a spur-of-the-moment performance, this kiss has got me hot and bothered. For a tiny thing, the impeccable rounded globes I clutch to maintain our lip lock are a handful.

I'm losing my grip—likely on reality—definitely on her ass.

The bulk of Paisley's slippery dress makes it harder to keep my grip on her than say if we were naked in my office. She slides down my body. Our lips don't part until her feet touch the ground. I stifle a groan, thinking about all the ways I could torture Paisley. That I'd corrupt her into tormenting me.

Her forehead rests against my breastbone. Her chestnut brown hair is coming undone. I had nothing to do with that. I only held her silky neck. My fingers purposefully dug into her hairline at the base of her skull, knotting into the curled tendrils. A spot I'm still massaging now.

Something comes over me. I pass it off as trivial. Simply my subconscious combating the achy loneliness that made me leave the tent while the party was in full swing and come back here alone to the deserted club. I kiss the crown of Paisley's head atop that vulnerable pile of curls. Right where it looks like something important has been ripped away.

Then I spot Paisley's crestfallen groom. He reminds me of a guy who has given me everything he has to take and then can't understand why I won't give it back.

Because I'm an ass and a cheater, that's why.

And where I have nothing else to lose except a nightclub my father left me to run when our lives went to shit, I swindle people for fun.

"I'm sorry, man. We're just uh, I'm sorry you had to find out this way." I lie, unsure of what, or who, I'm lying for.

The guy turns, his shoulders slump, and he bangs the long silver handle on the door. It slides shut behind him.

"Thank you," Paisley mutters into my chest. About four buttons down toward my stomach, I feel her breath and my balls tighten.

"I had to improvise." I press my lips to her head again.

Yup, lonely sap looking for love in all the wrong places. This time I'd shuck my pants for a woman who broke a guy's heart in front of a crowd, no less. No wonder why I've got my friends convinced that I'll never settle down. They're right, though. I don't plan to.

Paisley huffs and tips her chin up. Her eyes are misty and filled with regret.

"Drink?" I fall into bartender mode and scurry behind the bar to get two shot glasses.

I hadn't gotten far in drowning my sorrows when Paisley interrupted me. The bottle of rum I'd taken a swig from in my office lies on the table near where she's standing.

"Sure." She nods, wiping under her eyelashes and sniffling.

I snag a few cocktail napkins in case of emergency and pat my back pocket for my phone. Paisley's puffy princess garb is cute and whatever is happening is entertaining. However, the moment the waterworks start in earnest, the closest ride share is bailing me out.

"Why are you closed on Valentine's Day?" She sits when I motion to the table.

"You'll never believe it. I was at a wedding, too." The whole Sweet Caroline's crew received invitations. I'd do anything to make the bride happy, even shut my bar down on a night my staff usually makes excellent tips. Even give the bride away.

"Your own?" She laughs a little tinkling and misbelieving sound.

"Nah. This woman I'm not worthy of. Not that I think Cass is either, but that's who she married," I say, pouring for us both.

"Cary Cass? With the car dealerships and the *vroom vroom*?" Paisley pretends she's steering a car. Her arms flop to her lap and her nose scrunches. "Are you talking about Holly?"

"Perceptive. Does being a bride mean reading the engagement announcements in the society columns, or do you happen to know my former manager?" I lift my shot, pointing a pinky like I'm drinking tea. Empty, I refill the glass and toss the second shot like a man.

"She's in my store a lot. Holly doesn't buy much, but her girlfriends could keep the boutique in the black. They're incredibly nice."

"Girlfriends like Kimber… and Sloan Galloway. And you are *that* Paisley," I state.

"Yes, I am that Paisley." Her fingers make half a yin and yang symbol in the air the same shape as her shop's logo—something I have no choice but to know since half of my female employees also keep Paisley's boutique in business.

She slouches in the barrel-style chair cushion and lifts her forearms to rest on the semi-circular arm that flows from the back of the chair. I bought plush seats to keep my customer's asses comfortable. I wanted them captive, so they'd waive a cocktail waitress over instead of ordering drinks at the bar. But I can't help noticing Paisley has curiously short legs. Her skirt swishes as her knees move and bent heat the rustle of fabric her feet skim back and forth over the carpet. Then she makes an awkward harumph, pulls her dress up, and wiggles her coral painted toenails.

"I hope you don't mind. I stepped in a puddle." She reaches up her dress, rips a stocking off, and holds it up for inspection. The sole is shredded and I surmise the other foot is, too.

"So you didn't love him?" I ask while she fumbles

to take off the second stocking without giving me a glimpse of her wedding undergarments.

"I love him. I love him a lot."

What a damn dirty shame. "But you don't want to be married to him."

"No, I do. Well, sort of. We have a difference of opinion. If we got married, I'd lose the argument by default."

"A difference of opinion isn't a matter of life or death."

"Ha! That's your opinion."

"Had to have been something significant."

"It was. To me, anyway. However, Jake Ballentine doesn't need my sob story." A smug Paisley has heard all the nasty rumors of how I've used some of these stories against people.

My respect for her ticks up a notch.

"How old are you?"

"Considerably over twenty-one." She smiles, pouring a finger of rum.

"That's still too young to get married."

"How old are you?"

"I'm not dead yet."

"That's not what I asked."

"I'm an old maid—er, man? The hell would you call it?"

"Well, you're definitely too sinister to be a spinster." Paisley sees herself in a mirror and uses the reflection to pull a million little bobby pins out of her updo.

"Sinister… I like that." I nod with a wink and lift the rum to my lips.

"So why did you leave the wedding you were attending early?"

"Paisley, ah…" I point a pin in her direction, stumbling for her last name.

"Cooper."

"Paisley Cooper doesn't need my sob story."

"Okay then, why were you convinced your friends sent me here as a joke?"

She bends forward, shaking out her hair. When she flips back up, it falls over her shoulders in copper waves streaked with gold.

I decide to give her a reason to stay right there where she is, looking like a knockout compared to the primped princess that walked into my bar.

"They've all gotten hitched and believe I cannot commit."

Paisley leans her elbow on the table. She picks up her shot glass, letting it fall and spin, fall and spin on its base.

"I commit to the things that are important."

"But not women?" She fills my glass, then hers.

The freaky thing is, my parents raised me in this building surrounded by women. I caught on to which ones were selling themselves to maintain the status quo versus the ladies struggling to turn stripping into something better: the students who attend Pinewood State. I'm fully fucking devoted to doing anything for a woman who deserves it.

Take Holly, for instance. She was a single mom with the odds stacked against her. If it weren't for her son, I'd have passed her name on to my childhood best friend, Carver Galloway. He'd have found a room for Holly at the mill. She could have gone back to being a flight attendant instead of slinging hooch and having her ass grabbed at Caroline's. I probably would have settled into something longer-term with Holly until I'd fucked her senseless. But as great as the kid is, he was a liability for both Carver and me.

The last decade or so of my life haven't been what you'd call "child-proof". So I did what I could and stepped away when I would have rather kept Holly as my own. I transformed her into my own personalized version of a mill girl—the women who, at one point or another, live across the street in Carver's revitalized factory building.

A stretch of silence fills the empty theater. Paisley refills my rum, trying another tactic to get me to open up.

"Have you ever been in love? The real, true kind where no one else exists?"

My lips flatten to a line. It is Paisley's wedding day. The rum is three-quarters gone. I gift her an answer.

"She stole my heart from day one and, when she was gone, she took my dreams along with her."

"Which is what makes you a cynic."

"I prefer realist. Isn't that what you are, too?"

Paisley based her decision on the inability to see how her marriage could work.

"No. I'm a coward who didn't stand up for myself until there was no turning back. I dragged everyone down to a place none of us belonged. And I hurt someone who I honestly care deeply for. The stunt I pulled tonight was unfair. It cost a lot. More than money can buy to get back, you know?"

I cast a noncommittal shrug. As much as I'm enjoying Paisley's company, our trust is paper thin. Aside from the lone truth about being in love that I gift-wrapped for Paisley, I won't pour my heart out to her the way, at present, I regret doing with Holly.

Paisley isn't my bartender. The simple fact is she's another girl to get drunk on. Another beautiful woman I'd spend the night fucking if she used that "just go with it" line when the club was packed.

Women rarely share their problems with me. Maybe because our sum games when we start talking includes getting our tongues down the other's throat. The hot banter leads to a passionate encounter, not comes from it. Which makes what happened with Paisley different since there was no pretense in flirting before she kissed me. She was ballsy. It was a fucking amazing kiss. Paisley went right for what she wanted and she got the reaction she needed. I'm glad Gavin got the message so easily.

My heart thuds a little in my chest, and I mistake it for pride. There's no mistaking why my dick twitches under the table, though.

Holly would hate me if I fucked Paisley, I think as we slip into comfortable silence. I can't insinuate to Holly that she'd meant more to me and ruin the confession by taking Paisley to bed. If anyone found out, it'd turn me into a cliché and give the guys more ammunition against me.

Feeling the effects of the adrenaline wearing off and the alcohol settling in, Paisley lies her head on the table.

"Tired?"

She hums, popping up to rest her chin on her knuckles.

The high neckline of her dress stops me from peering between her breasts. I've only seen Paisley's toes and her arms. Intrigued by her bravado tonight, a glimpse of Paisley's tits would make it into my spank bank.

"I don't drink a lot and wedding preparations make for a long day." She sighs, sleepily. "When I convinced myself I could go through with marrying Gavin, I was also kind of looking forward to relaxing on our honeymoon. I haven't had a vacation in a while."

Images of Paisley in a string bikini, stretched out on a beach towel, fill my head. She arches toward my touch as I cover her with sunscreen. Paisley in my bed right now is a no-go. But I can still have my cake and eat it too.

"I tell you what; You help me get my friends off my back about not having a serious relationship, and I'll spring for your trip."

Chapter Three

Paisley

It's after midnight when I tumble out of the car that Jake stuffed me into. I wave at the driver, who Jake ordered not to budge from the curb until I was safe inside my home. Turning makes me sway along the path to my front door. I trip over my skirt without my high heels on, stumbling and skidding to a halt when Gavin's best man and a groomsman exit the apartment.

Each holds opposite sides of the sixty-inch television I bought Gavin for his birthday. The best man ignores me. I get pushed to the side. The frozen, dormant grass pricks the soles of my feet. If looks could kill, the local authorities would charge the groomsman with my murder. I watch them pass, noticing several open SUV trunks with Gavin's belongings stacked haphazard inside.

I tread lightly back over to the sidewalk. Entering through the open door, a second groomsman shoves me with the corner of a box he's carrying out.

Inside, the rooms of our shared apartment are

ransacked. They're removing everything of Gavin's that isn't nailed down. I didn't know what to expect. I wasn't even sure I could get into my home. So, I can't say I blame Gavin. In his shoes, I'd have taken my anger one step further and trashed some of his personal effects.

My former fiancé is on the ledge of the living room couch cushion. My mother sits poised next to him, clutching my purse on her lap and staring at my phone, willing it to light up.

About to stand, Gavin says something I can't hear to my mom. Her features pinch. She grabs ahold of his wrist, apologizing for my betrayal.

Apologizing *for me* as I'm positive she's done from the moment my mom and the rest of the congregation found out Jake Ballentine is my "secret lover".

In the deepest recesses of my black heart, I'm certain Gavin's whisper includes telling my mother it wasn't her fault. I'm fortunate he sees it that way. My mom did nothing wrong.

It's then that their eyes land on me. My mom sucks in a relieved breath, tears tumble down her pale cheeks. She glances between us, wanting me to set the story straight. To say Gavin was mistaken. The man she wanted to love and protect her daughter hadn't caught me in someone else's arms.

Gavin's intake is harder and unforgiving.

I'm drunk as a skunk wearing a wrinkled and soiled wedding dress. My ratty, unpinned hair gives the impression Jake and I took a tumble in the hay. Considering Jake's shirt and belt were undone, and I jumped Jake like a tick to suck his face off, Gavin has no reason to think otherwise. The chances he'll forgive me are slim to none.

And what's more, I'm not ready to forgive myself. So I won't plead for his mercy. Not when Gavin proved his compassion by staying with my mother.

I open my mouth, but Gavin cuts me off.

"No." He doesn't yell. His unwillingness to let me explain is matter of fact. "We had everything and now it's gone. So just... No."

Unlike the groomsman that shoved me with the box, Gavin leaves a wide berth as if I'm contagious. And unlike when he was in shock leaving Sweet Caroline's, this time the door slams behind him. His justified last word. Last action that screams how wronged Gavin was. He wants no part of the sullied stain of my duplicity.

It's a good thing. Since my double-life is fake and I couldn't explain it if I tried.

"You were so beautiful this afternoon." What mom is saying is that my dark insides match my tattered outside appearance. I'm not beautiful anymore.

I nod, agreeing wholeheartedly that I'm a miserable person for putting my mother through explaining my disappearing act to the guests, and for having to rely on Gavin for support.

"Honestly, Paisley, what were you thinking?" My mother rifles in a kitchen cabinet. She finds what she's looking for amongst the bevy of orange pill containers. Unscrewing a full bottle of pediatric electrolyte, thrusting it at me. "What would your father say? Jake Ballentine has no morals. He isn't even from a respectable family. His father watched and approved of his wife taking off her clothes for a living before he... Never mind."

I stare at the bottle, my vision tunneling in and out, as I check to see if there's a nipple or a straw that I'm supposed to suck on. My mother is treating me like a petulant child. I'd be offended if I weren't grateful that my mom is taking care of me, focused on me recovering from a hangover that, without a doubt, will keep me bedridden.

I should confess to Mom that I wasn't engaging in an affair behind Gavin's back, but the explanation for why I left the church won't be good enough.

She escorts me to my room, and while encouraging me to keep drinking the gross purple concoction, she helps me out of my ruined gown. The one she chose when I couldn't make up my mind. I drop my eyes from the dusty metal wall mount and bright square where the television used to hang and the sun has faded the surrounding paint.

Tears of shame prickle behind my eyes.

Out of energy, I flop back onto the bed. My mother snags the purple drink before I spill it. Gavin's pillow is by my nose. I bring it to my face, smothering my cheeks and breathing deeply.

Everyone said Gavin and I were a perfect match. I ruined that. I wielded a knife at the pretty picture of the newlywed doctor and his wife.

We were so close to having a down payment on the stately colonial with Georgian columns surrounded by a plush lawn and secured with the requisite white picket fence. Gavin kept saying that we had enough to buy the grand house that everyone aspires to. I told him we didn't, and I had a million excuses why. It was a seller's market. If we saved a few thousand more, we could afford renovations. If I pushed Gavin off from purchasing, we'd eventually see eye to eye on the big things that he kept insisting weren't a big deal.

For the past few months, I've held Gavin at arm's length. We'd been occasional partners in bed when his on-call schedule allowed and when I wasn't exhausted. Aware of my history, he didn't mind because he's a doctor.

Was I really tired, though? Or was I driving an invisible wedge so that I didn't have to admit the flaw in our relationship?

He was strong and I was weak. Incapable of finding my voice and standing on my own two feet, I'm responsible for hurting him.

Gavin will forever think I gave up on us for a perfect stranger. When what I'd done was give him back to the person he belonged with, and gave her a rightful chance at perfection.

Gavin was so good to me and he shouldn't have bothered.

My shoulders shake. I push the pillow away, sobbing. It finally hits me that what I'd done was attempt to hold off as long as I could before grieving this loss.

I've known for months that I wanted to be an adored wife. The woman who compromised while simultaneously having a husband who hushed her concerns with gentle, comforting words that spoke volumes of his love for her. I wish Gavin could have sacrificed for me, and that he didn't have to. I wish the lines between selfish and selfless didn't intermingle in cold shades of gray.

I wish someone, anyone, was on my side and said, "Gee, Paisley, I see your point of view and it's valid", instead of "You'll get over your reservations once you and Gavin are settled."

Meanwhile, I fed off of the trappings of my wedding to Gavin: the dress, the tastings for the cake and reception, the guests who sent RSVPs that I hadn't seen in forever, all the way up to how handsome Gavin looked in his tux. Everyone else's excitement lured me to the dark side.

What a lousy friggin' excuse to say I let them coerce me. All along, I wanted to do the right thing and marry Gavin. Until death do us part.

My mom rubs my back as I hiccup through my sobs. When I think I'm finally cried out, I reach for her.

"How could he ever love anyone as awful as me?"

"I love you." She hugs me.

"You're my mom. You ha-ha-hafta say that." I stutter.

"Can I be frank? Someday you'll understand that mothers can love their children, but not especially like them or the choices they make." She brushes my hair away from my tear-stained face. "What you did was horrible, but that doesn't make you a terrible person. Not to me, anyway. And there's still time for you to make different choices, Paisley. Better ones."

I cry some more and apologize for every transgression I've ever made against her. She only has me now, and Mom deserves to know how much I love her.

The following afternoon, I stop wishing for someone on my side and want everyone to be in full agreement with my mother. Getting involved with Jake Ballentine doesn't make me a terrible person.

Because all of Brighton believes it does, and they're not keeping those feelings to themselves.

I've had to hide and delete comments on the boutique's social media feeds. Customer requests to unsubscribe from the mailing list are flooding the store's email inbox. Other messages include things that I can't repeat in polite company.

When I woke up with a throbbing headache from sharing an entire bottle of rum with Jake, I thought the priority damage control I'd be in charge of was with my wedding party.

I couldn't have been more wrong.

"Paisley are you—" Greer is on speakerphone.

When her voice trails, it's obvious she's seen one of the more demeaning posts.

That I'm pregnant with Jake Ballentine's baby. Though the poster used a different "B" word.

"God, no!"

"Oh, I *um*—forget it." Greer, who co-owns the shop next to mine, was in the congregation last night. She called this morning, alerting me to open my laptop.

Greer has confided that she and her boyfriend, Byron are also actively not protecting. They want a baby. I'd be excited if Greer and Byron were expecting and she had a girlfriend to share being pregnant with.

"How long have you known him?" She moves the subject on.

"Not long." All broody and imposing, Jake sort of came out of nowhere. "Everything about Jake took me by surprise."

Or do I have it backward and that was me?

My heart skips a beat. I stop and swallow. Ignoring the sensation in my chest, but thinking back on the entire crazy encounter.

We actually had fun last night with the back and forth.

Nothing about our conversations seemed forced.

Jake hadn't pressed me for details when I refused to answer some of his questions.

For a moment, I forgot I was sitting there in my wedding dress with my ruined stockings rumpled into a wad next to Jake's pricey bottle of top-shelf rum.

He must be used to that. Women take their clothes off for Jake on a daily basis.

Strippers take their clothes off for Jake. He pays women to prance around in their altogether. He's a prick and a misogynist for taking advantage of them and selling sexual fantasies. I mean, who does that and then contends that they care about the opposite sex?

Except, he wasn't the least bit dickish... After the kiss, anyway.

Jake hadn't even tried to get me into bed. Again, the naked women thing explains a whole lot. I don't have anything Jake Ballantine hasn't seen.

Maybe he surmised that if I was dashing for a church wearing white, it meant I was a virgin and clingy inexperienced women aren't Jake's style. Maybe he wasn't interested in having sex with me because of what I'd done. Except, I am experienced, and the way Jake's arousal punched into my stomach when he was kissing me made it seem like sex wasn't something the man would brush off the table.

Not that I considered what sex with Jake would be like. Okay, not right away. But thinking about something doesn't mean acting on it. I may have kissed Jake with intention, but I have some pride. I've never fallen into the sack with a man I've just met.

Oh, my Lord. Who am I that I'm more concerned about the hours spent in Jake's company rather than destroying Gavin? Can I be any bigger of a detached bitch?

"Jake must be important to you if you called it all off, though, right?" Greer asks.

"Um, yeah." I hope the breathy tone disguises my underlying fear.

I'm not in love with Jake and I won't lie and say I am.

What I am is posthumously realizing I'm walking a dangerous tightrope.

Shaking on his vacation offer on a drunken whim, I created the potential for a huge mess. It's unwise to cross a man who exudes sex and power. I'll need to play it smart and use some serious smarts to get me out of the deal we made.

Overwhelmed, I wipe my ruddy face with the back

of my hand. "Other than shutting down the feeds, I don't know how to fix this."

"I understand the pressure you're under after doing the wrong thing. Don't make a rash decision about the store. Take some time away from Jake and everything else to think it through."

"I will." I *so* will. Avoiding Jake Ballentine is my top priority.

Chapter Four

Jake

Trig uses his palm to cover his face, which is stupid because I have the blackout shades drawn in my living room. They came with a remote and, seeing as sometimes my female company and I don't make it as far as my bedroom, are the best investment ever.

Sitting on my couch, every so often, Trig's eyes dart over to me. His chest rumbles and the corners of his lips turn up into a smirk. Sound comes out of his nose, he snorts, and a cycle of rolling laughter begins anew.

"You're an asshole." I chuck the hard pillow that came with my furniture at him. Those things suck as much as my buddy.

"Me? I'm not the one caught with his pants down." He throws it back. The rough fabric grates like sandpaper across my bare stomach and knee. The pillow falls to the carpet. I don't bother picking it up. Instead, I slide in my athletic shorts onto the throne behind my drum set and lean against the stool's padded backrest.

"My pants weren't down. You make it sound like I was fucking her when he walked in on us."

Thanks to the Google Alert that Trig set up for my name, he's blessed me with his company before I can flick the switch on the coffee pot.

"Don't you have better things to do? The wife…" I *rat-tat-tat* the stick on the symbol to agitate Trig. "…the kids. I could've sworn the two of you were procreating faster than rabbits."

It's a low blow. Trig and his wife Kimber, who was once a headliner at Sweet Caroline's and then my *former*-former manager before Holly, are the parents of three ankle biters. After Kimber gave birth to their first kid together, I'd lucked out. She came back to work and kept everyone in line. On occasion, everyone included me. They had problems conceiving their infant twins. Problems I could have continued to cash in on if Kimber hadn't up and quit when she got pregnant the second time.

"Better, yes. As entertaining? No." Trig answers.

Five hours post stuffing a slurring Paisley in a cab, it's apparent she and I are at the center of a local social media shitstorm. Thank fuck, there are no compromising pictures of our kiss, but Brighton woke up to news of the runaway bride and her deviant lover.

This is why I'm never getting married. All those guests were there to support Paisley and Dr. Douche. Yet, one of them set this ball into motion. A bitter cousin. A jealous bridesmaid. I spend my days around gorgeous, albeit often catty, women. I don't put it past them. Then again, it could have been a dumbass on the groom's side of the aisle thinking he was sticking up for what's-his-face and instead made things worse. What it comes down to is someone aired Paisley and her former fiancé's dirty laundry.

Normally, I'd eat this shit with a spoon. I'm

goddamn iconic at pushing the coats out of the way and finding the skeletons lurking at the back of a closet. I've made a habit out of cashing in on the secrets that interest me and turning others' misfortune to my benefit. A guy has to do something to stop the spark from dulling. And really, the only people I'm hurting are the people who intentionally hurt someone else.

Okay, or sometimes not. Casualties happen.

It's good for my ego when the citizens of Brighton whisper Jake Ballentine is someone to watch out for. But this go-around I'm not thrilled with them tweeting my name. That's going to make it harder for me to bank on the next guy who slips up when I get wind of it.

I don't know why Paisley hadn't registered on my radar before last night. Her shop's bags litter my dancer's dressing area and every business owner downtown is fair game. Since Trig barged in here, I also haven't decided if I'd have blackmailed Paisley over the affair the rumor mill says we're having. There's always the chance that I'd have Trig use his backchannels to hack her online bookkeeping account for a peek at anything out of sorts with the boutique's finances.

But because of that kiss, I have something on Paisley now that's valuable to me. Although when I hit the hay, I hadn't bothered to consider how our negotiations would play out.

"Give it to me straight. How long has this thing been going on between the two of you?" he asks.

"Long enough that she ditched Dr. Douche before the 'I do's'."

Ba dum dum. The symbol crashes.

"Come on, Jake. Are you serious about this girl, or did you tell her lies and screw up her life for fun? She was marrying a heart surgeon. That's like the gold standard, brass ring of husbandship. Unless the guy was abusive, why would Paisley back out when she did?"

"Why would I lie to my girlfriend?" I ditch the sticks, feigning offense.

Trig shoots me the "you're kidding" look "I've lost count of the *e-hem,* ladies you've taken home." He points to the front door. "I could go check the club's footage if you want a rough estimate for the last month. You're not dating Paisley Cooper. So the fuck are you doing to her?"

"According to the very colorful post you showed me on her shop's social media account, I very clearly am fucking Paisley Cooper."

"Prove it. Call your girlfriend to make sure she's okay. I'm sure the negative press has her pretty upset."

Shit, I don't have her number. "That's not the sort of relationship we have. Seeing as how Paisley was otherwise engaged, it's not as if I could text whenever I wanted."

"Yeah, yeah, it must've been tough keeping the fact that you weren't seeing his fiancée *at all* from the guy Paisley lived with. And while we're at it, why have you nicknamed Laughton, Dr. Douche? That's you, my friend. If I checked your phone records, I bet there won't be a single one for Paisley Cooper."

"You are exactly right. How do you think we kept it a secret this long? By not sending up any red flags to anyone. Whenever we met we set up the next time we'd see each other. Paisley's not used to me hovering," I lie.

"Uh-huh." Trig still doesn't believe me.

I don't blame him. The story I'm concocting is bad even by my standards.

"Listen, last night took a lot of guts on Paisley's part. She asked me to give her a few days to do damage control and I want to respect that."

"Because you love her."

I what?

"Of course, I do. What's not to love? Paisley is intelligent and attractive. She runs her own business. She's independent." I rattle off the few surface facts she opened up to me about while we shared my favorite rum. It's from a small batch distiller on the Outer Banks and hard to come by. Minus a periodic threesome, I'm not particularly the sharing type, so I throw in that we polished off the bottle for good measure.

"You are so full of shit. I'm going to enjoy bringing you to your knees on this one, man." Trig challenges me, adding. "Paisley, not so much. She owns Kimber's favorite store."

I relax the way I had in Paisley's company at Sweet Caroline's. Kimber's influence on Trig makes him hard-pressed to hurt Paisley in the process. I'm not sure why that matters to me all of a sudden, but it does.

Trig finishes giving me grief and goes home to his wife. It's sinking in pretending Paisley and I are together, and persuading my friends the novelty of our connection isn't tenuous at best, will be a lot harder than I gave it credit for.

Over the past few years, my friends—the kind of men, by anyone's standards, who should have remained confirmed bachelors—have succumbed to the fairer sex. Aside from Carver and Trig, the others are also married or plan to be soon. It's the reason why I avoid their social engagements; baby showers, birthday parties, etc...

Unfortunately, I couldn't pass on Holly's nuptials. Although, it wasn't as if I'd be okay without witnessing Holly step into the life she was destined for. Having decided as I walked off the dance floor at her wedding that she'll remain the single mill girl that I'll keep for myself, I'm glad Holly is the one I helped. I wish I could have been the man for her and I'm sorry for the shit I unknowingly put her through while working to get her where she and her son needed to be.

I've felt the stinging loss of the potential of more than a friendship with Holly for longer than I care to admit. In my weakest moments, I grabbed my bottle of rum and drunkenly poured my heart out to her about my personal failings. I'm all too aware of the murmurs behind my back that I have a tendency to fall for women I have no chance with. My friends aren't wrong. There's an inevitable demise to any relationship I've engaged in. So when I see the inescapable coming, letting the curtain fall before the final act beats getting the hook.

Maintaining a distance from Holly kept her respectable. I doubt I'll be seeing much of Mrs. Holly Cass as much anymore. It was the desired outcome all along, wasn't it? She's a woman I couldn't have when I could have her. Someone safe to open up to about my personal demons while she poured from my bottle of rum and listened to my sob story. Holly knows me best. Better than even Trig or Carver, the men included in the shadier side of my business. The more I've learned about Holly, giving up on anything romantic between us before it had a chance to bloom made perfect sense.

However, there's no way that I can show up once or twice with a runaway bride on my arm, say we're in a committed relationship, and fool anyone. I know next to nothing about Paisley. I'm also in a jam because the details I gave Trig about our coupling include that my girlfriend and I aren't tied at the hip, needing to text our every move, and gushing over our next secret rendezvous. We don't have an affair to keep hidden anymore. There's no trail of evidence unless I get off my ass and make one up. That seems awfully time-consuming for a woman I met less than a day ago.

So, I work with what I can: After making a monumental decision to ditch Dr. Douche on her wedding night, Paisley is highly emotional and confused. She asked for space. I agreed because I care about her. Since she's independent, me hovering isn't the right approach. Hell, since I'm an aloof asshole, hovering will look bad.

I have to accept her faults and there's no way my friends will believe we are together if she doesn't accept mine.

If you think that line is genius, lemme tell you something. The "Jake the snake" murmurings aren't for nothing. I've stayed hidden in the depths with my beady black eyes focused on my prey and my tongue darting out of my mouth, scenting their weaknesses. The same lovey-dovey scenario played out for Trig and Kimber all the way through Holly and her boy toy, Cary Cass. Apparently, once you find your soulmate, you'll let all sorts of annoying crap slide.

Chapter Six

Paisley

The boutique was hopping the entire time I spent tense and hiding out at home instead of relaxing on my honeymoon. It's midweek after most of my customers have cashed in their Valentine's Day gift cards from their significant others and exchanged gifts that didn't suit them.

I opened alone for my first official shift back at work today, figuring the trend would slow and inventory would garner my attention. However, I'm wondering which of my employees let the cat out of the bag that I'd be here. The foot traffic continues at a swift pace. Except it's without the unexpected and slight uptick of post-holiday sales it should have brought. The looky-loos outnumber the regular customers who've come in to browse. But thankfully an occasional regular winds up buying something.

Considering the nasty posts I hid from viewers on the store's social media feed, I'm grateful to have a shop at all. Although maybe the regular customers are ensuring they use up their store credits before I go under? I heard someone mutter they couldn't wait for a storewide clearance. Sure, the boutique has seasonal sales. But marking down everything in stock with a red slash through the price tag is something I've never considered. It's obvious because of the bad press, people expect a going-out-of-business sale.

The bell jingles. I look up from an exquisite pair of dangle drop earrings that a local artisan crafted. Keeping a good relationship with other small businesses has been key to my success over the years. I have a hands-on approach catering to my customers while they are in the store, too, and check in with them often. Some search racks and fill their shopping bags with scores of finds from the hangars, while others want the full personal shopper experience and for me to bring them new styles.

"I'll be right with—" the words die on my tongue when I see Jake Ballentine step inside.

Avoiding him in perpetuity isn't possible, but I'd done a damn good job of it so far.

"Take your time, *corazón*." He reaches toward the register and his arm skims the customer's whose purchase I am wrapping.

Unsure if Jake's here to empty the till or to make me squirm, I make an unladylike noise. I'm glad that neither of them notice because these are the same frustrated sounds I make in bed when I can't quite get there.

I'm polite, thanking Jake for whatever is in the Baked Beans cup and clearing my throat. My current customer is enamored with Jake's soft-spoken, but commanding appearance. I want her to remain happy and for Paisley's Boutique to be the first place she thinks of when she needs a new piece for her wardrobe. Two other ladies left in a huff when Jake entered. They must've been under the impression the rumors were nothing but. Now that they see it's for "real"—that I actually left flawless Gavin for faulted Jake—they won't spend their money here.

Another woman in her late twenties sidles up beside my demon lover. She flashes Jake a flirty smile and bats her eyelashes, saying she loves coming here.

"Then I hope you *come* back *often*," he replies, using the same tone.

The subtle innuendo grates on my nerves.

Jake holds the door for my last customer, flipping the sign in the window from "we're open" to read "back in five". I ring up the flirtatious woman without telling her to come back soon.

It's not my smartest move to bleed three customers in an hour. At present, word of mouth is not my friend and these customers can spout off that they had a negative experience in my store.

"Okay." I fold my hands in front of me and ease out from behind the checkout counter. "Why are you here?"

"I missed you, isn't enough?" Jake flips the lock, sealing us in. His gaze bounces from one security camera to the next, finally landing on me.

He puts one foot in front of the other, strolling a lazy line in my direction. The cocky grin pulling at his cheeks makes the cleft in his chin deepen. My back stiffens and my neck prickles with awareness. I'd forgotten how tall Jake was. Imposing with broad shoulders that stretch the limits of his blazer. Underneath his shirt, he's solid. I remember because, trying to hide from Gavin's reaction to seeing me with another man, I'd tucked my forehead to Jake's breastbone. The pads of my fingers pressed into his tight stomach muscles.

Like a complete idiot, I reach my palm to Jake's chest, intending to place it there to halt his advance. His stride stays steady, forcing my retreat as if we're dancing a Regency waltz. He cages me into the counter, resting his large hands on the glass-topped case. The top of my head hardly comes past the second open button on his shirt. Golden hair springs from his collar. Jake bends, tilting his chin to my neck, and my traitorous nipples harden inside of my bra.

Thoughts I've been trying to banish swirl in my mind. They start out innocent enough. The two of us laughing, making small talk a little over a week ago. The weird get-to-know-you that normally precedes a kiss. Then it rolls backward to the kiss itself. For a split second, I forget I was kissing Jake Ballentine.

Whatever I am thinking is not normal. I've been trying to make sense of it and have come to two likely conclusions. First, getting hot and bothered by Jake is no different than the appeal of the buff guy in a movie. It could be no different than the way Jake's customers react to the strippers. Lust may be a sin, but it's also human nature. Hell, if anyone I know, male or female, doesn't drool over a nice ass in a tight pair of jeans. Some are better at hiding lasciviousness.

And now, after twice seeing Jake dressed to the nines, I'm swiping at mental screenshots of what his rear view looks like encased in denim. *Thanks a lot, subconscious.*

Moving onto number two. My behavior screams "rebound". Not the I'll-jump-into-bed-with-any-human-with-a-third-leg rebound. But Jake was my emotional support the night I left Gavin. So—where I had to crush my heart to see that Gavin and I weren't meant for forever, before obliterating what Gavin saw as his future—I'm looking for love in all the wrong places.

Jake was present at an opportune moment, and I mistook his kindness for compassion.

Something he readily confirms when his warm

breath brushes the shell of my ear.

"Turn off the tape, Paisley. No footage for ten, let's make it fifteen minutes."

"I can't." I can't continue letting my body's reaction confuse the situation.

"Yes, you can. An app on your phone controls this system." Undeterred, he slides my cell over the countertop. "We need a little privacy for what we're going to do."

Jake's hard length presses into my belly. I swallow hard, fumbling to unlock the screen. He takes the device from me. With three thumb jabs and a flick, he turns off the store's security cameras.

Once disconnected, Jake backs off as if he's been burned. He unbuttons his suit jacket, stuffs a hand in his pocket, and kicks his feet up on a chaise lounge across the floor as if the room hasn't been matchstick hot with sexual tension.

"Here." He beckons, a white square held between his fingertips. "It is the original. I have a copy."

"Original of what?" I play coy. He jotted down the agreement we made on a cocktail napkin. I pretend to be Jake's girlfriend, and he pays for me to go on a vacation. "That was a joke." We were flippant and drunk. "It doesn't count… Also, I can afford my own trip. But thank you, nonetheless."

"What part doesn't count, Paisley?" Jake sits up, growling offense. "I'm guessing it's when you threw yourself at me so Dr. Douche would think we were having an affair."

"Don't call Gavin that! He's a good man."

Jake's eyes widen at my defense of my ex-fiancé. "Then tell me why you left him and I'll call it even."

"No."

The Jake Ballentine in my boutique is not the Jake I met in his nightclub. I don't trust this Jake to keep my secret when others find it absurd. Jake's and my sordid affair was the talk of the town before sunrise. I would rather die than for a sensitive guy like Gavin to hear the actual reason why I left him at the altar from someone else. And with the guilt I'm carrying, if Gavin forgave me, I'd get drawn back in. Trapped into marriage and trying to make his world right again.

"Then I guess you have no choice than to go along with our deal. Unless you're willing to risk your shop? People love rumors, Paisley. They feed off of the spectacle of it. Half of Brighton wants to see you fail because you chose me over Dr.," Jake pauses, surprising me by using Gavin's last name. "Laughton. I doubt when everyone hears what was going on between us was a big lie that my friends like Kimber and Sloan, who are still on your side, will remain that way."

Crap. Sloan Galloway is one of my best customers. I've special-ordered plenty for her and listened to her suggestions. Oftentimes they've sold like hotcakes. Nurturing the relationship has brought in additional sales. New customers tell me they've stopped in based on her recommendation they shop here. Unlike the ladies who were in the boutique when Jake made his grand entrance, I can't afford to lose Sloan… Or her girlfriends, for that matter. They've dressed for a ton of bigger occasions recently and shopped at my boutique first for the right piece to wear. The receipts following a Mill Girls' Day Out can be the difference between a good month and a great one.

I blanch, my stomach bottoming out. Jake's brow twitches. He's got me painted into a corner, right where he wants me.

This is the Jake Ballentine Brighton is wary of. I'm harboring a small secret of little consequence to him, and Jake's using it to his advantage. Without warning, the regret over ducking into Sweet Caroline's overwhelms the remorse for ruining

Gavin's happiness.

Showing Jake my back might mean I wind up with a knife plunged in it, but I turn from him anyway to hide the tears pricking my vision. I finger a display of anklets that arrived while I was at home tending to the wounds I inflicted on myself. One has the word FIERCE pounded into the rose gold metal with a decorative arrow next to it.

My daddy was of small stature, like me. Sharp as a tack, he'd been picked on as a kid, not chosen for teams, underestimated. Daddy empathized with my plight. When I was a little girl, he taught me that good things come in small packages. That I could achieve whatever I wanted. In my lowest moments, my father assured me time and again that standing up for myself would not only build my confidence, but earn respect.

The idea of backing down from a bully like Jake has my blood pressure spiking. He won't view me as anything but weak if I don't stand up for myself.

However, owning a boutique was my dream. These four walls are my future. I have nothing else, and I've worked too hard to see it go under.

"How long will this charade last?" I need to know what I'm getting into.

Unaware he has snuck up on me, Jake removes the anklet that's fascinated me from the rack. He has the gall to rip the tag off. Then he kneels, brushing aside the hem of my long skirt, securing the chain with the clasp around my ankle. Shackling me to him. "Six months seems long enough to prove we gave it a shot. Anything less and you'll give the impression of serially having cold feet."

"Six months!" That's too long to waste.

I'm also offended that anyone would find any truth in me having runaway bride syndrome if I left Jake Ballentine. On the contrary, they'd probably scream, "run faster!"

"You shout a lot. We'll need to work on that. The women I... *date* are more... docile," he remarks, rising from the floor.

"I am not changing who I am for you." Crossing my arms lifts my breasts. Jake hones right in.

"I'd also prefer it if you worked on the necklines. Showed a little more, you know." He nickers.

That's so not happening.

The evil eye I cast, Jake returns accompanied by a wicked mirth that makes my knees rubbery. I attempt to move out of his space. Jake catches me around the waist. Tingles slide down my hip as he touches me. Oh my lord, this corrupt man, with his immoral strip joint, has managed to turn me on... Again.

Chapter Seven

Jake

Paisley in my grasp, I pull a wad of bills out of my pocket. "This will cover what I've bought so far." It's a shit move making her think I think she's for sale. Paisley wouldn't whore herself out for anyone.

But fuck if I don't need to turn the tables to my advantage. I had it. Until the customers left, and Paisley and I were alone.

For a split-second, entering the boutique and seeing Paisley for the first time after so many days, I considered tearing up the napkin. Pushing her up against the counter was my first mistake. My dick might not have had the pleasure of pleasing her, but it definitely remembers the way she jumped me. What we could have done.

When she touched that anklet, I wanted her to fight me.

As her resolve wavered, letting Paisley off easy meant our game was over. I wouldn't see her be fierce. The opportunity to parade her in front of my friends, proving I could find a woman as good as they had, would fly out the window.

From her reaction to me calling Gavin Laughton names, there's no doubt Paisley's loyal to him still. Loyalty can't be bought. Not with the couple hundred I've fronted for a wardrobe upgrade to appear as my girlfriend, or even the bling of the extravagant wedding they were throwing.

The secret Paisley is hiding is meant to heal instead of hurt. That's not the kind of information I deal in. But I want that secret. Not to use it against her either. I covet a part of Paisley that the good doctor won't get from her. And I won't let her go until I have it.

"I won't do this unless you agree not to swindle anyone else."

She's cute thinking she has the power to negotiate that. Or anything, for that matter.

"Get a bikini for your trip," I order, intending to piss her off.

I like her riled up. She's a spitfire, capable of independent thought and knowing her own mind.

"Why? Is it part of the deal that I have to bring you?" Her neck and cheeks flame. Heat boils off of her skin, seemingly able to burn me through the gauzy fabric of her flowing skirt.

I'd take Paisley into one of the dressing rooms to find out where else she's flushed, but I won't break a new toy. It's been a long time since I've had one that I've wanted to keep playing with this badly.

"Not if you don't want to." *I'll make you want to.*

I grab Paisley's phone, praising her while she unlocks it without actually giving it to her. The security app is still open, but what I need is for her cell to text mine so that I have her number. Mission accomplished, I swipe back to the boutique's paused security feed.

"Smile pretty for the camera, *corazón.*"

Confusion mars Paisley's face until the point that I cover her mouth with mine. I flick my fingertip over the record button, reactivating the system. Plundering her lips, I leave a trail of evidence for Trig to find if he goes sniffing. To ensure whatever Trig sees proves Paisley and I are the real thing, I've already fucked with the audio on Sweet Caroline's footage from the night she unexpectedly showed up.

I shouldn't have to dupe my friends. Yet, I don't put it past them to snoop and I'm sick of the petty barbs. Settling down isn't for me. Nobody would put up with me asking why they didn't step out on their wives and girlfriends to sample a variety of pussy. It's a double standard.

With two hands, I grab Paisley by the chin, diving between her sweet lips. Sucking on her tongue. We're both panting when I pull back. Her body stretched to the limit from the inequity of our height, she has to drop her heels to the floor. I'm a bastard who gets off for the second time that she's chased me, not wanting the kiss to end.

"I'll see you tonight at Sweet Caroline's. Lock up and come by."

"I can't. Greer from Mind Your Own Beeswax invited me to go to yoga." She brushes a flop of hair off my forehead and scowls. Paisley sees the gears turn as if there is a window into my brain. "No Jake. No. Greer has been through enough. Everything anyone would want to know about her is public record, anyway."

"You're adorable defending people. Your nose does this scrunchy thing."

"It's called unveiled disgust." Paisley's unwillingness to pull punches makes me laugh.

I run my knuckles over her bare arm. We both watch the gooseflesh appear. Her lips press to a thin line. Paisley's fighting the way I make her body react.

I'm freaking enjoying every minute of turning her on, my latest hobby.

"Afterward then," I say, unwilling to argue. She can have an ally. "It's important we're finally seen around town."

"At a strip club?"

"At my place of business." I've given Paisley all the pretend time and space she's getting. "I'm done hiding for Laughton's sake. Don't keep me waiting."

I'm behind the bar with one eye trained on the ticking clock when the bouncer lets Paisley through the door. She stands timidly beyond the tables where my customers sit, cautious of the men facing forward. Lucky for Paisley, my clientele won't bother looking back. She isn't the only one leery of being caught at Sweet Caroline's.

Paisley clutches her wristlet by her thigh. She hasn't changed out of her workout gear. When she shifts her weight, attempting to look anywhere but at the dancer performing, the light from the stage glints off of the anklet I put on her. *Good Girl. Some battles I'll fight you for. Others I'll fight for you. Learn the difference.* Light pink yoga leggings cling to her calves. The tone of the second skin is so close to her own. Without the backlighting from the parking lot, the thick sweatshirt covering her ass seems like the only thing she's wearing. A racerback bra rounds her neck and the wide collar of the sweatshirt falls off her shoulder.

Dear fucking god, I'm going to see bits and pieces of this woman before I ever get a glimpse of her tits.

I'm positive Paisley didn't dress for me. If she thought I found this the least bit sexy, she'd have worn a cardboard box.

I'd accept the soft invitation to peel that top off and touch her if I wasn't raised around women who, through their harrowed experiences, taught me better. The choke of fear is real. Stopping doesn't require a scream, a slap, or a shove. Consent is a thousand yeses and understanding the body language of a single no. Confused? Ask.

Serving guests overpriced alcohol is what makes me the most money. The dancers attract the guests to Sweet Caroline's. And, while the club is unruly at times, my patience is always thinnest for those who consider hurting my bottom line.

Paisley brings a hesitant thumbnail to her mouth.

My instructions were to be here, not where to find me. The club has a decent crowd this evening. If I wasn't expecting her, Paisley's appearance tonight might become inconsequential. My newer entertainers cater to a diverse group. During my dad's day, beautiful ladies in the audience were a rarity. Nowadays? Anything goes.

She's safe, so I let my plaything stumble, insecure, a little longer. I relish witnessing the honest expressions morphing over Paisley's face and her body language. Then I bark at Kelsey over the din of thumping music and shouted drink orders. My new manager takes over the rest of the bar and I rescue the doe before the troublesome strobe lights and the next act overwhelms her.

I lace my fingers into hers. Caught unaware, Paisley hedges, pulling away until she notices it's me. I'm graced with a tentative smile, and I touch her cheek, appreciating how pretty Paisley is. She's flushed from her workout, and me putting her in an uncomfortable position.

Pausing the natural inclination to lean forward to capture her mouth, I'm suddenly possessive of

Paisley's reactions when we kiss. Her lips move in anticipation. I want mine on hers. But not in the center of the floor with all my customers able to watch.

We weave in and out of tables, taking the most direct route to my office down the back hall. Possession being nine-tenths of the law, it has the added effect of ensuring my patrons know Paisley is with me.

Pro-tip I picked up on from the shackled and enslaved: Trig planted his ass at my bar when he and Kimber started dating. Initially bad for my bottom line as Kimber was my weekend headliner, it wound up being a boon for her. A lot of her usual stalkers were quick to realize they were out-obsessed.

I close the door to my office and push Paisley against it. Her head bumps into the wood. Bending at the knees, I come up under to taste her. It's swift and short compared to any of our other kisses. Her guarded features are disconcerted, as if she worried this wouldn't happen. Machismo aside, I don't know why Paisley likes it when I kiss her, but she does, and I enjoy taking full advantage. Our lips meld and the magnetic attraction is the polar opposite of what you'd expect from someone who was planning on getting married less than two weeks ago.

Gavin's loss is my short-term gain.

"Is there a camera in here?" she whispers.

I nod. The entire club has security. Minus the restrooms, the dressing room, and a couple of hidden areas out back that a select few know the camera angles of. It's rare that I cut off the office feed. Mostly when Carver and I meet or Trig and I are talking shop.

"Can you turn it off so we can talk?"

Her request is a lot nicer than mine was this afternoon, making it easy to oblige.

"Do you expect me to be here a lot?" she settles onto the leather couch, tucking her legs up under her bottom.

"Are you asking for a schedule? Mondays, Wednesdays, and Fridays. The occasional bank holiday… I'm kidding," I say when Paisley rapidly blinks. "I hate being here." I sit on the cushion next to her.

"Then why are you here?"

A knock on the door interrupts before I can answer. I snap, "who is it?", and shake my head derisively when the bouncer takes it to mean he should enter.

"A group of college kids came in. Kelsey's slammed. She needs your help. The waitresses aren't serving quick enough."

Simultaneously slicking a palm over my scalp, I place my other palm on Paisley's thigh. The desire to touch her is ever-present, and I don't want Paisley aware of my weaknesses. With practiced nonchalance, I use the pressure on her leg to buoy me to stand.

"You'd think I didn't have barbacks that can pitch in and pull a draught beer," I growl.

"Don't shoot the messenger, boss. When I finished checking the frat boys' IDs, Kelsey called me over to the bar. She specifically told me to go ask you to come out." The bouncer shrugs.

I've been trying to give Kelsey the benefit of the doubt, but my new manager isn't as great as my old one. Kelsey can manage the bar or the strippers, but not both at the same time. On busy nights when the dancers get in a snit, I'm slinging hooch because the bar needs coverage. On slow nights, I'm filling glasses, too, since my other option is sitting around waiting for things to implode.

I don't dislike Kelsey. She's just no Holly, and it's

pissing me off that I fired Holly for her own benefit. No different from it rankling my nerves when Holly decided to take all of her fucking accrued vacation time when she started dating Cass. Holly might not have been a Kimber, but Kelsey depends on me showing my face at Sweet Caroline's, and she needs to get over it.

Chapter Eight

Paisley

He left!

Up and went.

No "I'll be back, Paisley."

Not a single word.

Jake closed the office door without a backward glance.

I sit on the couch, stunned and fuming at how rude this man is. I stood flustered in the theater, where I'm positive he watched to see what I'd do because the con artist who appeared in my store gave me no choice other than to show up to a strip club.

He may have kissed me, multiple times today, the same way the Jake I drank rum with did, but this Jake is a class-A jerk. It's clear whatever idiotic, romanticized thoughts that raced through my mind between when he pushed me up against the door and sitting down on this sofa were complete figments of my imagination. So, I'm glad I didn't shower after yoga and change into something nicer.

I own my own business. I get that emergencies

crop up. However, the bar is not on fire. And if it was, I would hope that Jake would mention where the emergency exit was, instead of acting like it's every man for themselves. Now I don't know who I hate more. Me for being the bitch with the audacity to ditch the genuine and handsome groom at the altar. Or Jake, the big brooding asshole, who doesn't have the courtesy to tell me when he's returning.

The minutes tick by with me expecting he'll pop back in and apologize. By the half-hour mark, I have nothing better to do than get sucked into a fast and furious text exchange with a bridesmaid at my wedding that didn't happen. She's the daughter of my mother's friend who's messages I've been avoiding. What the heck is a girl supposed to say to someone who is mad that they didn't stand up for you at your wedding? I might not have done the calling it off thing correctly, but I'm beginning to believe our guests would have preferred I marry Gavin just to divorce him next month. They're offended that I ruined their night out and an expensive, yet free-for-them, meal. Have they considered it was actually Gavin's Valentine's Day that I wrecked... Likely in perpetuity, but that might be giving myself too much credit.

Someone actually told me returning the gift they bought to the store was a hassle. Meanwhile, someone else commented that at least I had the decency not to steal the check from the personalized Mr. & Mrs. wedding card box and cash it.

That's what people think of me and, though a few weeks isn't enough for it to blow over, the negativity is getting as old as sitting on my ass waiting for Jake to reappear.

Do people not understand I'm doing a bang-up job of beating myself over the head about how wrong I was to let the wedding planning get as far as it did?

In all actuality, they don't because Gavin caught me *kissing* Jake Ballentine!

My split-second decision turned me into a two-timing fraud.

I'm so mixed up that I'm actually looking for validation from a con man because we shared a few toe-curling kisses.

Get a grip, Paisley. The attraction is all in your head. Jake's not popping a foot when *you* kiss *him.*

Angry, I zip my cell back into the wristlet and shove it to the side. About to storm out of the office to find out where Jake is, I glance up at the security camera. I see the reflection of me acting foolish by sticking my tongue out in the mirrored wall. It's papered with flyers advertising old performers. Then I remember Jake turned the camera off. I'm glad that the almighty Jake Ballentine didn't capture evidence of me being immature when I've been plenty patient staying put.

I could've beelined for the rear exit. Unless it's a trick and Jake didn't turn off the feed? Or Jake has more cameras hidden in here than he let on? Either option doesn't make a hill of beans difference, since Jake knows where to find me if I disappear.

Opening his desk drawer, I make a big deal of cramming my wallet in and slam it shut. I march to the door, intending on slamming that behind me too. However, I can't storm into the hallway.

Engaged in a heated discussion, Kelsey and a dancer block my escape.

"Fine. Kimber and Holly were in sync. I know I'm not either of them, but if you'd at least try to work with me, we can figure it out." I overhear the end of Kelsey's plea. Her eyes widen seeing me. The other woman rolls hers and makes a derisive "flavor of the month" comment about me under her breath. Something about high society serving vanilla.

I squeak a polite "excuse me" and move down the hall to where it opens up to the theater. There are a lot more people at Sweet Caroline's than there were when I got here.

Standing at the entrance of the open space, Jake is visible behind the bar. He's so tall it makes him hard to miss. He's swift at the pour. Bottles come off the shelf as fast as they get replaced. I lean against the wall, watching him fill multiple trays. Cocktail waitresses carry them to awaiting patrons at the small round tables close to the stage, and the process starts again. He barks over the head of a person helping him pull beers to the guy who came in to tell Jake that Kelsey needed help. Yes, the crew needs him behind the bar to keep things running smoothly. Yet, they aren't so busy that Jake needs to take out his frustration on anyone.

"I'm sorry. I didn't mean to bother him, or you. At least I had backup half of the time before Jake forced Holly to quit." Kelsey is at my elbow.

"Why would he do that?" I ball my fists.

"Got me. Sometimes it's like Jake is in constant reaction mode. Like he doesn't think things through… I, ah, I'm sorry, again. I shouldn't have said that. Not after ruining your night together." Kelsey sounds fearful that I'll tattle on her.

I scoff. "Don't apologize. The night wasn't so great before."

Jaw set, Jake decides to look up at that moment. Irritation pours out of his pores.

Kelsey steps forward, and I sling my arm through hers.

"Wait. Let him swing."

The thing is, Kelsey needs help. Real help. I'm appalled that Jake is unwilling to do more than get angry at her.

"What? No. I might not be as good a manager as

Holly or Kimber were, but I need this job."

"Why were they good at it?"

"Kimber was a dancer first, so I'm going with experience and she'd earned their respect. Plus, according to everyone, she and Hol were a team. The dancers who tested Holly's reserve when Kimber left didn't last. The ones who stayed also waited until Holly's shift and went to her when they had a problem. If Holly couldn't fix it, then she forced Jake to. Holly could literally yell at him and got away with it. It's only been a few weeks since she's been gone. But now the dancers go to Jake to complain about me when I've already been to him with their concerns that I can't manage on my own. But he doesn't budge." Kelsey shrugs. "I'm trying my best, but it's like they ran out of chocolate cake for dessert and all they have left to serve is banana pudding."

"I like banana pudding."

"You would." Kelsey lets out a nervous laugh. Jake is shooting dirty looks in our direction.

I get the impression the poor girl is walking on eggshells, as concerned about losing her job for poor performance as she is about spouting off to Jake to step up the way previous managers had no issue doing.

"I get what you are saying, though. When Holly left, they lost a confidante, an advocate. And so did you."

"Yup. And Jake tells each employee what they want to hear, but solves none of the problems. So then I get double-whammied when nothing gets fixed."

"Come on." Our elbows interlocked, I tug Kelsey toward the office.

"Where are we going? Jake is expecting—"

"Too much out of you. So you're going to tell me what you need and I'm going to take care of it."

My business mentality refuses to let my employees

swing in the wind. I can't accept that Jake does. If Kelsey hadn't approached me, I wouldn't have known about the former managers' stiff backbones.

Since Jake intends to use my disappearing act against me, I plan to do the same with whatever I learn about him. All the better if it helps Kelsey.

Back in the office Kelsey wakes up the laptop on Jake's desk and my fingers *clickety-clack* over the keyboard while she describes her job—it has a lot of moving parts—and what she feels like is missing both now and before Jake let Holly go.

Kelsey is sweet. I can see how hesitating to put Jake in his place makes her uncomfortable. She's also competent and thorough. From what I can tell, she's doing the job of one too many people.

I'm sure I have my story straight that teamwork accounted for so much of the club's success in the past several years. Though they hadn't worked together long, even Kelsey and Holly had a practical system. Except then Kelsey kicks my theory into overdrive when she comments on how Jake's friends also used to spend more time at Sweet Caroline's. In some instances, Trig, a younger man named Morgan who lives at Trig's house, and two others: Skye and Jasper, were here more often than Jake himself. But from what Jake said, most of these friends are now in committed relationships, which is how I got stuck here as the fake girlfriend.

Rooting out what details I can about Jake, I question where he was during that time and what would make him avoid his club. Kelsey looks like she wants to swallow her tongue when the man himself interrupts.

"Is there a reason you aren't out on the floor, Kelsey? I don't bring anything extra home in my paycheck when I do your job for you, and neither does my girlfriend." He cuts to the chase while staring me down for having the audacity to sit with the computer open on the desk in front of me.

"Kelsey and I were whipping up an ad for another manager. A co-manager." I lift and wiggle my fingers like I'm typing. "Thank you so much, Kelsey. I hadn't meant to keep you this long, but we have everything we need now."

Although Kelsey skitters by Jake, she leaves with more confidence than she had. I'm glad to be on her side.

Jake clicks the laptop shut. His annoyance at me for escaping the office and butting my nose into his business is evident. He presses a firm hand to the case. "I'm not hiring anyone."

"How wonderful for you. So, let me inform you of my refusal: I'm not stepping foot in your sleazy club again to sit here alone, twiddling my thumbs because you have yours stuck too far up your ass."

Everything that Kelsey mentioned about Holly getting away with yelling at Jake when he wouldn't listen swirls in my head, and his current curse-colorful grumbling spurs me on. I push a final button to see what I can get away with before Jake reminds me of the secret he's hanging over my head.

"It is almost like you want Sweet Caroline's to fail."

Less than thrilled that I'm speaking my mind, walnut-hard contours groove Jake's chin. "It's time for you to leave." His fingers curl around the bulk of my sweatshirt. Jake grips my arm, hauling me from the desk chair.

In agreement, I shove at his chest. "Do not manhandle me, you stupid giant."

He lets go, crossing his arms. We stare at one another for a beat.

"I thought I was leaving?" I quip.

"You are. But you'll be back here tomorrow night

to make up for the time we didn't get to spend together tonight."

"Face it, Jake, you're too busy and too self-centered a man to pull off having a girlfriend. No wonder why your friends have the impression that you'll never settle down in a real relationship. I don't even believe this." I motion between the two of us.

Jake shoots me a wicked grin. He bends, his mouth grazing the shell of my ear. I shiver when his lips press to my neck. "Believe whatever you want as long as you live up to your end of the bargain and act convincing."

Chapter Nine

Jake

I press my heel to the door and the thump of the music coming from the theater fades to a dull roar. Paisley is perched behind my desk. With her limbs tucked tight, she reminds me of a baby bird.

We're nearing the end of a full month that she's spent a few evenings a week at the club. I leave her sequestered in here often to prove the point that I get to do whatever I want. Sometimes Paisley stays put. Other times she goes out onto the floor and makes friends with my employees to prove the point that she gets to do whatever she wants. But what she's doing by making casual appearances in the club is exactly what I need her to do. I mean, how smart would it be to lock Paisley away so that no one sees my girlfriend and me in public?

She's gotten so used to being here that she doesn't seem appalled by what happens on stage. Though, I've seen her blush when a dancer has taken a guest behind a curtain. Her innocence is adorable, in as much as I have something extra to tease her about.

Tonight Trig is dropping in. All Paisley has to do is hang on me while we say our goodbyes. Something she's proven adept at in the past, so Trig gets a good show.

I drop a water bottle on the desk for Paisley and place a rum and coke on a paper coaster for myself.

"Thank you." Paisley is polite without glancing up from the word puzzle she's playing on her phone.

We engage in all sorts of games. This particular one is my second favorite, right after kissing Paisley until she's panting and then sending her home like nothing happened. The manic glimmer in her eyes when I pull away makes me positive that someday soon she'll go for my jugular and kill me for the number of times I've turned her on and then doused the flames.

That might put me out of my misery, too. I can't say pretending with Paisley is easy—I've taken my cock in my fist to work off some aggression—but having her around is entertaining.

Paisley ignores me for her cell and her water bottle for my rum and coke. I never stop her from sipping out of my drink. She gets off on the little power trip. She thinks she's driving me nuts since all she ever asks for is water, but I've compiled a collection of snide remarks.

"Don't hesitate to drink it all on my account, *corazón*."

"I won't." The corners of her lips lift, though she's trying to hide her smile from me. Paisley tips her forehead to the laptop. "Another response to the co-manager position came in while you were gone."

Ah, that's it. Paisley isn't a bird. She's the cat that ate the canary.

My pretend girlfriend thinks she's winning the new-hire argument since I allowed her access to the laptop Kelsey uses to schedule the staff. None of my unscrupulous activities are on this computer. Nor is it like I've given Paisley unfettered access to club business. In actuality, I told her to place the ad because I needed her distracted on an evening when some unexpected business cropped up.

I kick the rolling chair away from the desk with my wingtip and scoop Paisley up under the knees. Her shriek ends in an *oomph!* when I unceremoniously drop her ass onto the leather sofa. Then I sit in the spot she occupied, while she tries to keep the Cheshire smirk off her face. Sliding the desk chair back into place, I'm smug when I click on the notification and launch the program.

But my presumption that I can skim and click delete fades when I pull up the message and wind up focusing on reading it through a second time with ice in my veins.

"So?" Paisley can't bite her tongue any longer.

"They're from California. Clear across the country. I'm not paying for relocation expenses. And it's a man. The dancers here might take issue." I frown. If Paisley didn't think I was being picky about candidates before she will now.

The other applicants have restaurant and bar management qualifications, but none have had experience in entertainment, let alone adult entertainment.

"You're a man." She jumps up and walks behind me to scan the resume over my shoulder.

Paisley is relentless about treating my employees fairly. I know her well enough now than to close out the window before she can peek. So I stretch, looping my arms over her neck, and tugging her closer. If I have to endure this, I might as well get the chance to touch her.

This time Paisley's squeal is excitement. "Jake, this guy is an assistant manager at a club on the Sunset Strip! They have similar experience to what Sweet

Caroline's needs. If he's dealing with the demands of bands and producers, then strippers can't be that hard."

"That's what you think. Strippers make *everything* hard. It's in their job description," I wisecrack.

"*Ugh!* You had an assistant manager before. I heard Holly was a flight attendant before taking her role here. *Hmm...* Although, I suppose that gave her the wherewithal to handle handsy men." Pais leans to the side. In my peripheral vision, her fingertips on one hand lock together with the emphasis of a five-star chef describing a dish. "This person is per-fect-ly qualified. Why are you being such a pain in the ass and dragging your feet over hiring extra help?"

Paisley goes back to leaning on my shoulders. Reaching forward she slides the contents of the screen up and down.

Telling Paisley I don't want to hire anyone sounds priggish and cheap. I'd give my left nut to have two full-time managers. But the only people I'd hire are the women who made this place worthwhile for me to show up to. When I bothered to show up, since they always had everything under control. Kimber and Holly aren't coming back. Not that I blame them.

Okay, I blame them outwardly, but on the inside? Given the chance, I'd escape this place, too. I've only stuck around because Sweet Caroline's keeps Caroline—my mother—living the dream. I'm responsible for running the club to make up for the shit my dad pulled that ruined my parents' marriage. I'm the last person anyone would accuse of being a martyr for doing what was right. It also doesn't mean I like the lot life threw me. I fucking hate it because I literally learned to fucking walk crossing that stage. I had bigger plans than to bum around Sweet Caroline's my entire life.

I flex my hand, curling my fingers, and bouncing an

imaginary weight. The palm falls up and empty. "Want the job? I'll hire you."

"Not at all," she scoffs.

"Well, that sucks, being you are the most qualified candidate."

"Me?" She motions to her clothes. "The girls on the floor wear skimpier outfits."

Paisley must not have gone to yoga today since she is wearing ripped blue jeans and a sleeveless navy halter with a gray cardigan over it to ward off the March chill. She has her hair pulled up the way it was when we met, but not as fancy. I don't particularly like it this way. However, when she moves, the sweater exposes the smallest amount of skin between her neck and her collarbone. So, I guess I can live with it.

I wish the top had a keyhole view of her cleavage. Pais has great boobs. Full and lush, I'll admit I've pressed her chest closer to mine to feel them through the layers of fabric separating us.

Sweet Caroline's has a dressing room filled with G-strings and pasties. I can change Paisley's outfit in a heartbeat. Yet, right now, I like how my *girlfriend's* covered-up, sexy style allows my imagination to ponder over the entire reward of finally getting her naked. Meanwhile, I can still believe no other man is looking at her like she's one of the dancers when she's in the theater.

"It's not what you wear, it's how you wear it. What I really mean is, if you're stuck with me, at least I'd want to be here if you were here." Paisley is becoming one of the few people I can stand being around for extended periods of time.

"Okay, that was the weirdest backhanded compliment. Plus, you wouldn't have to be here as much if you had another manager."

"I'd love *coming* here, though." I bat my lashes the

way the flirty girl did at Paisley's boutique.

She snorts, covering her face. We agree the pickup line was awful. I lace my fingers into hers and drag her onto my lap. Our faces are close and, about to kiss her for no reason other than I can, there's an odd lightness in my chest.

We're interrupted when a bouncer cracks the door to tell me. "Trig Avery is waiting at the bar for you."

Have mentioned I hate interruptions? They mess with life's best-laid plans.

"Have him hold tight. We'll be out in a few minutes." I tap Paisley's hip to get her off of me. "That is your cue to go."

She rolls her eyes. "Why insist I even come tonight, Jake?"

"Because you're easy to tease and easy to talk to, Paisley. Which takes a load off of my shoulders while getting to know you so that my rat bastard friends stop hounding me about needing what they have. And look," I check my watch. "Tonight you're off the hook early. All you had to do was be your beautiful, cranky self."

"If I'm cranky, then you are stubborn. It's like you want us to be doomed to be stuck here when we don't have to be." She half whines-half sighs, exasperated.

"Us, huh? Where else would we go?" I cock a brow, adding with my best bedroom voice. "Give me a kiss and I'll ditch Trig and take you there right now."

"There's nobody watching."

"Pais, there's always someone watching." My eyes flick to the security camera.

"I think it's you." She mouths, finger pressed to a button on my shirt. "You go back and watch the recording to see if I'm using your computer to snoop."

"Are you snooping? Or after I shut the door, does the music seep into your bones and make your body writhe the way it does before you come undone? I'd pay good money for a private show, *corazón*. If I peeked at the videos, would you be dancing? I've seen you sway to the music when I've been covering the bar."

Redness seeps from under her halter top. Paisley's face flushes. I've made her uncomfortable. It's my favorite part of seeing how far I can push her.

"Do you want the position or not?" I ask, running a knuckle over her throat and around to the base of her skull, unclipping the barrette securing her hair.

She shakes her head. Golden brown locks tumble down. Have I mentioned I fucking hate her hair up? And that I love the way she arches catlike into my touch when I massage her scalp?

Her cheek brushes against my bare forearm and, knowing where it could lead, I want her to flick her tongue out of her mouth and taste my skin.

Paisley is as easy as any other woman who I've sat on my lap. And yet, not by a long shot. Because for all of our chemistry and banter, I've never dared kiss her while her ass hovers over my groin. And I've never had her body move against mine quite like this.

I glide my hands down her sides and use them to root her in place. My hips grind up out of instinct. Her little surprised moan is pure torture. I have to put an end to what's happening. My ego needs Paisley's secret more than my cock needs the satisfaction of being inside of hers. Even if I never use what Pais is hiding, even if she eventually confesses to Laughton, knowing it first means I'll still win over her ex.

Paisley

Jake's palm presses on my hips. Not for the first time, dampness seeps between my legs. He has me warm and flushed. I shimmy on his lap, uncomfortable with the arousal.

"Stop moving, Paisley, or in between appearances tomorrow, my headline act is teaching you the proper way to give a lap dance."

My eyes go wide and I stiffen at Jake's remark. My wiggling has had an effect on him. He bares his white teeth when he laughs, pretending like there isn't massive wood poking into my ass.

I need to stop acting like a cat in heat whenever we are close. I shove Jake's chest for being rude. He catches my hands, clutching them together between our bodies.

"Kiss me and I'll consider this guy's application." Jake puckers his lips and I give him a peck… on the cheek.

Because I've had a cold bucket of water dumped on my head and it's brought me to my senses.

Again.

Although the moment of lucidity doesn't answer the burning question, does it? What about this man has made me lose my mind since I... Well, since I put on that white wedding gown and lost my ever-loving mind?

I'm spending far too much time trapped in Jake's castle. I've tried to persuade myself that pissing him off is a fun way to pass the hours and that the back and forth, bantering over made-up and petty disagreements, are me bartering for my eventual freedom. However, my increasing attraction to a man who holds me captive is confusing.

"I'd pay good money for a private show, corazón." That's what Jake said to get me all worked up. Panting like I'm desperate to be fucked, when we both know the reality of this situation is I already am.

It's not even me trying to keep Jake away from my secret anymore. It's that sometimes I want affection from Jake that proves we are what we aren't and it's obvious he's using my weakness to his advantage.

My gut twists with disgust over the same comment that he'd pay to see me on stage. I worry about what that would look like. If he'd force me to dance for him the way he makes me show up at his bar. There have also been a few times that I've caught parts of a performance, wondering about the audition process, and how Jake chooses who makes it on stage. Could *vanilla* me take off my clothes with any sense of talent the way his strippers do? Would I be confident in my body? Does he get off on those dancers' flawless skin? Do their gyrating hips, and the snap turns they make when they strut in those sky-high heels, and not much else, turn him on? Has he ever touched one of them?

Would he want to touch me?

Not the way Jake insists on taking down my hair

when I've expended a lot of effort to get it up in a twist or how he clutches a hand like I'm an unruly toddler or even the way he cups my chin, angling for access to my mouth, demanding I play my part.

Dear lord, being around Jake is demoralizing. I can only hope he follows through with ending this deal and sets me free after another four and a half months. Although, I can't say I trust he will.

Jake lifts me up and drops me to my toes, following along by standing himself.

"Get your stuff. Trig is waiting. I plan to get out of here early tonight if I can." His voice is gruff, but Jake holds out his hand, expecting me to lace my fingers into his and assume the role of adoring—albeit idiotic for choosing him—girlfriend.

I need to book an appointment with a chiropractor for the whiplash he gives me.

In the theater, Trig is planted on the barstool he favors. I've noticed he's okay with engaging the customers, and cordial to the dancers, but ignores them on stage. I have a higher regard for him than some of the other people who come here. Okay, the men. Trig isn't stepping out on his wife, who is someone I know, and perhaps that's why it makes a difference. Although, I've had to mentally assess why I'm okay with the women who come to Sweet Caroline's to watch the shows, yet a man's intentions still feel shady.

Hello, hypocrite. Haven't I watched out of curiosity? I mean, it was morbid curiosity to start. But still, people in glasshouses shouldn't throw stones.

"Hi, Paisley. How are you doing?" Trig asks when we're nearly beside him.

"I'm good," I say over the music. "Thankful that you're taking this brute's attention so that I can go home and get some rest. The late nights are later than I'm used to, especially when I have to be up in the morning for my own shop." I mock-yawn, turning to glance up at Jake with a sugary smile.

His jaw ticks and he moves me almost into his body while Trig and I exchange pleasantries.

"I'm sure it's different. Kimber and I planned our schedules around this place. Now getting up with the twins at two in the morning seems like cruel and usual punishment."

"How are they? How is Kimber? I haven't seen her in a while."

"Everyone's great. Aidy says you're at Baked Beans every now and again," he remarks of his adult stepdaughter.

She and her boyfriend, Morgan—I was so excited to connect that dot!—live with them, and Aidy is a barista at the pastry shop.

"Aidy mentioned spotting someone else there." Trig mocks Jake.

"It's time for you to go." Jake grits out, manhandling me toward the entrance.

Kelsey waves the rag she's using to polish the bar. "Are you leaving, Paisley? Thanks for the extra hand behind the bar earlier."

"Me? I was more of a hindrance than a help! But it was really fun learning to mix drinks." I'd arrived at Sweet Caroline's during a lull and when I asked Kelsey how the gun thingy that shoots soda worked, she gave me a tutorial before Jake whisked me away.

Like he is now.

"Have a great night, Miss Cooper." The bouncer who interrupted us holds the exit open.

"You too!" I call over my shoulder, wiggling my fingers.

Jake scowls, escorting me out of the club under a possessive and watchful eye.

Seriously, what am I doing wrong by being nice to

people?

At my car, Jake opens the driver's side. He holds me by the elbow, stopping me from tucking into the seat. "You forgot something." Jake ducks his head.

I turn mine so that he misses. Jake's typical goodnight kiss in the lamplight lands on the corner of my mouth, though my lips react as if they want the heat from his against them.

He grunts, lifting a light brow and his shiny teeth make Jake resemble a vampire rather than a Norse God. "Not amused, *corazón*."

"Sorry, for a second I forgot I was around for your amusement," I lie. The truth is smack dab in my face. This man doesn't like me. He uses me.

Jake grabs my chin, but instead of kissing me, he grumbles, "Drive safe." Which makes me codfish since no one is around to hear that kind of sentiment.

In the rearview, Jake stays in the Sweet Caroline's lot until my car takes the left turn at the stoplight down the street.

I'm exhausted when I arrive at home, but flip-flop in bed, unable to empty my mind of the muddled thoughts zipping through it.

I should confess to Gavin and accept that the best-case scenario is he would have taken me back. Except that's among my worst fears. The best-case scenario now is that Gavin uses my perceived selfishness to turn me into a bigger fool. I can only pray that his reaction would fall somewhere in between.

I should concede that what's best for everyone else is best for me, too. But my heart breaks along with a damn of tears, unable to convince myself that's true. A tiny fissure takes root, widening my ribs and stealing my breath when I realize that telling Gavin also means facing an uglier truth. One I'd rather not accept.

If Jake has no power over me, I lose these nights

with people around to talk to. I lose him.

This complete asshole has threaded his way into my life in a matter of weeks. Unlike the demands of being the perfect couple, Jake and I fake our inadequacies without effort. Perhaps it's because the space we occupy when we are together isn't much larger than my kitchen and, other than Jake's employees and Trig a few times, no one actually invades our space. My demands of Jake drive him to negotiate. He never settles unless I fight back. And when I fight back, he does things like pushing me up against my car and kissing me goodnight the way that I refused to kiss him tonight.

I'm so fucked.

Because I let him.

I expected it.

And I would have driven home disappointed had he not tried.

Exhausted from lack of sleep, and frankly, with myself, I choke down a handful of vitamins and supplements in the morning. Then I stare into the mirror at the bird's nest that my chestnut-colored hair has become from rolling against the pillow. The copper highlights appear more like gathered straw rooting out from my scalp. I'd had my hair colored before Valentine's Day and that was over six weeks ago.

I twist it up into a messy bun, toss on slouchy clothes, and confirm with my calendar that I'll be seeing my stylist in the next few days. However, the universe likes to kick a girl while she's down on herself. On my way out the door to open the shop, I get my period. I have to change my loose-fitting jeans to a higher-waisted pair that, while retaining water, makes me feel more bloated.

On the upside? All the blubbering I did over my hot-as-sin rebound guy at four am makes a helluva lot more sense. I can't take the feelings I have for Jake seriously. The gushy girly ones, anyway.

Late for work, I'm fumbling with my keys, purse, and an icky, but healthy superfood shake when Greer pops out of Mind Your Own Beeswax next door.

"Oh, hey! I was bringing you some samples." Greer holds up what resembles golden pixie sticks. They're actually straws filled with honey.

"Make sure you have enough cards on the display, too." I remind her, even though her business and mine share a common wall.

We enter the shop together. Having a similar setup, she flicks the lights on before slipping the samples into a cute miniature tin bucket that's on the same table as her scented soaps. She pumps a tester of rose lotion, checking its fullness, and spreads the small white dot on her arm. "Do you like this one?" She smells it.

"It's my favorite." She'd given me a bottle in a bridal shower gift basket and I've worn the light creamy lotion or used the bath bar ever since. I'd have to buy out her stock if she discontinues it.

"Walk with you to yoga tonight?" She confirms while I'm firing up the register.

"Yep." I can use all the namaste I can muster.

Greer and I are close in age, with me being a little older. A decade older than the "over twenty-one" I joked with Jake about when he asked my age. She and I got friendly after her store's grand opening when I suggested having samples available at Paisley's Boutique might drive some foot traffic Mind Your Own Beeswax's way. When Greer delivered them, she had a lot of curiosity about my wedding. I'd invited her because she never attended one. I suppose her not knowing what to expect benefitted me. Greer is one of the few who sat in a pew on my side of the church, who didn't respond to my escape by immediately asking for her gifts back.

"How about a rain check?" commands a solid baritone voice that sends shivers down my back and makes my achy boobs throb with temptation.

Chapter Eleven

Jake

Paisley eyes me with suspicion. Weeks' worth of experience becoming familiar with her tells, I set a decaf green tea and a brown bag from Baked Beans on the countertop.

Both women pause what they are doing. They disregard me, gaping lustily at the sack.

"He didn't? It's the chocolate croissant with cayenne. I can smell it from over here." The one that isn't mine gasps as if I've done something decadent.

I guess the bakery's baked goods are as good as the mill girls say.

Also, say that three times fast.

The petite woman that is mine opens the bag. Her expression turns carnal, pulling out the delicacy. "He did. Want to split it?"

"No. I'm going to need my own now. And definitely yoga tonight, and tomorrow." She sighs and offers an introduction. "I'm Greer. I'm over there." She points. "My store is, anyway."

"Jake," I reply.

She nods. "I'm gonna go... back..." Greer darts out of the boutique.

A master at reading people, I don't get the impression that I make her nervous. It's more adapting to social norms and the world in general.

Paisley scowls over her croissant. "I told you—"

I motion for her to stop. "I heard."

And I rooted out every detail of Greer's life, which was simple. Her accident and subsequent jail sentence made the local paper. Not to mention, Trig and Greer's boyfriend, Byron, were Army buddies. It hadn't taken more than a crass prompt about what products Mind Your Beeswax carries—it's some impressive shit you can make from bees—for Trig to give me the same abrupt and irritated speech that Paisley had; Keep your distance.

What's been complicated is learning Paisley prefers hot tea over an Americano and Thai and Indian food over burgers and pizza. I can't use Trig to scope out the subtleties of her life that he's provided in the past for other my targets whenever I've needed it. To get to know my supposed girlfriend, I've had to get to know Paisley one-on-one. So, I defaulted to what initially worked best, cornering her and caging her in.

Not like a dog. Paisley's been free to leave the office and wander the club. I've given her leeway to get friendly with Kelsey and the bouncers. The club's staff seem to like Paisley a lot. More than they like me, that's for damn sure based on their reactions to her early departure last night. Which is fine, since I like Paisley more than I do most of them, too.

After a week or two, she could have stood up to me or shaken off my requests to spend our evenings together and I would have given in. But I hadn't realized that until last night when she wiggled in my lap and groused about us never going anywhere.

Like any other woman, there are parts of Paisley

that make me hard. But far fewer women that I've softened for. The key to my survival has been keeping those women in the dark. Being a wolf in sheep's clothing has its benefits. I won't shed my wool cloak. The days are too long and the nights are too cold, even in the company of the pussy so eager to surrender to me before Paisley came along.

Paisley doesn't seem to grapple with that, though. Her prissy pouting when I asked for a kiss aside, Paisley is an anomaly. She doesn't struggle to get away when I kiss her. Nor does she reach for my cock when she's well aware our close confrontations allow her the power to do so.

Maybe I'm as inconsistent. I don't want to be her bully, but I want to push her to fight. When she does, we both win.

"Give me a bite of that." I lean my elbows on the counter so that we're at eye level.

"Not. On. Your. Life." She dives into the flaky pastry. Her eyes roll back and she moans. It's the sound I want to hear when I'm buried inside of her. "Get your own."

I grab her chin and press my lips to hers. *I've got my own. She's mine.* The chocolate my tongue laps at tastes rich and sweet and the faint burn of the chili powder brings me back to how hot our first kiss was.

"We're going out tonight to Royce's."

Paisley puts down the confection. She wipes her mouth, avoiding my eyes. "Can it be someplace else?" Her tone begs *anyplace,* but I'm not yielding about the steakhouse. We've consumed enough Pad Thai from paper cartons for a lifetime.

"Trig and Kimber are coming with us. I made reservations for four. Six sharp." I asked them after Paisley said she hadn't seen Kimber in a while.

With Paisley opening today, she's not closing. I've been keeping her up all hours of the night. There are dark circles under her light amber eyes. She can nap all afternoon and I'll still have her home before what used to be her bedtime. I thought she'd like the break from Sweet Caroline's and go out on the town. Paisley is the type to appreciate a pricy meal, and I was trying to do something nice for her. Hell, any other woman would suck my dick for dinner at the most expensive restaurant in Brighton. I wouldn't turn Paisley down if she dropped to her knees, but that wasn't my intent when I made the reservations —Something I did before even asking another couple if they could join us.

"We could stay in. I'll cook."

Her timid suggestion raises my hackles, leading me to believe that it's me she's hesitant over being seen with in public.

"For fuck's sake, Paisley. You grumbled you were sick and tired of the club. Be ready on time. And wear this." I grab the nearest item with a low neckline and thrust it at her.

She lets the dress fall to the floor and, rage flaring, beckons me with a finger. The middle one.

I step into her space. She grabs me by the chin, forcing me to bend. "I will go out and play nice with your friends. But you can go screw yourself if you think you can tell me what to wear. I am my own person, Jake Ballentine. There are things you will not take from me. And no matter what it is you think you're holding over my head, this is my last compromise if you don't stop acting like an overgrown toddler."

Molars clamped shut, I bare my teeth.

Paisley? She's giving me the sweetest fuck-off smile that's ever graced a face. Tiny as she is, Paisley's not the least bit scared of me, and the lack of intimidation she's showing is highly attractive. If this were happening in my office, those tight jeans would be around her ankles, covering the chain she still hasn't taken off. The chain binding her to me.

At that moment, a customer walks into the shop. Paisley puts on the charm, directing the customer to new items in Greer's display in the rear of the store.

"I'll see you tonight," I grit out.

She blinks as I back away. "Jake, are *you* forgetting something?"

I step forward, pecking her on the cheek like a gentleman.

"That was nice. But I meant the dress. Pick it up and put it back on the rack. Unless you plan to wear it yourself?"

I dip to a knee, snatching the garment. On my way up, my opposite hand glides over the back of Paisley's thigh, grabs onto her ass, and tears her tee out of the waistband of the tight jeans that I'm jealous of hugging her curves. My fingers tickle underneath the anchor of her bra, caressing her soft skin. The way we bicker has my entire body throbbing with the need to pull her close. But as soon as Paisley settles into that warm spot in my chest, I do what she's demanded.

I move across the floor and put the dress back on the rack, adjusting the straps so the garment hangs nicely on the hanger.

I'm hanging on by a thread. One I won't let unravel. Paisley doesn't know what she does to me and I'm not about to tell her.

"Look nice." I bumble like a jerk, who is too dense to recognize Paisley has a choice of any outfit in the store she owns.

"Don't let my size fool you. I'm a big girl. I've been to fancy restaurants before." She bites into the croissant with a smarmy smile, booting me from her shop. "Thanks for breakfast."

Hours later, I round the hood of my coupe, helping Paisley out of the car. She's wearing a lacy pink dress.

The hem in front skims over her knees. The back is longer like a train, but it only goes to mid-calf. The natural tone in her legs from all the yoga is apparent. The anklet is still there, resting above her matching heels, and allowing me to forgive that the top of the dress is, again, a high halter. I'm pretty sure Paisley chooses this style with malice, but with her hair spilling over the bare skin of her shoulders, like it would over the pillows on my bed, she's incredibly sexy.

Bouts of stiff silence have filled the ride over. It is unusual for Paisley to be impolite and she isn't normally angry with me about anything for very long. I tuck her to me, noting Paisley's head barely comes below the joint that connects my arm and upper torso and the exceptional contrast of the tone of her dress to my gray suit.

"Seeing as this is our first official date, I almost brought you flowers," I admit, attempting to chip away at the ice.

"Why didn't you?" She peers up under thick brown lashes.

"It seemed trite and the last time I chose flowers it was for a funeral. White lilies reek of death." I didn't know what kind of flowers Paisley likes and I don't want to be the fool who gets it wrong.

"I like roses in this color." She denotes the pink she's wearing. It's the same coral hue as the paisley stamped on her store's bags. I file it in my brain that coral is likely her favorite color, and she looks incredible in it.

A valet takes my key and a doorman in a white coat opens the front entrance. Trig and Kimber are waiting for us inside by the hostess stand. We don't stand there long, though the hostess thanks us for our patience while she's sat other people.

I'm ready to show Paisley a good time, order a

drink, and enjoy our night out, when it becomes apparent I'm going to need to make it a double. The other people are people we know.

"Oh my goodness, I wish someone had told us you'd be here!" Sloan hugs Kimber.

"Isn't this a coincidence?" Carver remarks flatly.

"I didn't know the group of you were social," I scoff.

Pussy whipped by my former manager, Cary watches his new wife, Holly, convince the hostess and a server to push our two tables together. "We're mixing business and pleasure. Carver is in the market for a new car."

"Carver just got a new car." I remind the group.

This is unbelievable.

A vein in my temple flares when Carver pats me on the back.

"According to my wife, it's never too early to shop," he says.

"Stop!" Sloan bats at him. "I'm only this way because you spoil me."

"You deserve to be spoiled." Carver's attitude changes on a dime. He brings the pads of her fingertips to his lips. "Min-i-van." The syllables rush out in rapid succession.

"The specs for the new Maybach SUV are intriguing. Cary could order that for me." Sloan's lips playfully twist.

"The price tag alone for that car intones hiring a driver."

"What do you think you are? You hardly let me behind the wheel as it is."

We don't get along, but despite the bait and switch from a double date to a quadruple date, I'll cop and say something nice about Sloan. Having had a great mother myself, I know she would make a great mother. The problem is, as much as deep down they both want them, neither is willing to compromise about having brats.

Everyone gives a nice greeting to Paisley, similar to the one Kimber and Trig had for her when we walked into Royce's. There's no genuine need for an introduction. Everyone is familiar with the woman posing as my girlfriend. If I have to muddle through this fiasco, at least she's here with me.

I pull the chair out for Paisley, brushing her hair over her shoulder. The eight of us wind up seated: Paisley, me, Sloan, then Carver across from Trig, Kimber, Cary, and Holly. I want Paisley on my right, protected from the jackals. My friends showing their ugly mugs' at Royce's is a setup to see if we'll slip up. However, I spend most of the time we're sipping cocktails, reconsidering the arrangement. The girls should have either taken the middle or kept the second table as their own and put the men out of their misery.

Except, I'm not miserable next to Paisley. Once she and Kimber are munching their salads, they are happy to chat solo. I'm able to keep up the conversation with Trig and hear most of what Cary is saying to my far left.

Holly has a level of contentment with her new husband. They've held hands for the duration of the meal. The constant affection strikes me as odd until I realize I'm resting my palm on Paisley's knee. Unconscious of the action, my thumb brushes the pink lace, making sure she's real.

Chapter Twelve

Paisley

Owning a clothing store, the first thing I notice is someone's appearance. Holly has on a vintage red dress with an off-the-shoulder neckline. The collar is white with red polka dots and the same fabric is inset in the pleats of the skirt. Her unique throwback style is as enviable as Sloan's is posh and Kimber's is on-trend.

"Paisley, Cary and I got an invitation to the annual hospital gala. Will you and Jake be there?" she asks.

I forget for a moment that the three ladies have been pleasant all evening. They've unwittingly welcomed me into the fold, accepting me, *er* us, the way Jake and I need them to. Still, I worry about saying something wrong that will make them dislike the Paisley I was before Jake entered the picture.

Although I'm not in a rush to answer, anxiety makes me speed up chewing on the forkful of grilled asparagus.

So far the questions directed my way have stayed pleasant.

"How's the shop?"

"Have you seen Greer lately?"

And my absolute fave from Sloan, which always starts with, *"Can I special order?*

To which I want to scream like I'm having an amazing orgasm, *"Yes! Yes! A thousand times, yes!"*

From the outside, Holly's question is innocent enough. But I should've expected the mill girls to put the squeeze on Jake's and my romantic entanglement sooner or later.

Jake, who removed his hand from my knee when the waiter served the entrees, turns away from where Holly sits at the far side of the table. He wipes his mouth on the linen napkin, places it back in his lap, and puts his hand where it rested while drinking cocktails. We swallow in unison; me thinking on my feet as Jake's pinching stare makes me feel like I've gone and done something horribly wrong.

"I actually just found mine," I lie. "It had to have slipped out of the stack of mail and... Well, long story short, with so much upheaval I'd forgotten the gala was coming up, so Jake and I haven't compared calendars."

I smile at Jake, playing my part in this charade. While I'm certain he's aware I'm fibbing, softness washes over the usual stoicism. His flat brows that never give away a hint of incredulity relax. I wouldn't have noticed the slight change in his features had I not spent so much time with him recently.

"I hope you can make it," Holly chimes back in. "This is my first year, obviously. But Sloan's been invited a bunch of times."

"I go every year," I say for Jake's benefit, though skipping the back-tie soiree this year is much more palatable.

My mother invited me as a stand-in the first time I attended. My father was sick. The following year, the hospital held the event in honor of my dad. And the year after that, one of my dad's colleagues introduced me to Gavin. Which means Gavin will be there.

It's already proving impossible to avoid the things my ex-fiancé and I did together for the rest of my life. But how do I walk into the ballroom with my head held high? How would I feel if Gavin brought a date, flaunting another woman in front of a crowd of my colleagues so close to our breakup?

"Carver sends his regrets when our invite comes," Sloan tells Holly.

"They don't miss us as much as they'd miss our donation to the cardiology research center," Carver cuts in. "But where your friends expect they are going, we can as well."

The food in my stomach rolls, and a sour taste fills my mouth.

The men seated around us at the table would do anything for their wives. Gavin would have, too... mostly. His department at the hospital needs that money. There are times I felt like Gavin's arm candy. That my presence sweetened the deal right before donors pulled out their checkbooks. However, there are patients depending on the generosity of others toward cardiac research.

Going will make my mother happy. It will make Holly happy. I'll be happier if Carver attends and his contribution is larger than usual, which is awful to admit but entirely honest. But will Jake consenting to go for my sake, the way I've envied while watching his friends dote on their wives, make Jake happy? Or would Jake decide to go to one-up Gavin? Or worse, for a bigger opportunity to line his pockets by sniffing out dirt on Gavin's colleagues?

"Paisley?" Jake looks at me like I've missed something someone has said.

"We'll go if you're free," I blurt, all of a sudden

feeling more caged than a captive animal. "I ah—If you'll excuse me, I'm going to powder my nose!"

Jake stands along with me. His mammoth knuckles brush against my arm. "*Corazón?*" His voice is low, trying to deflect attention from my wild proclamation.

My yelp sounded too loud to me, too. Pretending I'm not creating a scene is stupid to attempt. He's a freaking Viking and I'm akin to something you pluck out of the heather by its wings while chasing after a pot of gold. We're like night and day in human form. As subtle as a carnie sideshow exhibit. The lawbreaker and the good girl. *Former* good girl.

"I'm fine." My voice wavers with false bravado. I bring a hand to my throat. The back of my neck is sweating.

"I'm going as well." Kimber winks in Jake's direction, following me towards the ladies' room when I'd rather be alone.

Locking myself into a stall and leaning back against the floor-to-ceiling walls, I take a moment to recover in the bougie water closet. I find three solid things; the tiles, the awkward industrial toilet tissue roll, and the rounded lip of the wainscoting. Then three colors; porcelain white, the terracotta under my coral rose high heels, and the rich mahogany staining the wood. I control my breathing and let my lungs settle from the sharp pattern that stopped me from getting any oxygen.

I stand glued in place until I hear a flush and the sound of the door swinging on its hinges. Sloan's voice combines with Kimber's in friendly, idle chit-chat. I wait another minute with my ears perked before pretending that I've finished.

The loud swirl of water down the drain echos as I exit the stall. I wash my hands, noticing Kimber is lazing on a chaise like the one I have in the store. She must like them since it's similar to the way I've seen her sit when the mill girls shop at my boutique. It's also close to the way Jake kicks his feet up, but feminine. Her body language is far less sloppy.

Sloan, who has been admiring her reflection, twirls. "So what does he have on you?"

I glance between them blankly.

"Oh, sweetie, we're going to make this easy on you because we like you," Kimber assures as she creates space on the couch.

"And because Jake doesn't do this." Sloan fluffs her fingertips for me to sit.

"What's this?" I lower myself, playing dumb.

"He doesn't do relationships, Paisley. He doesn't do anything long-term. Jake has never once asked Trig and me on a double date. I don't even think you can consider what he does with the woman he sees dating."

My stomach tightens. I'm not dumb enough to believe that a strip club owner has turned down pussy.

"Oh—the intervention has already started! What did I miss?" Holly pushes into the small room. "Have we told her we like her yet?"

"Yes," Sloan confirms.

"Have we told her *he* likes her yet?"

"We were getting there," Kimber replies, patting my knee.

"I honestly don't know what any of you are talking about," I say firmly.

Also in the sense that I'm his fake girlfriend, Jake is supposed to like me. Except I'm not supposed to fall for a fake boyfriend the way my rebound guy has me acting like I am for his friends' benefit. If it takes a ruler to my knuckles to remind myself that Jake and I are not a thing when we are alone together, then so be it.

"He's not conning *any* of us," Sloan begins.

Damn, she's including their husbands.

"He may have started it out that way," Kimber continues.

"But as of tonight, the only person Jake is fooling is Jake," Holly concludes.

Kimber picks back up. "We agree it's cute, though. Jake telling you to order what you want, but suggesting his favorites. Offering you a sip of his drink before dinner. Touching you when he thinks none of us notices." He was hoping they'd notice. "The man has hung onto every word you've said. Hell, Trig nudged me whenever Jake deferred to you."

"Why wouldn't he? It's polite, right? I mean, why would anyone put up with someone mistreating them?"

Each time I stand up for myself, Jake backs off... Only to come to me again from a different direction, which is bothersome. However, standing my ground, it has felt as if his respect for me has increased a smidge.

Why do I want it? My subconscious trills a warning bell.

"A litany of others have gotten off on him treating them like crap as long as they got bragging rights. *Ugh,* I'm sorry I even brought that up because it's obvious Jake is special to you. Forgive me, Paisley?"

I nod, ignoring that hearing about Jake taking other women to bed makes me green. Although I can't decide if what I'm feeling is disgust or envy.

Holly removes a tube of fire engine red lipstick from her clutch. She puckers, training her heavily lined eyes on the mill girls. "From my perspective, maybe Jake's met his match?"

"Perhaps all he needed was a challenger who put him in his place." Sloan titters with sadistic glee.

"I don't understand any of this!" I blurt.

The three of them keep talking around me.

Sloan's comments are succinct. "The thing about Jake is, he wouldn't have let you get as far as the altar if he wanted you. That whole 'if you love something, set it free' ideal isn't in his makeup. Giving up on something Jake has in his possession isn't a common occurrence. He has to have it ripped from him. So, we know Jake has to have dirt on you for you to have left your fiancé."

"And we know that whatever has happened since… Well, suffice it to say, Jake's a sure thing for you, Pais." Holly grimaces. "He's going to test you, though. The things he's pulled so that the other boys wouldn't fall in love are un-freakin'-believable— especially what he did to Carver and Sloan by posting pictures of her."

"He what?" I gasp.

The other girls agree the images were awful. Sloan shrugs without apology, making me doubt she's forgiven him.

"You can't change Jake. These men never do anything they don't want to do, and they have no remorse for certain things they do. Yours especially," Kimber advises.

"Mine?"

"Jake's a hard nut to crack," Holly interrupts. "If he's really stubborn, I suggest the rum on the top shelf at the end of the bar."

"The label has a ship on it?" I query, surprised.

"One step ahead." She casts me a glowing smile. "You've got this… if Jake is who you want. However, if you can't manage the bastard, like Kimber said, good luck getting him to leave you alone."

"Why are you telling me all this?" I laugh, uncomfortable with their candor.

There are three women, shining a bright light on Jake's deepest flaws.

"Jake may be an asshole. But he's our asshole," Kimber says.

Holly adds, "In a perverse way, he loves us, too."

"Speak for yourself," Sloan chortles, but her expression softens. "Jake and I don't get along. But he is important to Carver and to my closest friends. The loyalty he's shown them makes it easier to set aside our differences."

The other two ladies' sighs make me certain that's not the case. Jake's friends are wise enough to keep him and Sloan in separate corners so that they don't duke it out. Their concern highlights all of the things I haven't learned about Jake and everything I try to ignore when I let my feeble heart take the lead.

"FYI, we actually don't expect you to answer about the blackmail. Everyone is entitled to their secrets, Paisley. We just wanted you to understand we're already on your side. Because you're good for him and, when Jake finally figures out he's in love with you, he's going to fight it tooth and nail."

Chapter Thirteen

Jake

Cary and Carver's conversation ebbs almost as soon as Holly ducks down the hall towards the ladies' room. The table grows quiet enough that my ears pick up the clinking of silverware used by the occupants of the few tables spaced away from ours in the same section of the restaurant. My friends and I regard one another, not saying what each of us is thinking: Their wives are ganging up on my girlfriend in the bathroom.

Although I'm not worried that Paisley can't hold her own with the mill girls, it still leaves a sinking sensation in the pit of my belly that Kimber, Holly, and Sloan are testing her.

Cary clears his throat. "Do you only do your own dirty work, or is what you do for hire?"

Trig sips the last of his bourbon.

I roll the ice in mine.

It's a ballsy question for such a public space. But we're all aware that Trig dug up plenty for me to blackmail Cary's father with before the shitbag kicked the bucket. Not that Cary cared then or even cares now that I could take down the man who raised him. Rex Stanton made an enemy out of Cary as a boy.

"That all depends," I reply in a bored tone.

"On what, exactly?"

"On how it affects Holly." Trig bends his head, speaking into his empty glass.

"It wouldn't. In this case, she's aware there are things I'm not telling her."

"Good for her keeping you on a tight leash," I mock.

"We trust each other."

"So who don't you… trust?" Trig bites.

"I'm working on a deal with my half-sister, Adelaide Powell. Addie did her homework on me."

"And you want to return the favor." I lean back in my chair.

Trig turns his attention to Cary. "I can handle it for you. The basics of what financials she might be hiding. The personal shit, like with your old man and where he was sticking his dick, I'm not touching. Find someone else." Trig cuts my favorite part, the potential scam, out of the mix.

My jaw ticks, enraged. Despite this, my stomach loosens when I see a light smudge of lipstick on the rim of Paisley's unfinished glass of wine. The two sensations are disparate and combined, they are uncomfortable.

Leaving Holly and Cary's wedding, I'd considered leaving my worst habits in the past. However, I revel in the power of owning secrets. It's why I infused Trig's security company with capital when he needed an investor to get it off the ground. At the outset, he'd gone to Carver, but Carver's money was tied up. I had plenty to spare and a hankering to put myself on top in this town quickly. The impetus was to save

Sweet Caroline's reputation for my mother after my father had forsaken their marriage and the business they'd built when he got arrested.

At the time, Trig merely found the various ways to investigate amusing. He didn't mind using his surveillance company as a front on an occasion when I asked him to tap into a rival's security feed. For years now, he's navigated the reaches of the dark web along with my cousin, Skye. But what once was a game has become a bother to Trig. He's bored with it, and since Rex Stanton's stroke, we've argued.

Trig wants to sell out to some conglomerate in Minnesota. I'm his investor. He should listen to me.

"I don't give a crap about Addie's personal life unless there are any sordid details that might rain down and fuck the deal."

"I'll let you know what I find." Trig knocks the table twice.

The motion alerts our server, who stops to clear plates and offers the dessert menu. By the time we spy the girls coming back from the restroom, it is as if the tangential discussion never happened.

I stand. Paisley waits to meet my eyes. She's hiding whatever has gone on during the too-long-to-be-gone gab session. The one that they've grilled her during. The corners of her lips curl up as if to assure me the ordeal wasn't awful. Paisley will reveal all on the drive home. Warmth spreads in my chest. She is about to take her spot next to me when the clip-clop of another set of heels interrupts.

"I can't believe you have the nerve to come here with Jake Ballentine!" A stony, irate woman points a dangerous finger at Paisley. My name is a curse on her vicious tongue.

Paisley cod-fishes, her face growing white and then bright red.

"You brought the man you were sleeping with

behind my brother's back to Gavin's favorite restaurant. To the place where you held your engagement party!"

I place my palms on Paisley's shoulders. She's shaking from embarrassment and the scene that the disdainful woman is creating in the swank establishment.

Paisley doesn't interrupt Gavin Laughton's sister. What she does is take every insult without defending herself or trying to explain.

How could she, though? This was my idea. I'm the one who forced her into going out to dinner with my friends at Royce's.

The good doctor's sister swipes the half-full wineglass from the tabletop. Cabernet covers Paisley's coral dress. It spatters on the floor and droplets hit the white tablecloth and stain the cuff of my shirt. The glass falls over when Gavin's sister puts it back on the table and the bell cracks.

"You think you can shatter Gavin's heart and then have the audacity to rub it in? All you've proven, Paisley, is that you're trash. Just like the whores dancing at his club."

This morning I'm the trite guy who brings flowers. All because of a three-word text from Holly.

Bring her flowers.

I trust Holly. It's me no one should trust. The only best interests I have at heart are my own. Even now when I'm making amends, it's not because it's what anyone else needs.

I usually relish the role of asshole because it means I have the upper hand. But today I'm not the pompous asshole who gets his way. I'm the remorseful one.

A heavy weight has lodged itself where Paisley lays her head when we're standing close. Or right where she would, if we stood closer more often. I don't know what to do with this feeling. The one where I let her down. The one that makes me feel like a failure for not having the innate knowledge of how to love her, when mostly what I want is for us to spend enough time eating takeout and drinking rum that eventually my girlfriend will forget who we are to one another and let me fuck her.

I pace the sidewalk outside of Paisley's garden apartment with a dozen long stem roses biting into my palm. I've gotten to the door and lost my nerve before knocking too many times to count. The buds graze my knee. Petals swipe against my jeans, falling and littering the ground. I'm ruining the delicate bouquet by holding it upside down.

But that's me, right? Jake Ballentine is the giant ice god who lifts people up by the leg and shakes them until coins fall out of their pockets. I wreak havoc on lives for entertainment's sake. I throw a monkey wrench in their destiny, to destroy their goals the same way mine were. And then I watch, amused, while they scramble to put the pieces back together.

There's satisfaction in disrupting what they've got planned out. My motives are insignificant. I'm cursed. Evil. The son of a sinner. A sinner in my own right. This Jake Ballentine is someone I never wanted to be, but it's who I became.

Forever ago, the spark ignited. Wanting to be a better man for *her* momentarily lit me up.

Charismatic.

Caring.

A charmer. That's what the dancers at Sweet Caroline's dubbed me when I was a teenager. In my youth, I believed this compliment would take me farther than it did.

Until *she* broke me by choosing *him*, snuffing the embers out.

Her decision wasn't even on a whim. Their meeting seems preordained. It hadn't mattered that I saw her first. That I'd spoken to her and encouraged her to stay. That I'd actually told her upfront that he was different. His appearance spooked other women, and I wanted their introduction to go well. For my sake. Because I wanted her to understand that he and I were close. And I wanted her.

I don't think she needed my warning at all. She saw into people's souls, and she must've seen the traces of blackness already taking root in mine.

If I hadn't encouraged her to stay, she wouldn't have met him. I wouldn't have had a backstage pass to see them fall in love, get married, and have a kid. I wouldn't have lifted as many skirts in plain view to make her aware of what sex would have been like between the two of us. Not that it made a difference. I was his friend, and out of respect for our friendship, she put blinders on for everything I did. Greedy bastard that I am, I ate up any attention she gave me, hoping she'd see me as her friend. And when that wasn't enough, I flaunted even more women in her face.

Maybe I wouldn't have driven him to the florist after their car got totaled. Or, when he couldn't speak, agreed that adding those fucking white lilies to the arrangement on her casket was fine. I'd known from the instant I saw her she was the kind of perfect that deserved the entire thing covered in roses.

But what did I really know? For years, she reappeared like an angel on every corner I turned. I'd been grieving losing her before she'd ever died. Her death wasn't the precursor to everything going to crap. That shit snowball began rolling the instant he fell in love with her. Because he'd do anything to make her happy. And since his love for her was instinctive, she glowed, happy with anything he did.

I'm still pissed about a lot that happened back then. Everything he did continues to seem above reproach. He clammed up and made me choose those reeking lilies. So now he can blame me that she didn't get roses... And where I'm burning in hell anyhow, so can she.

My indecision and pacing has brought me halfway back to my car. I spin on my heel, grinding one of the pinkish petals into the concrete, and face the apartment complex.

Paisley has cracked open the door of her unit. I see a single eye and then her whole body emerges, clad in fleece pajama bottoms and a t-shirt. She sets a hip to the frame.

"Are you going to be doing this much longer?" Her fingers walk back and forth, pantomiming my pacing. "My neighbors started texting me. You're creeping them out." She grimaces as she tightens her ponytail. Her arms cross over a form-fitting top, and she stares beyond me to where I parked my car on the road.

Paisley gets a kick out of doing that. Tempting me to look. Making me wonder how full and ripe they'd feel pressed in my palms but never giving me a view of her skin.

My obsessive thoughts of Paisley are a constant intrusion on my day. They are as flagrant as fucking a groupie in front of my friend's wife before she passed away, and as blatant as the whip-fast sting when Kimber sidelined me for Trig. The difference between the two being by the time Kimber came along, I had moved past showing my manager the dick she was missing out on. I fucked out those feelings in private. It taught me how to hide them when Holly applied for a job at the club. I kept my distance from Holly. But with Paisley? Not only can I not stay away, I don't bother trying.

The evidence is the bouquet I thrust toward Paisley because Holly says I need to make amends.

Me, the guy who previous to Valentine's Day would go full bastard and spit that what happened last night when the girls came back from the ladies' room at Royce's wasn't my fault.

"They're peach. I couldn't find coral," I grunt, hating that I have one more thing to be remorseful over.

I went to three goddamned florists whose limited selection included pastel pink or red. Finally, I had to respond to Holly's text to get a recommendation. She gave me the name of a grizzled old man who had them growing in his yard. These roses smell like her, too. Paisley, that is.

"They're beautiful. Thank you." Paisley tucks her right hand behind her back and reaches out with the left. She brings her nose close to the petals, still refusing to meet my gaze.

She's stoic but polite, speaking to me the same way she'd spoken when I'd picked her up and driven her to the restaurant for our date. I'll go as far as to say she's ashamed of our association and what I've forced her into. Laughton's sister intended to humiliate Paisley with her rant, so I'm not sure why I expect a different reaction from my girlfriend. But it rankles me, nonetheless. The only reason Paisley should be thinking about Gavin Laughton is the same one I have. Had Paisley not run, then she wouldn't be mine. But maybe that's exactly what she is thinking...

Paisley should run away from me.

Chapter Fourteen

Paisley

"I want you to know that, when you refused to go to Royce's, I should've asked why you hadn't wanted to go there."

My lips twist. Trying to avoid the Nordic God from seeing my eyes water, I pretend the herringbone pattern of the sidewalk pavers is interesting.

Apologies don't come easy for Jake, so I didn't expect he'd flat out say he was sorry. He's not especially great with sympathy or empathy either. I watched when one of his overwhelmed dancers cried recently. His reaction was annoyance surrounding dealing with any "bullshit".

Yes, that's what he called it.

And yes, it's on their behalf.

Except whatever emotion someone else's troubles evoked from Jake, they washed away the instant the dancer left Jake's office.

Out of sight, out of mind.

And that's what I thought happened when Jake's car pulled away from the curb after he brought me home last night.

That Gavin's sister's tirade didn't affect him. It only affected me.

I mean, Jake can buy a new white button-down. I have, *had,* one favorite dress that's ruined. The red wine stains haven't come out of the delicate lace no matter how long it has soaked or how gentle I scrub.

Overnight I laid in my bed, awake for hours and angry. I hadn't stood up for myself and told Jake I wouldn't go to the restaurant Gavin chose to celebrate our engagement. Although Gavin's sister's lack of maturity aggravated me, and I was perturbed Jake hadn't defended me.

I'm supposed to be acting like Jake's girlfriend. Even doting fake boyfriends defend their girlfriends, right?

All eyes on us—including the aghast looks from the mill girls—Jake merely escorted me in my sopping dress out of Royce's, telling Trig they'd square up the bill later. The whole sordid scene seemed to prove Sloan's theory wrong.

This man doesn't hold any affection for me.

He has feelings of self-preservation, which includes avoiding unnecessary attention, for himself.

Staring at the dashboard when he dropped me off, Jake didn't even lean in and force a kiss. For show or not, it's rare he doesn't kiss me anymore. I hate that I've come to rely on how reassuring his touch is. I got out of the car, muttering a simple, "goodbye". It hardly felt like we'd spent the past months becoming acquainted to enable us to pass off our relationship as real. The rideshare driver on Valentine's Day was friendlier.

And now Jake is standing on my doorstep with soft petaled peach roses that have deeper coral tips, appearing contrite. I'm stunned he went out of his way to try to find my favorite. His thoughtfulness adds to my cluelessness over what to think about the past twenty-four hours. My neighbors were curious why skinny Thor was pacing outside. Coming up with a response has me embarrassed all over again.

How long am I supposed to continue this charade? The one that makes me not only look like a cheater to the entire town of Brighton, but a woman who can't hold down any relationship. Rumors spread like wildfire. It seems anyone who was in the boutique yesterday or peeking out their windows this morning believes that Jake and I are in the middle of a fight. A big one at that.

Thank you, social media, for once again headlining my personal life on my business's page.

"Don't cry." Jake uses the tone Gavin had when my ex did something heinous. It has a crackling edge that denotes, "It's my fault". This makes me wonder if Jake knows how bad things are for me and how genuine his concern is.

My fake boyfriend steps into my space, cupping my cheek. I sigh into his touch, wanting something, though I'm not sure what it is. I allow him to tilt my brown eyes to his icy blue ones. They are softer today, more like the sky. I swallow and the action sends tears tumbling over his thumb.

I huff at my weakness and inability to follow his order, sliding a foot behind me, inside of the threshold. Jake wraps his arm around my waist, tugging me to his chest. My fist gets trapped between us and the roses. The cellophane crinkles.

"You're going to crush the flowers if you aren't careful," I protest, feeling guilty that his hug absorbs my anguish.

"If they wither, I'll buy you a dozen more." His fingers thread behind my ear, into my hair. Jake kisses the crown of my head the way he did the night I ran to him.

I mean, the night I ran away from Gavin.

He scoops me up with one arm under my bottom. Moving us into the house, he kicks the door shut and walks us to the couch. Jake settles me onto his lap. I tuck my head under his chin. He pecks my forehead.

"I suck at this, Pais."

The funny thing is, if Jake is trying to make me feel better, he's pulling out all the stops. Little broken pieces of my heart fuse back together, thinking he's acting like a real boyfriend. Just to shatter again when I remember this is all for show.

I laugh at my stupidity. Yet, I can't help snuggling closer. Which proves not only are my signals crossed with my hot as sin rebound guy, I've also contracted an acute case of Stockholm Syndrome.

"I would have changed the reservation, *corazón*. Found a different restaurant to eat at. Why didn't you tell me that Royce's was where you had your engagement party, or that Gavin's sister was your maid of honor? Nothing like our first official sighting looking like the runaway bride was thumbing her nose at the good doctor." He sighs.

I sit up and cock my chin. "You don't want to hear my explanation."

"Sure I did."

"No, Jake. You didn't and you still don't. You want everything your way..." He also enjoys when we argue. Because at some point he wins. "And what difference would it make if I gave you specifics, like telling you the names of every one of my bridesmaids? You don't care about the life I was leading with Gavin and—" I pause.

"And what? Do you think I'm going to use what you have to say against you?"

"Whatever, use it... My bridesmaids don't talk to me. It's not as if I have friends the way you do to worry about what they think of me." Nor with them living out of state was it as if we were in each other's back pockets. However, all of our interactions since I called off the wedding have been ugly text messages and uglier voicemails. They are angry they spent a lot of money to travel and on formal attire for nothing.

"Plus, the rock through the boutique's front window solidifies my place in the court of public opinion."

I hold up my gauze-wrapped hand, which I've had cradled in my lap underneath the bouquet.

"Hold on, you got hurt because someone threw a rock through the store's window?" His jaw drops.

So, he didn't know.

Jake grabs my fingertips in his.

I wince.

"Are you okay? Did I hurt you?"

"No. At first, you moved so fast that I was worried you'd squeeze it." My reaction was as reactionary as his.

The alarm went off, alerting me to the fact that a vandal had tried breaking into the boutique. It was still dark out when it happened and they didn't steal anything. I was already exhausted filing the police report. My single-mindedness had me intent on cleaning up the mess before maintenance showed up to screw plywood into the open window frame.

I sliced near my Mount of Venus picking up a jagged piece of glass.

"I put aside the broom and dustpan to place the biggest pieces in the trash bin. I wasn't thinking it was sharp enough to cut me, and it took a while for the bleeding to stop." Probably because my blood pressure was elevated.

"Let me see. Do you need stitches? I'll take you to the ER."

"Don't worry about it. My dad was a doctor. I used a butterfly suture on it. It'll be fine." Once it stops throbbing.

"Did I do this? Ruin your life?" He brings my fingers to his mouth, pressing his soft lips to the pads.

"No Jake, I did this. I'm responsible for the few friends I stayed in touch with over the years not sticking around, the boutique's dwindling sales, and replacing the plate glass."

The shop is closed for repairs. It only seemed right to give my employees the day off. I'd rather stay in bed than be at my shop, and no one else should have to clean up my messes.

"I'm paying for the window," Jake objects.

"What for? To prove some omnipotent power? So I'm indebted to you? Maybe I don't need rescuing, Jake. Maybe everything that's happening with my reputation and my business being in the gutter was bound to happen if I hadn't run into Sweet Caroline's."

"But you ran into the club, so we won't ever know. And now you're stuck with me. Guilt by association." The frown hasn't left Jake's face. But the crease in his brow is more pronounced than ever.

"I'm a pariah either way. I'm surprised the people who work for me haven't quit. *Guilt by association.*" I shrug, repeating the same words he uttered.

"Pais, do you want to be unstuck?"

I stammer. I honestly didn't think Jake would offer me a choice.

"Because I have a problem, I don't... want to be unstuck from you, that is... The nights go by faster when you're at the club. My employees like you, so it's not shocking that yours are standing by you during a tough time."

"Um, but—" I shake my head, never mind.

Jake nudges. "Yeah?"

"Do you like me?"

"I said I'd have the window replaced. I thought the rest was inferred."

"Not really."

"Not even when I offered to take you to the hospital?"

"Nope." God, why do I want Jake Ballantine of all people to say it?

"I like being around you, *corazón.*"

Is admitting to liking the way he feels when I'm around, but not actually liking me, what Sloan meant about Jake fighting tooth and nail?

I refuse to read into it and use Jake's perceived selfishness as allowance for my own.

Even if I'm using this man to forget my fiancé, since encountering Jake, I've been too busy for the loneliness I experienced before we met. The foundation of our relationship is wrong. But, out of necessity, I've looked past that for weeks. Can I now? Can I use Jake to make myself feel better about where my life is at this moment?

It isn't as if he's professing he loves me or asking me to assume a bigger role in this farce than I am. Jake is only saying he wants to keep me around. But I sort of want to keep him around, too.

Jake

"If we're sticking together, we have a few details to iron out."

Paisley hasn't agreed yet. In fact, her bewildered brown eyes stare at me unconvinced, and her parted lips exhibit her confusion. My fingers glide into the tendrils at the back of her neck, bringing my forehead to hers. I hate Paisley's ability to look into my mind and see the cogs moving. My current thoughts betray how well the strategy of her posing as my girlfriend is working with my friends. Although I'm more afraid she'll see the other tiny gears shifting. The ones that keep my pulse moving and my heart pounding in my chest every time I think about Paisley when she's not around.

I don't want her to see how the idea of someone vandalizing her shop throws me into a rage. Nor the concern that her cut won't heal without medical attention. I'm not ready to offer everything I have to Paisley on a silver platter. Everything I have is tarnished. She deserves more than the heaping crap of baggage I've felt compelled to continue carrying. But I also want her to understand that I'll do anything for her to make up for the callousness I showed her yesterday.

"I'm sorry, *corazón*." I nip at her lips. "So. So sorry for not listening." My tongue swipes at the seam. Paisley opens for me, completing the velvet stroke as our mouths combine.

You can tell me anything. I want to say. *You can rely on me*. But I don't know how to express that other than with the fierce determination of kissing her harder. The language we began with is the one we're best at.

I move the roses so that we don't crush them any more than we have. Light as a feather, it's easy to shift Paisley to straddle my lap while our tongues tangle. She moans when I deepen the kiss. Unlike yours truly, Paisley doesn't hold back. Perhaps when Paisley kisses me it's because she doesn't want to. More likely because I won't let her. I want all of her and, sadistically, I don't want to give her all of me. Not when, from the moment she ran into my arms, I was already aware she was worthy of a better man than I'll ever be.

And my biggest fear is becoming that Paisley understands this, and no matter what I try, I'll never convince her otherwise.

All I can do is keep kissing her as a method of persuasion, hoping that she rides the high as long as I do between kisses.

She rocks with practiced perfection over my hard length. Teasing my dick. Reminding me of what, at any other time, I've been brave enough to ask for. Yet, with Pais, there are strings attached and the last thing I want to do is rip her heart out.

I reach under her short shirt to cup her breast. It's covered by a sports bra.

I groan. "You're killing me with the spandex."

Paisley pulls back. Our noses mush, but I can still see her tooth sink into her swollen lower lip. The one my teeth are jealous of her biting. She lets me palm her tit. Through the tight fabric, I pinch her taut nipple. She takes a sharp inhale, moving her mouth back over mine. When I skim my hand higher toward her collarbone, Paisley grabs my wrist and forces my hand back to her hip.

She grinds against me. Although her panties and pajama bottoms and the thick denim of my jeans and cotton boxers separate us, the way she moves against my throbbing erection is the reward for letting Paisley control the pace. She's not a cock tease. I simply haven't shown Paisley what she's missing. When I do, I'll have her naked under me, right where she belongs. The thought makes my balls tighten.

"*Corazón,*" I whisper with one hand cupping her ass and the other her cheek. "We have to stop or I'm going to blow in my pants."

When she laughs, my thumb slides to rest on her chin.

"You think it's funny turning me into some horny kid?"

"I can't either. We can't. I'm—It's that time of the month." She shakes her head and her unbound hair flies everywhere. The scent is intoxicating. I love the way she smells.

I brush an errant lock away. The need to touch her overpowers all else.

"Not lying to you. That excuse has never stopped me before." Paisley's eyes widen when I slide my thumb into her mouth.

In the dressing room, Sweet Caroline's dancers hold nothing back. For instance, I learned at sixteen that sex is amazing for menstrual cramps. And depending on how much hot water versus the sting of cold that you're into, not much beats the easy clean up with shower sex.

"You tell me what you need to make you feel better, *corazón*. I'll listen. From now on, I'll listen. Nod if you understand me."

Her head bobs and my thumb slides between her lips. She sucks on it. Doesn't that paint a pretty picture of the other things Paisley can do with that mouth?

I roll her to her back, letting Paisley lie flat on the sofa. I tickle her neck with my nose and kiss the soft spot behind her ear while her legs are still wrapped around my waist. My dick hates me as I take us down slowly. But this way I have an image of what her hair might look like spilling over the sheets of my bed or the cushions of my couch, should we not make it that far.

"It seems a little mean of me to leave you like you are," she says once we finally start using full sentences again instead of single words.

"Consider it my comeuppance for acting a fool. Next time, I won't be as kind."

"Next time?"

"Oh, yeah. And I have a little secret I want to share with you. Next time, you're going to come. On my hand, my fingers, or my face, I don't care. But I'll get you there. It'll be your just desserts for the number of times you've made me hard."

Paisley inserts her hands into my back pockets, grabbing my ass. "You sound awfully sure of yourself."

"Are you arguing with me?"

"Maybe. Maybe not, if you get off of me and walk across the room."

"Why would I do that?"

"Because I'd like to see you from behind in these jeans."

"From behind, or *my* behind?" I ease off and my

feet land on the floor.

"I thought you said you were turning over a new leaf and listening? Do as you're told."

I place a hand on her thigh, using the leverage to boost me up. "There's a difference between hearing what you say and taking orders from you." I waltz across the room, looking over my shoulder when I'm near the kitchen. "Is my butt everything you wanted it to be?"

A smile dances on her face. "Yep. Now come back over here and tell me what exactly you think we need to figure out, since we're stuck together, Elmer."

I'm surprised by the throaty chuckle that escapes me, and we bicker through laughter about whether Pais can nickname me after glue. She lets me win. She'll keep calling me "Jake" to my face and "asshole" under her breath. This woman.

I order us lunch, not giving her an option of restaurants because I've grown to know what she'll choose, anyhow. Waxy cartons of lo mein won't make up for the meal we didn't finish at Royce's, but staying home makes sense.

We sit on stools at Paisley's kitchen island. The cut on her hand stops Paisley from using the wooden chopsticks that came with our takeout. We have another amusing tiff. I tell Paisley it's a sacrilege to get a fork from the utensil drawer and feed her noodles and veggies out of my box. Taking bites myself while she chews.

"I want one of those," she says of the mini corn I've popped into my mouth.

I root around, finding one. She wiggles the vegetable between her teeth. I lean in to kiss her, snapping off half, and tasting the sweet and savory sauce.

I feel a twinge of guilt for buttering her up.

"I'm glad you're feeling better." Her full belly

makes the news I'm about to deliver palatable. "I messaged my guy, Dusty. He should have the boutique's window replaced in the next hour. We can go downtown to take a look at his handiwork." While we're at the shop, I'll make sure that nothing else needs tending to.

"I notified maintenance to take care of it. You went behind my back!" Her voice is sharp, but Paisley's features are soft.

"We're going to have to compromise somewhere, *corazón*. It'll be easier if you let me take care of you… When you need me to."

"That wasn't me. It was my business."

"That got a brick through the window because of me."

"Again, you give yourself far too much credit." Paisley takes the chopsticks. With effort, she manages to wind a noodle around it. Holding it up, she eats it like a shark.

A cute, little, determined baby shark.

But damn, she's gorgeous with her messy hair and pajamas covering every inch of her.

I glance at the bouquet I brought. A tad worse for wear, it sits in a crystal vase nearby. She explained how to trim the stems at an angle and we worked as a team on a mundane task. Everything about the past hour feels domestic and the only way I can describe the current vibe is bliss.

"Do you think Sloan and Holly will find anything at the boutique to wear to the hospital gala?" I change the subject.

"I don't cater to Hol's style much." Paisley shrugs. "Sloan could go either way. Prom season is coming up, but I'm not stocking floor-length formal wear. Women go glam for the benefit. Even I order my dress from someplace else."

I bop a rosebud. "Well, I owe you a new dress, so

whatever you pick out is on me. You can even put your personal shopper skills to use and find my tux. But only if you have the time."

"You want me to dress you?" she asks with incredulity. "And hold on, we never agreed we were going to the gala."

"You've attended every year you've received an invite, and after everything that happened last night, you aren't going this year without me beside you. If there was anything on my calendar, my priorities have changed."

"To protect me? Enough of other people will be there. Sloan and Carver. Holly and Cary. Gavin will be there, Jake! I can't flaunt this!" Her hands move in every direction and Paisley comes close to stabbing me with the chopsticks. "My mother will be there. I can't take a spectacle of myself after putting my mom through the wringer when I called off the wedding."

I hum in agreement with everything Paisley has said. She can't. And we won't. And I'll match Carver's fat donation to ensure all parties take my girlfriend's dedication seriously.

"I'd like to meet your mother."

"You would?" She looks shocked.

"Of course, it's only right that I meet her when you've met mine."

"But I haven't—"

"Caroline wants to meet you and I've put her off long enough. If we're going to continue to pretend we're stuck like glue, the devil is in the details. It's time we level up and meet the parents."

Chapter Sixteen

Paisley

Previous flames have introduced me to their mothers before, and putting my best foot forward has been relatively easy. However, what exactly is the appropriate attire when meeting the mother of your rebound guy/con artist/fake boyfriend when said mother is a former stripper?

After emptying the contents of my closet onto the bed, I've   concluded that I have zero to wear. Nothing.

Me. The boutique shop owner.

"Why did I agree to this?" I lament. Talking aloud to myself is something I do far too often.

The reason that sticks in my head above all else is that Jake spent an entire day making me feel squishy inside. Not only when he handed me the roses and apologized but also when he said he'd listen and then got me all hot and bothered. When he put the brakes on, Jake still made me feel crazy beautiful with my bandaged hand, messy hair, and frumpy pajamas. He also took care of me. I've been doted on during hospital stays. Except, no one has had the patience to feed me a whole container of food since my mother spooned prunes into my mouth as an infant.

By the time Dusty called to ask Jake if I wanted to go downtown and inspect the new store window, Jake convinced me that he was looking out for my best interest by escorting me to the gala.

It's flattering to hear that Caroline Ballentine knows who I am.

Me. The fake girlfriend.

Though, suppose everyone in Brighton is well aware of the story about the local runaway bride and whose arms she was caught in. So it would be hard for Mrs. Ballentine to miss that those were her son's arms, now wouldn't it?

I slump on my bed and the pile of clothes slides onto the floor. I kick it with my foot and the hangers become tethered between my toes. I lift my foot, deciding that the garment that sticks will be the one I wear.

The top of the simple white cotton dress has a crew collar with small capped sleeves. The bottom ruffles flare. It's a super cute look leftover from my inventory last spring, and it still has the tags on because I haven't found any place to wear it. I guess meeting Jake's mother today is as good as any occasion.

The concession pays off. Twirling in the mirror, the short flirty hem spins like a ballerina's tutu. I pair it with flats in case the afternoon goes south and I have to make a hasty exit. Don't accuse me of not learning from my mistakes.

And while I'm on the subject, I hope finding my Jimmy Choos lying on the sidewalk turned around Valentine's Day for whoever it was who found them, and that they are in love with those shoes.

Jake arrives and anxiety still grips my stomach in a

solid knot. He's the type of man who uses the word "date" as a euphemism for "sex". Before I landed on Sweet Caroline's doorstep, this guy—who I keep kissing without a care of what I might catch—*dated* the way people exercise: daily. I probably need an abacus to tally the number of partners I assume he's had. Yet I'm hopeful I'll make a favorable impression, instead of being perceived as his newest, and uptight, fuck-buddy.

Not that we're fucking, nor will we. I mean, unless Jake endures an honest discussion about his status because I'm clean. But again, fooling around isn't fucking and I'm not planning on having sex with Jake Ballentine, so why I don't know why thinking about this even makes a difference.

"Nice jeans," I quip when he arrives.

Although casual, Jake is dressed as dapper as always. Damn, the man has style.

"This woman I've been spending my time with mentioned she enjoyed the rearview." He shoots me a cocksure grin.

I like Jake's appearance in his dress pants, too. Since our make-out session on the couch, I have to admit I've watched him prowl toward me at the club with as much anticipation as I have when he's walking away. Whatever Jake is hiding under his clothes is likely as beautiful as seeing the long length of him in his tux.

"You look pretty." Jake flips the script, making me feel squishy all over again.

He bends and I expect a peck on the lips, but Jake has other plans. By the time we come up for air, the air itself is cooling the exposed part of my butt cheek Jake's palm isn't keeping warm. He's got the dress bunched up in the back and my underwear elastic invades my crack.

"In case you were curious, I've become partial to

your rearview as well." He squeezes my ass. "Wear a thong."

"Not with this short skirt." I play-slap him away, reaching for my clutch.

Jake wraps his massive paw around my wrist. He circles around me, tightening our arms around my waist. His thumb grazes the underside of my breast. "Buy them," he instructs, his breath whispering by my ear. He holds me so close that his body becomes a hard shell protecting mine.

"Okay, but not today." My voice quivers.

Jake hasn't won by a long shot. I own sexy panties. The ones I have on are adorable. I chose them for myself. A thrill zips up my core, tugging at my belly. I lean into Jake, pressing my thighs together, thinking about what panties I'd pick out that I'd want him to see me in.

OMG really, Paisley?

And…

Did I do that for Gavin? I pride myself on my appearance, but when I used to get dressed to go out, did I do that for me or for my fiancé to find me sexy? It's been so few weeks since taking off my wedding gown and I can't quite remember. What I do recall is my mom made the final decision about what I wore that day all the way down to my underwear. Not because she took the choice from me, but because I didn't care enough one way or the other to decide.

When it comes down to it, I spent longer worrying about Jake's mother's perception of me than I did about if Gavin found his bride beautiful. And it is a cop out to say I assumed all grooms are knocked out by the sight of their brides coming down the aisle.

Shaking off the less than innocuous realization about my behavior, I tell Jake we'll be late if we don't leave soon. He assures me that Caroline Ballentine's home isn't far from where I live.

I'm surprised when we pull off a busier road and into the wide circular drive of a two-story Georgian. It's a creamy yellow with bright white columns. The boxwood hedges, trimmed high, are stately without being pretentious. The fountain in the center of the lush green front yard—a six-foot marble statue of a naked woman—makes me giggle when I notice that it's the focal point for anyone attempting to peek past the landscaping who passes by the home.

"That was intentional." Jake's comment widens the smirk on my face.

"I had a feeling."

"When my dad bought the property for my mom, the neighbors spread a rumor that they intended to start a brothel. What my parents really wanted was a nice house to raise kids in. The more work mom and dad put into the place, the worse the harassment got. So, mom had the fountain imported from Italy to thumb her nose at them."

"I'm surprised she didn't have to remove it."

"Believe me, they tried. But the house is private property and since the ordinances allowed racists to put up white crosses and the Confederate Battle Flag, which others found as objectionable, then mom could keep her, albeit massive, objet d'art. The city council members passed by the house a dozen times before they could even identify which residence was offensive to the complainers. You have to crane your neck to see it when you drive by."

"I noticed. Clever."

Set back from the road, the elegant fountain blends into the garden. If this were a historic site, no one would've batted an eye.

"Let's get this over with," he says in a tone akin to "it shouldn't hurt too bad" that I heard as a kid from doctors when something wound up being quite painful.

We chain link our index fingers on our way to the door. Once inside the foyer, I can't contain my awe.

"This is beautiful!" The house is a dead-ringer for what I'd hoped to purchase with—*moving on*! "Did you enjoy living here as a kid?"

Jake shrugs. "I dunno. When Carver squatted here for a bit, I guess. Mostly it was like a gilded fortress, so I stuck to the club. Everyone worth talking to was there, anyway."

"But you don't like the club now." It's a fact Jake has shared.

Jake's jaw twitches. "I do. When you're there."

Trepidation over making a good impression has me forgetting to ask about the co-manager applicant for Sweet Caroline's.

"Jake, is that you?" a melodious female voice calls.

"It's him." Carver pops out from behind the staircase carrying a silver tray.

"Speak of the devil." Jake huffs a laugh. He shakes his head, tightening his finger around mine. "What are you doing here?"

"Sloan never turns down Caroline."

"And you never turn down Sloan."

"Sure I do. But I also concede that I'm able to give my wife the finer things that she should have had before we met, and spending time with Caroline makes Sloan happy. How lucky are you that Paisley had a good life... Until she met you, of course. Then it all went downhill." Carver winks at me.

"Play nice, Jake. Carver is the closest thing to a brother that I'm giving you." As she approaches, I latch onto a slight rasp in Caroline Ballentine's voice.

She's a striking blonde. Her sharp cheek lines mirror Jake's and she has the same blue eyes. If they change color the way Jake's can depending his mood, no wonder Caroline captivated men. I haven't looked away from her face to notice her body and, even past her prime—a phrase that's the least befitting as most women nowadays could pass as years younger than I presume Caroline is—it's not as if her attire hides her curves. Jake's mom radiates a level of gorgeousness that the women I dress aspire to.

"Thank god for that, Mom. You know, it might boost my confidence every now and again if you took my side and told Carver to play nice with me."

"Oh, baby. I do." She cups a manicured hand on his cheek, patting lightly. "Just not when you're around because you have such big issues with that over-inflated ego of yours."

Carver lifts his knuckle to his nose and snorts. It's obvious around Caroline the men treat one another like siblings.

I can't help giggling.

"Gee, thanks," Jake says. A sarcastic smile etches his face, making the cleft in his chin more pronounced. He's sexy when he's broody, but he's truly handsome when he's happy.

"I'm glad to have both of you boys home whenever you want to come over and whatever the reason is for." Caroline hugs her son. It's the first time Jake has let go of me since we exited the car. "I love you. It's good to see you." She pulls out of the embrace and steps back on her high heel. "You must be Paisley."

I roll my lips between my teeth, nodding. "It's lovely to meet you."

She takes my hands and looks me up and down. "Oh, Jake. Something tells me you finally got it right."

Jake

"Only the five of us?" I ask my mom.

She shoots me the "don't start" look and sits down between my girlfriend and Sloan. Carver sets a silver tray of finger sandwiches on the coffee table. The tea service is already there. Mom has pulled out all the stops. Like Pais, my mother wants to make a good impression.

Caroline Ballentine doesn't lack male companionship, though she's never introduced me to anyone. I wish she'd "get it right". I wish she would move on. My dad's been gone a long time, longer than he's been dead, and what he put her through was wrong.

I don't understand how loyal she is to him. I don't get how she can still love him, focus on the good times, and act ignorant of the bad.

I've seen firsthand how love destroys a person. First with *him* and *her* when he gave up his dreams after I picked those godforsaken lilies for her casket, and then when my dad betrayed my mom's trust. My mother stood by my father when he went to jail. While he was on the inside accused of dealing, she was dealing with the mess he'd created on the outside. Fighting to keep the house that the good people of Brighton had already tried to take from her, and to not surrender the club that bore her name.

Do I want her to have stars in her eyes over some dude who wants to pretend he's my daddy? Nah. But I don't want her spending the rest of her life so hung up on my father that she can't bear inviting anyone to join us.

"Paisley, I was downtown and saw that Dusty did such a wonderful job replacing the store's window. I especially like the logo decal he added to the glass." Sloan says to my girlfriend.

"That's my favorite part, too." Paisley holds up her finger, making the half yin and yan symbol. "When Greer saw them, she asked Dusty to make a honeycomb design for Mind Your Own Beeswax. The credit goes to Jake, though. The decal was a surprise. He asked Dusty to do it. I knew nothing until we went to inspect the window."

"What a sweet gift." Sloan turns to face me, unbelieving I'd have the chivalry to do something so simple.

I get hot under the collar from her attention. Sloan and I mix like oil and water. I'm not used to her compliments. She's kind to everyone but me. Although the reasons why are my fault. Carver's wife has an uncanny resemblance to *her*. Except the similarity is only skin deep.

Sloan was nothing more to Carver than a pretty face until she weaseled her way into his good graces. The shift I saw in him—how he began relinquishing the desire for money and influence he'd sought since we were kids—was reminiscent of witnessing how others had given up. It's why I did what I did when it was obvious he was going to break his own rules and allow Sloan to stay at the mill. I tried to talk Carver out of starting a relationship with Sloan. She had the roughest upbringing of any of the mill girls. Carver smoothed out her sharp edges.

I don't like liking Sloan even in a platonic way, and I don't like it when Sloan graces me with any compliment. So, I can't utter a "thank you." Hell, I'd be remiss for taking credit for doing something nice for my girlfriend when her association with me was the impetus for the boutique needing a new window.

"Oh, I heard about your troubles." My mom pats Paisley's knee. "Do you know who threw the rock?"

"Trig is looking into it," I say in a firm "let's drop it" tone.

"You should stop in, Mrs. Ballentine." Pais extends an invite to my mom.

"We could go together, Caroline," Sloan suggests. "Paisley has such nice stuff…"

I lose track of the ladies' animated conversation. The fact that my girlfriend's business is female-oriented doesn't mean I'm disinterested. It's that Sloan and Caroline are monopolizing Paisley, and Carver and I are relegated to silence in the wing chairs opposite the spread on the coffee table. I offer to pour Carver a drink from the wet bar. Glasses in hand, we rove about the room rather than endure a sit/stay command.

"You know who did it?" He subtly revisits Trig's investigation while the ladies are otherwise occupied —Now with chatter over the upcoming gala.

My jaw clenches. I move the sheers and look out the window at the fountain. My lack of acknowledgment to Carver's question is an answer in itself, and we move on to another topic.

Paisley comes up from behind me, warming my back. "Caroline is going to give me a tour of the house. Want to come with in case there are any naked baby pictures you want to hide?" Her hand slips around my midsection, resting below my shirt pocket.

I chuckle, placing mine over hers. I don't know when the simple touches stopped being for show. I don't know why I crave all of Paisley and, when she can't give me her full attention, I pout in the corner like a jealous fool.

"I'll wait here, *corazón*. You go and enjoy."

The corners of my mouth perk as she leaves the room.

"Never thought I'd see the day Jake Ballentine was bamboozled."

I sigh as if I'm bored of their second-guessing my commitment to my girlfriend. "I told every last one of you it was for real."

"Yeah, but, Jake. We know in the beginning *you* didn't believe it. So, what is so beguiling about Paisley Cooper that she has the finesse to do what no other woman could; stand to be around you for more than five minutes?"

I haven't the foggiest. Nor do I get why Pais doesn't annoy the crap out of me the way my previous lady company has. I wouldn't have let anyone before Paisley get away with what she does without getting my dick wet.

The rules are changing for her.

It's dusk when we say goodbye to my mom. Pais yawns in the passenger seat next to me. I should bring her home, but I pass the turnoff for her neighborhood and head to my place.

"Why are we here?" Paisley tosses her clutch on the couch.

She circles my living room, checking everything out. Her feet pause by the drum kit. When she lightly spins the crash cymbal, I don't bark for her to get the hell away from it. Then two fingers stroke the counter hoop on the closer of the Tom Toms. I stop breathing and watch her trace the metal. I feel like she's touching my bare skin. It also feels like having her here is the absolute best bad idea I've ever had.

I clear my throat. "You wanted to see more than the four walls of the club. This is another place I haven't brought you."

Her head bobs from right to left on her shoulders, agreeing with my logic. I give Paisley a mini-tour since she seemed to enjoy that at my mom's. We end in the kitchen. Dinner is light since we've been picking at hors d'oeuvres all afternoon. I open the freezer and hold up two green boxes, giving Pais first choice before popping hers into the microwave. She jokes about my bachelor life.

"I tend to have more in the fridge. But somebody has wanted to eat out." I lean my elbows on the counter so that it puts our faces at the same level and tease her back.

"*Ah*, I cook. I just haven't been home to cook."

"Oh, is that your excuse? Then our next outing should be to the grocery store."

"I'd like that," she whispers.

"Me too," I reply.

A co-manager to take the pressure off of Kelsey keeps seeming like a better idea. It affords the opportunity for nights like this.

Finished eating, we retreat to the sofa. I sling an arm around Paisley. She plays with the fine hair on my forearm, commenting on how it's sticking up like I've seen a ghost.

I'm beginning to wonder if I have. Whatever is going on between me and Paisley is reminiscent of my past. When she enters a room, the tunnel vision I had seeing *her* for the first time returns.

"What did you mean when you said you didn't enjoy growing up in your house?" Paisley asks me.

I don't see a reason to lie to her.

"It's not the house. It's what surrounded it. My parents had enough money to fit in. They should have had country club memberships, but each board rejected their applications."

People hide their immorality. Ours was in the open for all of Brighton to judge.

"Their kids were complete assholes, too. By the time our hormones caught up with us, most of them were taught sex was sinful. None of the girls' fathers could cope with them having me as a friend, let alone the fact that I could be the guy they waited on the porch for with a shotgun. In high school, the boys were all convinced the band geek was out to steal what they had."

"Band geek? I can't imagine you in a uniform with the feather on the cap." She draws her hand up from her forehead as far as it can go, indicating a plume. Her knuckles inadvertently hit the wall. "Oops, sorry. I got carried away."

"Take two feet off my height, fifty pounds off my weight, add a full set of braces to my teeth, and dot my face with acne."

"Did you play the flute?" She giggles.

"Percussion. And I caught what you did there. Bad form." I tickle Paisley to keep her smiling, though I tire of anyone questioning anyone else's sexuality.

Those same holier-than-thou kids were as likely to question what I was doing with Carver—a kid from the wrong side of the tracks—when he lived with us as they were to say I fucked strippers. Shy of forty years old, I haven't been in a situation with creative people; dancers, musicians, artists, who only lead traditional lifestyles. Hell, a majority of Sweet Caroline's female guests are there to watch the shows, not to pick up anybody.

That one couple when Cece Wescott hung up her stilettos notwithstanding.

"I won't be as kind if you say that again," I warn her between her gasping breaths.

"Okay!" she squeals. "Okay, I was rude and wrong. Now stop!" She regains her composure. "Oh, is that why you have the drum set?"

"You wanna go off on that tangent now or finish the discussion we're having?"

"Keep going. With the growing up part, I mean. Although if you played the drums in high school, I can see why a teenage boy would worry about keeping a teenage girl's attention. No matter how old you are, drummers are sort of sexy."

"I'll keep that in mind."

"Am I allowed to be curious about your father? It surprised me how many pictures your mom has of him."

"You can ask whatever you want, *corazón*. That doesn't mean I'll always answer... But in this case, Caroline holds a torch for him."

"Why? Everyone said—Well, I guess I was too young then to know what everyone said."

"My dad got involved with the wrong sort. It was disrespectful to my mom and their marriage, but she says it wasn't a matter of infidelity."

"It still bothers you." She leans her head on my chest.

"How could it not? When the ATF took the ring down, the business they built together was a casualty."

"But you still make shady deals."

There's no sense in denying what Paisley already knows. The difference between me and my dad is what I do has no fallout. I came back to Brighton and made sure Caroline was set financially if the club goes under. I have no family relying on me. My dreams went up in smoke, so the fuck do I have to reach for anymore? Paisley won't stick around and my mom got used to visiting day at the corrections institution. I'm sure Caroline can do it again.

We stand up, dusting our palms on our thighs. In the awkward silence, I calculate how much time I have left with her if Pais cuts bait at the first sign of trouble. I've tried my best behavior on for size since we met. It's yielded mixed results.

"Stay here tonight." I tug her toward the bedroom.

She hovers in the doorway. "I'm not sleeping with you, Jake."

"Yes, you are. In my bed. And I get to touch you." I unbutton my shirt and toss it to the side. "I'll bring you home in the morning."

"Then I'm wearing my dress to bed."

"Without your panties."

Pais lifts her index finger. It twirls, zeroing in on my crotch. "If the belt stays buckled."

"Jeans and a belt? That's not uncomfortable." I reply sarcastically, giving her a smarmy face. But secretly I'm enjoying her negotiating. "Pants on. Belt off."

"Pants on. Buttoned. Belt on. Buckled. Or no deal. I'm not a damsel in distress, relying on the hospitality of strangers anymore. I have my phone with me this time, and can call for a ride."

"Belt buckled. Panties off." I agree with a devilish wink.

I don't know what Paisley thinks she's won, but it's not this argument. I hadn't minced words a week ago when I told her that the next time she came, it was going to be on my face. She doesn't realize I've officially charmed the pants off of her. If there are no other options for me while my face is buried in her sweet pussy other than to hump the mattress, then count me in.

Chapter Eighteen

Paisley

A shirtless Jake flicks a switch, lowering the same style shades in his bedroom that I saw in the living room. He turns down the bedcovers. "Are you standing there all night, or are you getting in?"

My thumb hikes the skirt of my dress, slipping underneath the side of my panties. They slide to my knees and I shimmy a bit for the lacy scrap to fall and puddle at my toes.

Jake's tongue finds his back molar while he watches me. I don't know if I did it right. Boldness I'm familiar with. Being seductive isn't my strong suit. At least not from what I've gathered about myself watching the dancers at Sweet Caroline's.

I climb onto the mattress first. Jake follows suit, flipping off the lamp on his bedside table and bathing the room in darkness. I hear him bunching a pillow between his head and bicep. He faces my side of the bed, curling his large hand, positioning me how he wants me. It comes to rest on my hip.

The blackness leaves me nothing to concentrate on

other than what I can hear and feel. My long hair is trapped between my cheek and the pillowcase, creating tension on my scalp. His belt buckle notches into my back and my feet touch the scratchy fabric encasing his legs. I want to rub the bridge of my foot over them, outlining the muscle beneath.

But I try to stay still, warding off a shiver when I wonder how demanding he'd be, how tight his fist would pull at my brown locks if I... *If I...*

Why did I demand Jake keep his pants on? Exactly what argument was I winning?

I'm not stupid.

I know what's about to happen.

Frighteningly enough, I *want* what's about to happen. I may even want more than what I agreed to tonight with Jake.

The growing feelings I have for Jake could be construed as me wanting not just his package, but the whole package.

And that makes me feel like I don't know myself anymore. Sure, there are choices I've made that I stand by. However, the person under my shell isn't the person I thought I was.

The woman in Jake Ballentine's bed is risking getting her heart broken. Willingly.

I doubt I'm special. Logic has me convinced his persuasive techniques are the same for every woman. But sound judgment has flown out the window by the time a girl's panties are off, even when she's smart enough to overrule a man and make him keep his pants on.

I lie still with my eyes closed.

"Did what I say about my dad scare you, *corazón?*" Jake's nose nuzzles the back of my neck.

"No." I revel in the soothing softness of his lips. "I had a vague idea of what happened to your family when we began whatever this is."

There's something relatable to his parents' story. Mine lived for each other, too. Although my dad was sick before he died, the way it ended was as tragic for my mom. I don't blame her for not being ready to move on. Jake's dad isn't around anymore either, and maybe for Caroline, the time her husband was incarcerated parallels my mom's experiences learning how to love someone who won't be around any longer. Teaching herself what she wants in the future when half of what made the past worth living for is gone.

Jake's palm glides from my hip to my belly. His lithe body cocooned around mine, I'm safe surrounded by his powerful shoulders. As if nothing could hurt me, not even my own bad decisions. Apart we are two parts of the same circle. Joined, we're the complete ring.

I chose every step of my life on my own. I've never felt *incomplete* without anyone else. So why do I have these feelings for Jake? And what do I do with them if we find ourselves un-stuck? What happens if Jake's priority becomes me, but his past choices tear us apart?

I'm forced to reevaluate why I was fine with my decision to let Gavin find his perfect person. I accepted the idea of remaining alone. But despite his surly imperfections, I'm falling in love with Jake Ballentine, and that scares the shit out of me.

"*Corazón?*" Jake's thumb glances over the underside of my breast. "You're never this quiet."

"Touch me."

Please, touch me. Show me what we have is real. Lie to me if you have to. The truth is, I'll keep your secrets—and I'll keep mine as well—if you'll pretend whatever intimacy happens in this moment is what a glimpse at forever would be like with you.

Jake palms my tit, pinching my nipple through my

dress and bra. I moan a desperate, quaking "Yes!" at the luscious pressure. He manhandles me, rolling me to my back. My skirt bunches at my waist.

I can't see anything, only sense his actions, as we move and the mattress shifts. He uses his solid hips to spread my legs. His nose brushes mine once. Twice. Before he covers my mouth. I whimper at the invasion of his tongue. My knees pull up of their own accord, and my core rocks against the hard length bulging at his zipper.

He grips my neck, sucking and biting and then cupping his hand around my breast. His hair brushes my chin when he moves his face to bite that, too. I wish we were naked and his teeth were sinking into my sensitive skin, drawing the rosy flesh hidden by my bra into his mouth.

The other hand travels further, to the juncture of my sex. Dampness that's seeped from me is all over Jake's jeans. It slickens my thigh when he adjusts his lower body and uses his forearm to hold dominion over me. A knuckle spreads my folds, tracing from my clit backward.

"So wet." His whisper is cocky and unabashed. "Do you want to fuck my fingers or my face?"

"I want to fuck all of you."

Jake's chest rumbles. He leans back on his haunches. "Oh, no. You've already put me at a disadvantage. The rules of this game are clear: Panties off. Pants buckled."

"I could—" I fumble in the darkness, searching for the buckle. He dodges and my hand retracts, empty.

Jake has a self-assured demeanor whenever our opinions don't match. I sense his trademark coy and sexy smile playing on his lips. "Consent goes two ways, Paisley. And I do not consent to getting fucked over on a deal you insisted we make. You want my cock between those pretty lips that love to argue with me, or stretching your sweet cunt, that's a new negotiation."

"You want to fuck me," I sass boldly into the darkness.

"I'm going to fuck you, just not with my dick. I hold the power tonight. You gave it to me. Willingly. Now, decide before I do. Fingers, face, or nothing at all. I have a shower and I have a hand of my own that I've gotten used to using…"

Jake plants a seed that makes my hips roll. "I swear Jake Ballentine, if you don't shut up, get your tongue between my legs, and eat my pussy I'm calling for a rii—"

My weight is on my shoulders and Jake is holding my ass in the air before I can finish what I'm saying. His wicked tongue swipes my slit and he fastens his lips around my clit. Deep rhythmic draws tug on the pearl of nerves. I'm so wet, his slurping and groans bounce off the walls, hitting my ears alongside my panting and pleading. A slick trail of saliva and my juices drips toward my asshole. Jake would take me there. No negotiations. All I have to do is beg. He'd give in with a single plea. I know he would. And I file that little power trip in my brain to use when I'm needy for him and Jake needs more than I've given.

My fingertips crawl through Jake's blond hair, pressing his face to my exposed cunt, and bucking toward his lips. My voice has grown louder, shriller. An expert, Jake's holding my pleasure at bay. My orgasm is right beyond my reach. I want his cock. I want his fingers. I want whatever Jake has in mind to do to me to make me come.

Anticipating my every desire, he holds my butt cheeks in a vise and shimmies a pillow under my hips. His ministrations never cease.

"Give me more. I'm not done. I want to drink you down to the last drop." His grunt is gruff and crude.

Although they aren't the words he speaks, inside I'm certain Jake is demanding more than I've given to any other man, not only the man who had me previous to him. Jake doesn't share and he won't leave anything he thinks belongs to him for anyone else. Not even my cum.

His hot breath blows against my damp thighs. Jake slides two fingers into my tight channel. The realization of what he wants and the thrust of their curl causes me to explode. I grip his hair harder at the root. Sealing his lips to mine. And while I fall back to earth, he continues lapping until I'm sure the next experience with Jake and little death could almost kill me.

I demanded a ride... And Jake's giving me the ride of my life.

My thighs are tight and sticky this morning. My lady bits are also chafed from Jake's stubble and, as of last night, I don't recommend dry humping without a protective layer. At least, not the second time. Denim is sturdy and I'm sore.

I suppose the discomfort finally got Jake as well. Sometime between sleep overcoming us and me waking, he slipped off the pants he'd come in and put on a pair of athletic shorts.

When I get out of bed, the drying evidence of our escapade greets me. Bushed, he left his jeans and boxers in a lump on the floor. I sigh, thankful for birth control since accidents happen, and relying on my inner grown-up to be mature because all that jizz is, *ew*.

"I'll toss those in the laundry." Jake bends, places a

hand on my hip for balance, and chucks them into a basket.

The floor is immaculate. His place is borderline pristine for a single guy.

I stare at the hamper, making a lewd gesture with my hands to stop them from wringing. "If we'd… Are you?"

Jake towers over me, grinning like a wolf. "Yeah. Rest assured, I've got one thing going for me that's squeaky clean."

"Can I use your shower?" The boutique opens at ten. I have time to wash up and go home to change into fresh clothes.

"Knock yourself out… On second thought, watch your step, and stay upright." He jokes, planting a kiss on the crown of my head.

I turn on the water to warm the tiles and find extra towels rolled into fluffy tubes on a shelf. It's nice they aren't hidden in a cabinet. I don't want to be accused of snooping, but then I worry about why the towels are readily available.

"Not helpful, Paisley," I mutter, taking off my rumpled dress. "Jake doesn't care who you've been with. And you need to trust his word. Don't make a big deal out of a decorating idea you saw dog-eared in a hospital waiting room magazine."

Yet the ground is always shifting with Jake and I don't trust it won't come up and swallow me whole. That's why I argue. That's why I stand up for myself and show him I deserve his respect.

I stand under the spray, letting it loosen my sore muscles.

The door opens. Jake walks in. Lost in my thoughts, I yelp.

Steam coats the glass shower door, but I cover the front of me. He's a blurry mass on the opposite side of the bathroom, sifting through a drawer between the double sinks.

"What are you doing?" I face the tile.

He chuckles at my modesty. "Hiding doesn't change the fact that I've seen it all, *corazón*."

Not my *all*.

I peer over my shoulder. "Are you done yet?"

His mass shifts, leaning against the sink with his arms crossed. "The real question is, are you? How long do women shower alone? The only time my bathroom has seen this much heat is when I've used the double heads for their intended purpose."

"Thanks for the visual, but that's not exactly sexy." Why is Jake planting other women in my mind? Did I miss the memo? Am I not over the towel thingy? Did we not spend the night messing around like two virginal teenagers?

"How do you know it's not sexy? Have you thought about everything we could do together with that shower head? I have. I am right now." He saunters across the room with his lazy signature swagger.

My belly tightens and the small space—perfectly comfortable before—becomes over-warm.

"If you let me come in there we could experiment." Jake reaches for the door handle.

"No!"

"Okay. Your loss. So that you are aware, there's a massage setting."

"Why are you still here?" I ask when Jake doesn't go back to his bedroom.

He's standing with the opaque barrier separating us by less than an inch. I can feel his cocky smile as if the steamy fog is non-existent.

"Did you hear me say there was a massage head?"

"I'm not deaf."

"Neither am I. That's why I'm waiting for you to flip that lever and use it."

"While you're in the room?" I laugh sardonically. As if I'd ever do that in front of... Anyone. Warmth spreads into my lower belly. My bare thighs rub together. Oh, God, would I?

"Exactly."

"Wh-why?" I cannot believe he's serious about staying!

"Because you're my guest and I want you to enjoy the shower head. And because after listening to all the sounds you make in the dark when I stuck my tongue between your legs, now I want to hear to you pleasure yourself."

"But you can't see anything."

"Pais," Jake's outline closes in on the door. "I'm not leaving until you do, which means at some point the water will run cold, and I'll be watching you. Not. Just. Listening."

Chapter Nineteen

Jake

"That all of it? Everything you found." I confirm with a clean-shaven man standing on the opposite side of my desk. Tipping back in the chair, I fight the urge to pace my office.

Trig sits on the leather couch with his dog sprawled over his lap. He's stroking Tallulah's ears. It's early. There's no bass from the sound system pumping or music to disguise the conversation we're having. But it isn't as if we're unaccustomed to speaking in code or talking around subjects.

The clean-shaven man huffs. "You lucked out, most of the stores downtown have internal cameras only. Nothing watching the doors from the outside. I only found two cameras monitoring the sidewalk near the boutique. One tape we confiscated from the owner after Ms. Cooper filed her police report. The other is the town of Brighton's CCTV, but the log files were corrupted around the same time that Miss Cooper's store was vandalized. Funny how that happens."

"Hysterical," I agree.

Trig meets my gaze. He shrugs. It wasn't him who messed with that video.

"The evidence you confiscated from the other store owner?"

"What evidence? No one can pinpoint where that store's external surveillance footage disappeared to. But I don't recall mentioning our investigation found any evidence of wrongdoing."

It's my turn to laugh. They lost it. Intentionally.

"Trig?" My attention is back on my business associate.

"What he's saying matches the sources I have," Trig says.

I open the drawer and toss a fat envelope onto the desktop. The guy reaches for it. When he opens his jacket light glints off his badge on his belt. He stuffs it into his breast pocket.

"I appreciate your department's thoroughness and your discretion."

"Anytime," he replies, showing himself out.

Trig and I remain silent until we are certain he's off the premises. I look at Trig, waiting.

Trig has things to say. Things I don't want to hear. Trig has made choices he regrets and moving his business assets under another surveillance firm will give him a measure of security.

There's a guy Trig met while he was serving overseas. A muckey-muck with family connections at some big corporation with government contracts. I own part of Trig's company and all it takes is my signature for him to gain the peace of mind that the shit we've done won't come back to haunt him.

"You paid off a cop," Trig hisses.

I nod, tipping my chin and raising a brow.

"Where does it end for you, Jake?"

I thought it would be over by now. In a moment of weakness, I'd convinced myself when I fired Holly while dancing with her at her wedding that I was ready for a clean break. An hour later, I insinuated to Gavin Laughton that his fiancé and I were having an affair, setting the ball in motion again.

"You kept secrets from Kimber. I did what I did to protect Paisley." She's loyal. I can't bear to see her trust broken.

"Don't bullshit me."

My tongue finds my back molar. I'm finished talking about my girlfriend. I may not be the reason Paisley left Gavin, but it was because of me that he wound up in front of her store that night.

"If you sold out to Walsh right now does that mean you'd drop Cary's inquiry about his sister?"

"The sources I'm using to scope out Addie Powell's background are perfectly legal. None of the info I agreed to share with Cary is stuff he can use against her. You heard me. I'm done. I've been done since Rex Stanton and Holly's deadbeat ex, William, blew back on us."

"You're being ridiculous. That was small. It didn't blow back on us."

"It could have hurt people I care about, Jake." Legs spread, Trig leans forward and puts his elbows on his knees. His hands loosely clasped, he stares me down. "Where is the line? When did we move it? And what happens when we cross so far over it in your quest to make Brighton's elite pay for treating your parents like crap that *our* families pay the price? Doesn't this shit with Paisley teach you anything? When she finds out, what will you have left?"

"Stop bringing Paisley into this. She's smart. She's heard enough rumors to know what I've done."

"Your *girlfriend* won't stick around, Jake. You didn't let your need for payback die with Stanton when it could have. You won't be able to use Rex's advances toward Caroline as an excuse with Paisley. It won't matter anymore that he took out the restraining order against your dad, or that Rex planted the evidence that sent your old man to prison for accepting that gun shipment. As soon as Rex Santon was six feet under, the crap you dug up on him over the years became moot."

I know Trig is right, at the very least about Stanton. I never quite got the dirtbag where I wanted him. Any patience I had I used up biding the years, waiting to put the final nail in his coffin. I won't use Rex's transgressions against Cary. Not when Cary suffered at his father's hands and if it means making Holly miserable in the process.

I actually mulled over the offer Walsh made to Trig. He could buy me out with the proceeds. But I've dicked my buddy around, saying that I want my investment back first. He's got the cash. We all do. It's never been an issue before now and Trig has every right to lose his temper with me. Yet the guy is dead calm, always. It must've been his tours overseas that made it so that it takes a lot to throw Trig off. He doesn't get mad. Although I know the real reason behind the dog on his lap is that Trig suffers from PTSD. I haven't seen a bruise on Kimber in a while. She deserves the best Trig can offer her.

And I'm standing in the way.

If Trig accepts the deal with Walsh on my terms, the money still has to get laundered through Sweet Caroline's. He can't do that without me.

So how long am I going to hold him over a barrel, and if the stress breaks Trig before I relent, what is the likelihood Kimber becomes the victim? He'd never do anything while he was awake. But over the years, his nightmares from stress have caused Kimber pain.

The night I bolted from the wedding, I decided I wasn't following the path I was on any longer. But then I met Paisley and everything changed.

I don't answer Trig's rhetorical questions. We're beating a dead horse and have nothing left to say to one another. He's made his position about conning any more of Brighton's elite, as well as his intention to take the buy-out, clear. He and his pooch leave without a backward glance. I stick my thumb and forefingers into my eye sockets, trying to relieve a tension headache.

I really hate this club, and almost every single life choice I've made up until this point. I'm ready to get the hell away from the club the way I used to, but Kelsey needs backup. Not being able to head for the hills whenever I want anymore makes my skin crawl. Unless Paisley is here to soothe me. At home, I sit at my drum set. Instead of my sticks flying wildly through the air, I find myself tapping out the steadier beats of old love songs.

Ones *he* wrote for *her,* and we practiced for hours until we played them by heart in front of audiences that came to hear them. Just because it happened to stroke my ego on the occasion that we massaged the perfect tune into what could've been a chart-topping hit, doesn't mean a damn thing. I've rarely played them in a decade. The past is better left behind me, right where it belongs.

Those songs are melancholy no matter the pacing. However, the familiarity of the lyrics I hear carrying through in my mind strikes my soul differently nowadays. They're not his loving words written about her anymore. I'm no longer focused on gaining his wife's attention or seeing the glowing pride on her face when we exited the stage.

What I want is to see Paisley walking through the entrance of Sweet Caroline's with that expression. The lyrics have become my poetry and the way my sticks interpret them has changed the murmured song into one I'm singing for someone else now.

Someone who is coming to mean far more to me than his wife ever did when she was alive.

A woman who, if I'm not careful, could lay waste to the rest of my life.

As if I've conjured her out of nowhere, my cell rings and Paisley's number flashes across the screen. "*Corazón*," I croak with a lump in my throat.

"Would you mind if I didn't drop in at the club tonight?" I hear her reluctance to see me as loud as I heard her shallow pants from behind the foggy glass door.

She did it. Paisley used the shower massage. She let me listen to her get herself off and as a reward for exposing herself, I tossed my bathrobe over the stall. Flushed, she pulled the collar up to her chin, glancing everywhere but at my face until she saw how hard she'd made me. Shocked—I'm not sure why. Paisley knows her hot little body turns me the fuck on—that was the last time Paisley met my eyes until I kissed her goodbye. Even then, she was shier than usual.

So I'm not certain what made me conclude Pais wouldn't try backing out of seeing me.

I made her uncomfortable. Pushed too far. She was set to marry a guy Trig called the gold standard of husbandship. A man I have to play nice with when we attend the upcoming benefit that is so important to Paisley.

And what am I to her? The shithead who doesn't care that he insisted she do something dirty as fuck. I gripped my cock and jerked off while she touched herself, too. Hot as fuck, that level of degradation wouldn't have crossed her ex-fiancé's mind.

She's never going to believe she's anything to you but a pawn.

"It's that Greer asked me if we could stop at Baked Beans after yoga." Paisley snags my attention, bringing me back to the present.

"That's fine." I blow out a deep breath.

I don't want Paisley's lame excuse. This call is telltale of her priorities. Seeing her friend is more important.

Plus, I hurt her feelings. She should be able to hurt mine. That's how this relationship works, right?

I clear my throat again.

"Hey," she coos. "Are you feeling okay?"

"It's spring allergies. Maybe a cold. You're sort of a germaphobe so you can take the week off."

"The week off of what?"

"Me."

"Oh, it was only for today."

"I've seen the supplements you take, and you commented on how clean my microwave was for a bachelor before I made the TV dinners. You even wash your hands as soon as Kelsey wants your help at the bar."

"That's a health department code. You want your waitresses using the restroom without washing afterward?"

"You're missing the point. I'm not feeling great." I'm evasive. "We have the gala coming up. You shouldn't be sick for that."

"If you insist." She doesn't argue.

I don't know how to take Paisley backing down so easily other than realizing she really doesn't want to see me.

Chapter Twenty

Paisley

Dodging tables to find a quiet booth, I juggle my hot cup, the change from buying Greer's drink and mine, and the receipt; *why did I need a paper copy?* I make the silly remark to Greer.

We've been on both sides of the register and agree that no matter which way it feels rushed trying to stuff all that crap away and make room for the customer behind to move up in line.

I place my wristlet on my lap. Then I take the to-go lid off of my steamy drink and bob the bag up and down, darkening the hot water. "I'm surprised you wanted to come for tea so late."

Yoga with Greer has become a favorite of mine. The downtown studio is a short walk from our shops. It's nice to support another local business owner. My muscles feel great afterward. I'm relaxed. It also gives me something to look forward to besides seeing Jake because I don't hang around Sweet Caroline's every night.

This is the first time Greer has asked me to do

anything since she suggested joining the yoga studio. She'd been cautious when she brought up coming into Baked Beans after class. Almost reluctant to bother me, so I hadn't wanted to push her off. The years of solitude turned Greer into an introvert. I'm sure most people consider her an outcast and underestimate her ability to contribute to the town. However, Greer is actually quite capable and is becoming less apprehensive of people since her shop opened.

Greer shrugs in answer to my comment. "I needed a friend. Byron loves me, but there's only so much I can say to my boyfriend without burdening him with all my girl stuff. It feels weird discussing anything that's intimate in our personal life with Karen, where she co-owns Mind Your Own Beeswax and her husband is Byron's boss. I mean, I know that you probably have a bestie that you open up to about things..."

My heart skips a beat and my brain latches onto Greer's comment that I have a best friend.

Do I?

I have female acquaintances and women like Greer that I've met because I'm a store owner. Gavin's sister was my maid of honor because she was an appropriate choice. My bridesmaids were women I grew up around whose mothers were honorary aunties and whose parents were close with my own. Except all those friends got was my highlight reel. I'd never share my worries with them. *I didn't share my cold feet over the wedding with anyone.*

The only person I've let my guard down for is Jake. Aside from the increased comfort being obstinate towards him when we bicker, I tell him silly things no one else wants to hear. Backorder inventory woes and shipments I'm excited about arriving. Even finding new local suppliers for niche products like what

Greer sells.

While Jake doesn't care about my hopes or dreams, which is to my benefit since I don't have many, he listens with intent—and not in a malevolent way. I've never once felt a gnawing in the pit of my stomach that Jake intends to use those trivial details against me. Seeing as he's a business owner as well, Jake has a frame of reference and he "gets it".

Not to mention, I'm past worrying about being on my best behavior with Jake. It isn't like what I think of Jake concerns him. So I'm free to fly my flaws like they're a flag flapping in the breeze.

I have a goofy grin plastered on my face an hour into our conversation.

"Is it weird that I don't care if we get married?" she asks.

I scoff. "A piece of paper doesn't make you any less committed. I suppose getting married makes it more difficult to end things. I might not be the right person to ask, though." I run my fingers over the tabletop.

Greer blushes like it hadn't occurred to her. "Don't get me wrong, Byron isn't pressuring me. We both had parents that were married and stayed together for the long haul. And I want to be with him forever. A wedding feels hasty? Obligatory?" She sighs. "I'm not explaining myself well."

I wrap my hand over hers. "Have you considered the world changed while you were away and nothing anyone does has to be linear anymore? My mom and dad met, married, *then* moved in together, and tried for a baby. I bet yours did it the same way. So, so what if you and Byron lived together and are now putting the rest out of sequence? What if you skipped a step everyone expects in its entirety?"

"Like having a wedding."

"I proved to you when you attended your first wedding that weddings aren't what they are cracked up to be." I raise a self-deprecating brow.

Greer nearly shoots coffee out of her nose. "Oh, I'm sorry. That was gross." She laughs, wiping her face. A broad grin stretches over her cheeks. "Can I say something without you getting offended?"

"Sure."

"I figured you were under a lot of pressure deciding between Gavin and Jake. But even if Jake's sketchy, I'm glad you followed your heart and called it off with Gavin. You seem happier now."

"Yeah, I… am." I hate lying. My relationship with Gavin ended because of me. Jake had nothing to do with my choice. But looking back on the past few months, I feel more alive than I have since I signed the lease for Paisley's Boutique.

Greer hums, sipping her drink a slight bit more tentatively. "Is it serious? Between you and Jake?"

My lips twist. "I met his mom, and he's supposed to meet mine at the hospital's annual fundraiser for the cardiac unit."

Her jaw drops. "That's big—Okay, maybe not in this day and age. What do I know considering I put the cart before the horse with the whole baby thing? —But I doubt Jake Ballentine holds a meet-and-greet with anyone's mothers, especially his. And *wow*! Isn't this the benefit they named after your father?"

"Renamed. It existed before."

"Still, Paisley, I can't imagine introducing Byron to my parents at an event of that magnitude. It was nerve-wracking enough driving to my mom jond dad's house for a simple barbecue." Greer has anxiety riding in cars to begin with. However, she makes a valid point. "We're talking hot dogs and hamburgers, not coq au vin."

"I'm counting on it taking a lot to rattle Jake. He's um—"

"He's? Paisley, you're blushing!"

"Jake enjoys doing things that..."

Greer cocks her chin to the side.

I squeeze my eyes shut, blurting, "Have you ever had shower sex? But on your own. While he's in the bathroom telling you what to do." *With a massaging shower head. And while he's getting himself off.* I leave out.

"Well, that's kinky. No, but now I'm intrigued and might want to try it. Also, do you mind if I go get a croissant? I'm starving."

The tight coil in my stomach releases. I've never shared details of my sex life with anyone and Greer's nonchalance, excusing herself to get a treat from the bakery case, makes it less awkward.

I can't imagine giving a play-by-play comparing Jake's prowess to Gavin's. I had no complaints in the bedroom with the man I was supposed to marry. I was marrying him after all. Gavin wasn't the first man I fucked, but getting to the point where we were naked in bed wasn't as much of a challenge as keeping my clothes on with Jake seems to be. It's as if I'm always on a slow burn, waiting for Jake to stoke the flame, instead of waiting for the spark of life to be snuffed out.

Chapter Twenty-one

Paisley

I screw the backing onto my diamond earring, dashing for the door as the bell chimes. On the other side, Jake's arm is bent up and his forehead rests on his fist. Blue eyes like a melting ice cap meet mine and his irises flare.

In the other hand, Jake holds a small plastic box. A corsage of three coral roses rests in a bed of champagne gold tulle with sprigs of baby's breath with pink-tipped petals.

He says nothing, casually offering me the flowers while taking in my appearance as he strolls inside.

I must say, for as many times as I've seen Jake Ballantine in a suit, I'm speechless, too.

Clothes make the man, and Jake has exquisite style. That he was adventurous with his wardrobe and did not require I purchase him the uniform dark suit every other man will be wearing tonight made my inner shopper ecstatic. He was as fun to outfit as Sloan can be. Though I won't risk telling Jake, I'll tell Sloan that when I see her.

He has on his typical crisp white button-down paired with a salmon-colored tie. His spring line tuxedo trousers are a shade lighter than the tan jacket I picked out and had the tailor he uses send over. His broad shoulders are a beacon my eyes can't resist. Not a strand of his blond hair is out of place. Not a speck of lint is caught on his coat.

He's sublime.

I slide my hands over his chest and touch the handkerchief in his breast pocket.

Jake sucks in a breath. "You look incredible," he says.

His knuckles brush my bare arm, sending a tingle throughout my entire body. However, deep lines groove his forehead. Jake appears to be concentrating too hard at keeping is hands off of me.

I frown, unable to understand his hesitation after the ways we've touched one another. The anticipation of being with Jake after a hectic week flows away and I'm left wondering what I've done wrong.

We've exchanged brief text messages since the day I had coffee with Greer. Jake had club-related business, and one of my employees took bereavement to travel to a family member's funeral. I covered her shifts and the extra hours at the boutique kept me on my toes. I hoarded the things I wanted to tell Jake in person for tonight.

The main thing is something I realized after spending the evening with Greer. I've wrapped a lot of myself up in making my store a success, but it's been at the expense of any other dream. Or anything else, really.

I thought I'd find someone eventually. The whole time I was with Gavin, I thought that someone was him. But it wasn't.

Gavin was the man my mom wanted for me. He was the man I intended on making her happy by marrying. I needed my fiancé to love me for her sake. When we were engaged, I was forsaking the happiness the person I might get to grow old with would bring. In the same way that running away gave Gavin back to his perfect person, I was giving me back to mine.

Well, my imperfect, perfect person. If that makes any sense.

With all his bitter flaws, I crave Jake's company. I love the way he challenges me, like he wants me to call him on his assholiness. Jake on the other side of my front door gives me a rabble of butterflies. Jogging into Sweet Caroline's, I can't wait for those first moments when he traps me in the office and the rest of the world ceases to exist.

I can't explain why. Logic has completely flown out the window. Every time I've tried cajoling myself out of thinking this could be love, I recognize whatever I'm feeling is something I haven't felt before. I've fallen for Jake Ballantine.

It's inevitable our schedules will fill up like this again. However, I don't want another week of separation. I want to admire Jake in his fancy suits and I want him to look at me in the desperate way he is right now—like he could lose me. Like he could cherish me. Like someday he might even love me.

I hope after tonight I still feel the same way.

I turn for my bedroom, telling Jake I need to retrieve my matching clutch.

"You rearranged the furniture," he calls after me.

"I did!" I shout. "It was time for a little update."

Gavin pushed the living room furniture against the walls, saying it made the space look bigger. I decided that an intimate conversation area was nicer. So I moved the sofa from in front of the window and pointed the back to the door. The jury is out if I'll keep it this way, but I'm embracing change.

"Are you ready?" Jake asks, resigned.

"Are you?"

"You don't believe me. That you look beautiful." He changes the subject.

I spread my palms over the evening gown I'm wearing to the gala. The slim cut makes me feel taller, and the silk is soft against my skin. After I tried it on, I couldn't resist and wound up spending a fortune. It's the second dress I've done that with and I'm not sure where else I'll be able to wear it. I won't repeat my wardrobe at the annual benefit and it isn't like I expect to RSVP to any black-tie weddings soon.

"I'd be apt to believe you if you didn't look so sad. You're like a bull who has got a ring in his nose and I'm using it to lead you to a slaughterhouse."

Jake laughs but the light doesn't touch his sorrowful eyes.

I grab his chin. My thumb fits in the cleft and I pull his face to mine. I get another rush of power when his long, lean form bends to my will. "What is going on?"

"I don't think I can manage this, Paisley."

"Sure you can. You're Jake Ballentine." I grasp the knot in his tie and cover his lips with mine. Like a moth to a flame, his hands find my hips, his fingers sinking into my ass like there's nothing between us.

He cages my lower half against the rise of the sofa, pushing his legs between mine until I'm perched on the couch. Holding me steady with one hand to the small of my back, Jake raises my silky skirt up over my thighs. His fingers dance under the lace of my stockings. "Did you wear these for me?"

I swallow. And nibble his lip in response.

"These things are so goddamned sexy. When you stuck your hand up your gown and took the ruined pair off, I wanted to be the one taking them off of you." His thumb brushes close to the apex of my sex.

"After the gala, Jake." Holding dominion over a powerful man gives me a thrill. I love the way Jake's kisses make me hot and needy and alive.

He grunts his acquiescence, but not before erasing the inch between my thigh and where my panties cover. The lace is damp and Jake finds out how wet his talented mouth alone makes me—even when it's not centered on my core.

"Christ, *corazón*. What am I doing to you?"

I palm his hard cock. "The same thing I'm doing to you, apparently."

"I can't, uh, I can't be seen at a charity event like this." He glances around circumspect.

"No, I guess you can't, can you?" My toes dip to the floor and I push at Jake's midsection. My fingertips grip the button on his jacket, flicking it open. "Nice belt." I smirk, unbuckling it and undoing his zipper.

"You can't be serious." His hands halo around my form when I drop to my knees. "Now?"

"Why not now?" When have I had the time to repay the favor from our sleepover? "By the way, ruin my hair and I'll kill you."

"What if I smudge your lipstick?" He chortles, lightening the mood.

I prefer this version of us. The sexually charged challenges. The contrary exchanges.

"We all make sacrifices, Jake."

I take him out of his pants and he's every marvelous inch of what I expect. I stroke his thick velvety length and my tongue darts out to taste the pre-cum at the tip.

"The hell did I do to deserve you?" He groans when my lips encircle his cock.

Jake jerks back at the first drawing suck I make, watching the color I painted on when applying my make-up smear from root to tip.

I look up at him under my eyelashes and make a leisurely show of pumping my fist and taking him as far to the back of my throat as possible. My eyes water. I blink back tears, continuing the rhythm.

Jake's hips sway forward, chasing the warmth of my mouth the way I know I fall victim to when he pulls away from one of our breathless kisses.

His hands grow closer to my shoulders. My hair is down the way I've learned from the times he's taken it out of clips and ponytails that he favors. He plays with the tips of my locks, running them between his thumb and forefinger as if they are as supple as the silk I'm wearing.

"I don't know how much longer I can stay standing and still follow your rules."

My knees dig into the carpet and the front of my dress fits snug to my upper legs, in danger of ripping. Yet, I moan around his dick. I have zero intention of stopping. Control slipping from a control freak makes Jake vulnerable, sexier.

I may not have had my fill of fighting with Jake, but I'm done arguing with myself over how much he turns me on. It isn't too much to ask of the man that he stays upright while I have my way with him. The next episode of this little fantasy includes Jake losing it completely, gathering my hair to the base of my skull, and fucking my face. But he doesn't need to know that right now.

Jake brushes my hair to my back, conscientious of the effort it took to curl each tendril.

"Fuck," he says, on the verge.

His palm covers my neck, his thumb strokes the underside of my chin down to my sequined collar, and it rises again. The light pressure is intense and there's a rush of wet warmth in my already damp panties.

He rides the hollow of my hand. Glides between

my lips. Pushes through my pursed cheeks. The pace is frantic at the very end, when the fingertips of my other hand skim the underside of Jake's balls, and the sensation tips him over. I swallow, taking something he's withheld as my own.

Chapter Twenty-two

Jake

Paisley's mother has been boring a hole into my forehead since her daughter made introductions. If I were in a snarkier mood, I'd tell her I've had my fair share of practice with this technique. People in this town have been staring me down since I was a kid, so her laser vision doesn't hurt. I actually took off for a few years while I could. The breather I got from not having to keep my defenses in place did me good. Although I was prepared for everyone's negative reactions when I returned.

Part of me doesn't blame Mrs. Cooper. I'm not the catch that Laughton is, given the crowd of men he's lightheartedly cajoling into making bigger contributions with his too-wide smile, glad-handing, and boring ass stories about medical innovations.

There is also the fact that the server just set my cocktail on the tablecloth atop a napkin that has an embossed heart with an intersecting zig-zagged line. The frantic up and down of my pulse matches the staccato rhythm of the design. In bright red lettering,

"Brighton General's Cyrus P. Cooper Heart and Vascular Disease Foundation" surrounds it.

"You failed to mention this charity ball is named after your dad," I say to my girlfriend.

What we did, what Paisley Cooper did to me an hour ago to make me relax, seemed very real. The disjointed place we are with one another right now—not knowing certain things about what makes the other tick—puts a strain on our connection.

"It wasn't always. He started the ball when he was the head of the department. The board renamed it after his death." Paisley plays with the corsage on her wrist.

There's an overarching sensation that we're out of place.

Or I am. Not that I don't know why. I'm waiting for the other shoe to drop.

I'm playing along that our issue is my introduction to Mrs. Cooper wasn't as pleasant as the welcome Paisley got from Caroline. However, the hair on my neck stands on end each time Laughton diverts his gaze to us. It was futile hoping he'd remain in his court while we shuffled in ours.

Eventually, he approaches where the three of us sit. On the inside, I'm begging that he leaves the shop out of whatever is about to come out of his mouth. Laughton apologizing won't make the legitimate reasons I had for doing what I did to protect Paisley any easier for her to accept.

"Paisley, could I speak to you in private?" Gavin bends, talking into her ear.

I rest a hand on her knee. "Anything you have to say, you can say here."

"I suppose that's true" He snuffs. "I was sincerely sorry to hear about your recent trouble and wanted to reassure you that my sister had nothing to do with shattering the boutique window. She was planning to join me as my date. When I saw your RSVP on the guest list, I decided it was best if I came alone. Accepting that you've moved on has been even more difficult for me since her outburst at Royce's. My career, my professional reputation, treating my patients has gotten me through the past three months. I wouldn't want to see anything improper happen for a third time when what we're here for is to focus on solving problems much bigger than our own."

"Thank you for being sensitive and putting your patient's needs first, Gavin. I appreciate it." Paisley replies with grace. "I don't deserve your forgiveness. I apologize for not being honest about—" She stops and sighs. "Everything. You are a good man, a wonderful physician, and an asset to the hospital. I'll stay out of your way tonight for the sake of the gala."

"That's a slight problem for me. I could actually use your help."

"Mine?" An apprehensive Paisley squeaks, looking between Gavin and me.

I would have expected her voice to have raised based on the way her eyes land on mine. She's practiced tamping down the shrill exclamations that used to shoot out of her because I told Paisley when she agreed to be my fake girlfriend that she needed to work on being more docile. The thing is, I'm not a huge fan of her falling in line with my demands.

What Paisley wants is to make amends, but she's also tethered to my side. That I do like. But Paisley is unsure if she's supposed to ask my permission or do as she wants, risking me balking and her supposed cheating on Laughton causing a scene in the ballroom.

"You should help Gavin, Paisley.' Mrs. Cooper chimes in, creating a new level of angst.

Our friends haven't arrived. If Paisley leaves the

table, it's her mom and me flying solo. I can handle whatever Mrs. Cooper throws at me, but I have doubts Paisley thinks I can remain polite for her sake.

We're in an indelicate place. The eyes of several donors prove they are fixated on what will happen between the three of us. Whether Paisley recognizes it or not, the time she spent on her knees, talking me down with her precocious, pouty lips was exactly what I needed to get my ass in gear and deal with the consequences. She needs to believe I can man up and do what she needs me to do as well.

"Perhaps Paisley should hear Dr. Laughton's request?" I'm formal, addressing Gavin. Not to be an asshole. He's the heart surgeon. This is his soirée we're crashing, and frankly, this is as close to burying the hatchet as we're ever going to get.

I'm grateful that Laughton approaching our table hasn't ended in an uproar. Pais admitted she made a mistake. She deserves for her ex to treat her with the same respect she's giving him.

Laughton clasps his hands. "Do you remember Mr. Crowder from the benefit last year?"

"Yes, the older gentleman. He was quite generous."

"He was. Because of you. You spend a good deal of time—"

"Schmoozing him?" Her lovable laugh is like a tinkling bell.

Laughton's head makes a round on his shoulders. "I prefer: indulging his curiosity. But, yes. Mr. Crowder inquired about you when he arrived and it was clear his contribution level was on his mind. He's interested in having his name engraved on the wall in the heart unit as an ongoing contributor, but I suspect he might need a nudge. I understand if you aren't willing to speak with him. However, based on how candid he was when he asked me if you'd be here, I don't get the impression Mr. Crowder was ever aware of our engagement."

Her tooth sinks into her lip and the heat of uncertainty surrounding my behavior pinkens her cheeks. A mental war rages inside Paisley's head. Being outgoing is in her nature and it makes Paisley a great store owner. This is an important event for her. She knows she can encourage Mr. Crowder to donate if she aligns her interests with Gavin's.

It's me that's the problem... Except I'm not. Laughton seems to have enough coolth to avoid the reason behind why his sister's outburst is a sensitive topic for him. And for as territorial as Gavin's presence makes me, it isn't like I'm going to piss all over Paisley and mark her as my own.

As a matter of fact, it's her lipstick staining my dick, which gives my girlfriend a claim on me.

Paisley and I didn't fuck out our insecurities in the beginning. We haven't yet because I get that she's at a point in her life when she expects a commitment along with sex. I may have been trying the idea on for size as well. So, I trust this woman isn't a bed-jumper.

"I won't stop you, *Corazón*." I have no reason to be on the defensive based on Gavin's current demeanor.

On the inside I want her to go. On the inside I want her to stay. Holding opposing emotions confuses the hell out of me, but my gut says that if Paisley goes, she will be back. We're like magnets; the same ornery poles face one another and we repel, but it's hard to separate us when we get it right.

"It's fine, Gavin. It won't hurt me to kill Mr. Crowder with kindness." Her grip on my hand tightens as she stands. "Thank you." Her features soften with gratitude, similar to the way she peers up at me when I have her tucked to my chest.

I pat myself on the back for managing to get being a good boyfriend right, but there's an unexpected level of missing Paisley when the soft silk of her gown brushes my skin as she turns to walk away.

I watch the swish of her hips. How commanding her presence is despite her size. Across the ballroom, it's Paisley that snags Mr. Crowder's attention before Gavin has the opportunity to present her. Laughton stays put, but it is my charming girlfriend doing the hardest job since Mr. Crowder is rapt on whatever Paisley is saying.

Damn, she's beautiful. The way she smiles. The confident way she holds herself. I wonder why I haven't seen it before. Yet there's an air of familiarity to it, as if I've been drunk with blinders on to how much positivity Paisley brought into my life when she launched herself at me.

It seems I'll do anything and everything to make her happy, even surrender her attention.

"She's in her element," Mrs. Cooper boasts. "Last year, the foundation had record donations. People were generous the year my husband died, but since Paisley and Gavin have increased their involvement, it's exceeded expectations."

"Are you more afraid that I wouldn't let her come, or that I'd stop her from interacting with donors?"

"I'm more afraid that your mere presence ruins an event that Paisley loves."

"That I will further corrupt her reputation."

"Correct."

"And in doing so, the contributions to the cardiac department dry up."

"This gala connects her to her father, Mr. Ballantine. They were extremely close. Paisley doesn't deserve to feel like she failed my husband if the foundation's goals aren't met."

Fingers pinch the shoulder of my suit. I glance up to see Carver standing behind me. I tell him I'm glad they made it, going as far as complimenting Sloan and offering her the seat next to mine. Then I return my attention to Mrs. Cooper and make polite introductions before conceding.

"I agree and can see how memorializing your husband is difficult, no matter the circumstances. Except what I've heard is it appears Mrs. Galloway has quite the positive influence on your daughter's business. And although it's poor form to point out, Mr. Galloway, who decided to attend because Paisley and I would be, has as deep pockets as anyone else."

"My wife has already instructed me about how many zeros we're parting with." Carver chuckles. "Sloan is quite the philanthropist with causes she has a connection to."

"I misspoke, and it was offensive," Paisley's mother blanches.

Wanting the higher road for myself, I latch onto Mrs. Cooper's apology, though it isn't directed at me. She's eating crow in front of Sloan and Carver.

"You got off your chest what you needed to, but I hope that by the time the evening ends, you'll give me the benefit of the doubt."

Mrs. Cooper nods. Distracted, her eyelids stretch wide. "Perhaps the rest of this discussion is best held for later on. Cary Cass is here."

"Lovely. I'm so glad we didn't have to wait long for them." Sloan sips some bubbly.

"This is the first time the board sent an invitation to Cary. Now that he's the face of the automotive dealership and married, it seemed appropriate to include him on the list. Paisley mentioned we'd be sitting at the same table," Mrs. Cooper mentions, tamping down the excitement that would make her daughter squeal.

Ah, so that's where Paisley gets the idiosyncrasy from. Now, I wish I knew what Paisley inherited from her father. Maybe it's the animated way she speaks with her hands?

My ears remain on Sloan and Mrs. Cooper's conversation, but I return to watching Paisley. What Mrs. Cooper said is true, Paisley is in her element. She'll convince this guy to become a benefactor and has the charisma to do the same with whomever else she speaks with. The foundation's endowments don't need my friends to cover lost contributions.

"Cary's wife is a good friend of ours, Mrs. Cooper. Holly managed Jake's club." Sloan links her arm in mine. I shift my stance, shocked when Sloan pats my forearm. "Personally, I always thought he'd act exactly the way the rumors about Jake Ballantine describe him. But Jake is full of surprises. He's been supportive of Holly's new nursery since he found out Cary had purchased it for her as a wedding gift. You've even gotten Paisley flowers from there, haven't you, Jake?"

"From the former owner, yes. He lives next door, and Holly knew he had coral roses." My mouth, agape from my best friend's wife touching me, clamps shut.

Sloan walked into a situation where she could tear me limb from limb and is sticking up for me instead. Hell has frozen over.

"Aren't those her favorite?" Sloan asks Mrs. Cooper.

"They are."

Chapter Twenty-three

Paisley

Stealing looks at Jake while I spoke to Mr. Crowder became addictive when I caught Jake's eye. Each time we've glanced at one another since, my heart has done this silly little flutter. Because he's always looking back at me. Not with a scowl or his jaw set sharp, demanding that I shower him with attention and be a doting girlfriend. His expression is something warmer. He's actually blushed when our gaze has lingered too long.

Yet, for as much as I feel the pull to Jake's side, the way your fingertips itch to touch something expensive and decadent—or sinister and off-limits—after I've spoken to Mr. Crowder, I schmooze other potential donors.

Whatever is happening between Jake and me tonight is a game with no losers. His often lopsided grin when he's laughing at whatever is happening with his friends at our table reassures me he's doing fine. Swift donations to the foundation pour in over the next hour passes. And our separation, though it's only across the ballroom, emboldens me.

The months of problems while fighting the negative social media posts that tore me down and the fear I'll lose my business have flown away. It's as if struggling has helped me bloom. I have the confidence to ask for what the hospital's patients need. Even more so than in previous years when I've encouraged donations above and beyond the hefty per plate fee we've all paid to be here. In the past, I pleaded for everyone to empathize with a situation they'll never endure. When all they needed to hear was a personal thank you for the good they were doing.

I also wonder if I sought their pity. Their condolences. Their good favor. A glimpse at something I'll never witness the way I was present for the community's outpouring of support at my father's funeral.

Which is also odd since I'm relying on these people, whom I hardly know, to replace the friends who should be there in the end.

I cast a final look at my date. Jake's rough edges are no longer jagged enough that I live in constant fear he'll hurt me.

Will he be there? I think. And it hits me all at once that whether we're still together or not, Jake would. He might hide behind a gravestone and wait for the crowd to disperse so that no one saw Jake Ballentine express emotion, but *my Jake* would be there to say goodbye.

The pitter-pat in my chest shoots up and out of my shoulders. As if carried by wings, I'm weightless. My dad's presence surrounds me as I give into the inexplicable draw to Jake.

Sloan and Holly's hugs intercept me from my target. I'm glad they are here. The way the mill girls have their brunches and shopping trips, I have the uncanny notion that this could be our thing. The three of us could get dressed to the nines and enjoy a triple date for a good cause.

When they return to their seats, I don't stop to worry if they'd be sad—or even notice—if I weren't here. I'm simply happy they are.

Standing behind Jake, I don't have far to lean for my breath to blow over the shell of his ear. "I'd like to dance."

"With me?" There's a hint of sarcasm, but no hesitation.

"No. With Mr. Crowder. Yes, with you!"

"I thought you'd never ask."

He sweeps me to the parquet, tucking me into the safe spot in his chest I adore.

What an odd coupling. The big man and the tiny lady. The carnie act was the opposite, but we're still a sight to behold.

Jake interrupts my thoughts. "There's something I want to tell you, and I don't want you to get an inflated ego."

I stop swaying and pull back from his embrace. "I'm sure that's my line." I wink.

"Ouch, *Corazón*. You think I have a big ego?" He tugs me back and I have to crane my neck up to see his brilliant blue eyes.

"Along with a few other parts of you." I lick my lips. I can't not be aware of the heat from inside Jake's trousers intensifying. His belt presses against my belly, no matter what.

He laughs and I reach up to cup his face. To hold on to this gruff man's gentle smile.

"I wanted to say I'm proud of you."

"You are?" My voice cracks.

"It's quite a con you pulled tonight, separating all these rich socialites from their money. I'm impressed. I could use a talent like yours."

"Jake!"

"*Shh*… I'm kidding, Pais. What you did was remarkable, though. I'm glad I got to watch it, even if it meant losing out on the time I'd wanted to spend with you."

"I missed you so much this week," I whisper.

"Now there's an ego boost." He makes me laugh. "I should have asked if Greer was okay."

"Can you keep a secret?"

"King of secret keeping at your service."

"Greer and Byron are having a baby. She needed someone to talk to and chose me."

"You seem surprised."

"I thought there was someone she was closer with who she'd share such important news with." I frown.

Jake's chin wrinkles. "You like kids, *Corazón*?"

His endearment may have started out to fool others, but I know what it translates to. My heart.

Jake has mine and, if I'm not careful, too soon it will get broken.

"Mm-hmm." I hum my answer.

Jake swallows, wrapping me tighter in his arms. The lightness I felt before we stepped onto the dance floor fades.

He kisses the crown of my head, his lips lingering. "There's something else I want to say, Paisley."

"Careful with the compliments, Jake. My ego might get as big as yours."

I look up and those blue eyes are dark and serious. "I'd do anything for you.

After he says it, Jake's features soften as if his admission astounds him.

"Okay." I set my thumb into the cleft in his chin. "Repeat after me. I don't just like being around you, Paisley Cooper. I like you."

He brushes my hand away and places both palms over my cheeks. Before kissing me, he says, "I don't just love you, Paisley Cooper. I want to take you home, lie you down in your bed, and show you exactly how much."

If anyone surrounding us hadn't heard the rumor that Jake and I were together, they'd have figured it out when our lips parted after he used the L-word.

I, for sure, wasn't saying it first. Jake zipped right past what I needed to hear to what my heart wanted.

The flutters are back. A million wings beat inside my chest.

I'm ready to risk wanting Jake in all the ways I denied myself from wanting him. I want his body covering mine and to feel him inside of me. I want to hear him tell me he loves me again as we undress. I want to give him my secret and hear him say he loves me, anyway. That I'm perfect the way I am. That his strong shoulders and that soft place I always seem to land against his chest will protect me.

"Why are we still here?" I ask, as Jake nips at my lower lip.

Jake and I leave the dance floor and make our goodbyes. I feel awful that I haven't spent enough time with our guests, except my blood is on fire thinking about the promise of Jake in my bed.

My mother touches my forehead. My flushed face concerns her when I mention that I have a slight headache. I'm certain that Sloan and Holly see through my excuse. Both apprise Jake with knowing looks and lean into their husbands as if they hope the night ends on the same note.

My feet weren't touching the ground before Jake scoops under my butt and carries me into my bedroom. We kiss with reckless abandon and my fingertips make fast work of the buttons on his shirt. I'm drowning in his scent and living off of the euphoria of not having to hold back.

Fucking is Jake's idea. Don't get me wrong, it's a

great idea. I'm all in. But no matter how much I want him, I can still maintain that I had no expectations of going to bed with him tonight.

The worst lies are the ones you tell yourself. I should have been truthful with Jake.

I kneel on the bed, watching a brutally sexy Jake shed his coat. His wrists catch on his cuffs and his shirt is wide open, exposing smooth skin that covers hard muscle. I unbuckle that pesky belt and his trousers fall to the floor. I grip his long length, my fingers hardly completing a circle around his swollen shaft. Jake lets out a painful groan when I tug. His lip curls and his white teeth flash an arrogant smile, proving he likes me taking the lead. Rolling a condom on, my impetuousness makes me wonder if it will cover his entire shaft. Jake is well-endowed and we're not having sex without protection.

The jeweled button securing my dress at my neck is undone. The frantic need to see how amazing sleeping together will be puts a stop to our undressing. We fall backward onto the mattress. Jake's heavy paw eases up my leg, bunching the trapped yards of silky fabric at our waists.

"I wanted to fuck you so hard the night you ran into the club. I wanted to take my cock out, lift your lily white dress, and lay waste to your pretty pink pussy," he says gruffly.

"Why didn't you?" His words have me soaked.

"Lust makes a man weak." Jake licks down my neck, intending to dip his mouth closer to my breasts.

I whimper when our chests separate. Again, when he grabs my thigh, pushing it up and my slick core feels the first sensation of the mushroom head of his cock sliding against my slit.

"And love doesn't?"

"No. Love lets me claim your cunt as my own and

vow to never let another man near you again."

My back arches as Jake thrusts his cock inside of me. The searing pain of someone as tiny as me accommodating his size subsides with the gentle rocking motion of his hips. I swallow virginal words I never understood until I saw how well-endowed Jake is. I worried it would never fit. But it fits. We fit.

I open my eyes. Watching Jake's awe. Listening to ceaseless dirty thoughts tumble unbound from his mouth, telling me how much he likes how tight and wet I am. I feel every inch of him and, each time his hips jerk, the last thing Jake makes me feel is tight.

The conflict between us these past few months morphs into the struggle to remain as close as possible. Perhaps that's why we fight. We've been trying to make sense of everything so we can be together.

Jake brings me to the edge and backs off until the rumpled silk of my gown is damp with sweat and perspiration drips down his temple. Giving into pleasure, I've all but forgotten that he's-not-to-be-trusted Jake Ballentine and I'm can't-be-honest Paisley Cooper. The way I tumble over the edge, my thighs clamped around Jake's waist and my pussy pulsing around his breathtaking dick, is the most genuine experience I've had. I swear I see stars when Jake gets me there a second time as his own orgasm overtakes him.

His hips keep riding the slow rippling waves that leave me incoherent. Mere inches from suckling on my nipple, I anticipate the sting when Jake beads it between his lips and teases it with his teeth. I want to make love to him all night. But everything comes to a screeching halt.

He stares at the flat white scar over my sternum. His expression is as horrified as mine.

I yank the bodice over my exposed front. "Jake, I

can explain."

I should have told him about the surgeries I had when I was a kid. About how I have a congenital heart defect passed on by my father. A father who dedicated his life to research and cardiac patients, and whose legacy was organizing a charity benefit so that people like me have a chance to live a long life. Because he wasn't just a doctor, my dad was a patient, too.

There was no reason to reveal this part of me to Jake when we met. I'm flawed and Jake has his choice of sexy and flawless strippers at Sweet Caroline's. Sex wasn't a reality between us. He wasn't winning me over with his devilish charms. We weren't supposed to keep kissing one another. I wasn't supposed to fall in love.

Jake has already scrambled off the mattress and grabbed his trousers. He's halfway out the bedroom door, clutching his clothes like he's woken from a siren song as I'm about to lure him into the depths.

I begin to shake, my heart aware of his revulsion the way only a few moments ago my body accepted him inside of me.

This man was the means to my end with Gavin. Then faking our relationship was to put a stop to Jake's friends harassing him about settling down. We were using one another. I was an easy target. An easy lay. But Jake didn't get the sensual, beautiful, perfect woman he made one last bargain for. I did my best to dazzle him and dupe him into taking me to bed.

It's obvious omitting the truth disgusts Jake. When he dares a last look at my tear-stained face his features harden and he says the last thing I'd ever expect.

"I threw the rock."

Jake

I'm familiar with the feeling of getting in the car and driving to a destination, but the middle part—the actual travel—gets lost. Autopilot it's called. But for that to happen, I figured a person needs a mental roadmap of the streets they're traveling to get to the destination.

I've never been where I am. Although an internal compass led me here; down a two-lane country road, past a well-maintained Tudor mansion surrounded by a tall fence. I turn the wheel right. The tires bump over gravel. In my rear view mirror, yellowish orange dust kicks up. Through the translucent plume, I can still make out where I came from. The problem is, I can't see what's in front of me, and I haven't been able to see where I'm headed for a long time. A haze of uncertainty has obscured the road in front of me for years.

Peeking from between the trees to my left, I spy a round turret of a Victorian. It's not as old or as big, yet it is as elegant as the Tudor I passed and even the

Georgian monstrosity I grew up in. To my right, there are stables and a veterinary office. Straight ahead are row upon row of vines. Perched in the midst is a massive barn-like building, marked: banquet hall and tasting room.

I pull into the winery parking lot, kill the engine and sit there, a witness to the surrounding greenery and expansive vineyard that has the pull of heaven.

"What the hell are you doing?" I ask myself for the umpteenth time. My fingers grip my unwashed hair.

I've been alone with my thoughts since bolting from Paisley's.

For as much as I wanted to fuck her from the instant she leaped into my arms on Valentine's Day, I'd been waiting for Paisley to be ready for us to be intimate. Our chemistry was off the charts, so when we finally fell into bed, the experience was bound to be explosive.

But I've avoided what I've known on a deeper level, too. That the sizzle between us is more than sex. It made lying to my friends effortless, and our connection an easier pill for me to swallow.

I'd decided when Liz died that relationships, girlfriends, and especially wives were a burden. I wasn't tying myself down to any woman. But something about Paisley being brave and stubborn—and fucking crazy enough to pass off an asshole like me as her lover—gave me no choice.

I can still feel her baby-soft skin under my fingertips. The way strands of her silky brown hair glide between my fingers when I massage the base of her neck. My dick has tried to punch through my fly the number of times I've thought about the way her lashes fluttered when she sucked me off. I was seconds from bailing on attending the benefit, and it wasn't Paisley's lips wrapped around my cock that convinced me to stay by her side. It was every moment I'd spent with her until that point.

On the way to Paisley's house, I'd come to the conclusion that she should go alone so that I didn't have to deal with any fallout from Laughton. Gavin has to have known I was the one who broke the boutique window. How was she going to stay with me if he let that slip? And if he didn't? If Laughton acted more like I would have when I held any power? The last thing I needed was for Paisley's ex to laud that information over my head.

I'm convinced Laughton is the better man for Paisley. She was a rockstar at the gala. I was so turned on. So tuned in to her. I don't remember the last time I saw a woman with the immense poise and sophistication to let bygones be bygones.

To ignore anyone's shit.

Yeah, I do. She left this earth too early. And, when I didn't get my way, I was an ass to her, too.

I'd let bitterness and my emotions overrule all else.

Paisley has a flat white scar over her sternum where a surgeon stitched her back together. She's healed.

But as I disengaged our bodies, a decade of scrambled memories flooded my consciousness, making it obvious that I'm... *not*.

Still out of order, the flashes of Paisley and Liz have me squinting like I'm staring it into the sun. They continue making my head hurt. The shock hasn't worn off.

Guilt swells over my horrible reaction and the irrational need to put distance between me and the woman I was sure I loved.

What if it's her *heart?* Echoes between my ears. *Who is the woman that I've been with all these months? Why weren't you man enough to stay there and ask her about the scar?*

The pinch of another migraine rushes at me as the

memory of my confession replays.

"I threw the rock."

It was out of my mouth almost before it was on the tip of my tongue. I couldn't stop it.

If Paisley has heart problems, then she belongs with Laughton, a cardiologist.

And in my current state of mind, the last place I should be is in Texas. This is where Cris escaped the band, L.A., and the Sunset Strip, after I put those reeking lilies on Liz's coffin. Kingsbrier is his haven. I deserve to suffer a lifetime of purgatory for bringing my wretched troubles to his doorstep.

As I'm about to restart the car's ignition, two kids run out from between the rows of grapes. The older boy has dark hair. The younger one is a towhead. They shout with glee, chucking handfuls of something at one another the way kids pelt one another with Nerf guns.

The blond boy dashes the way he came, using the vines for cover. About to give chase, the older boy pauses. He looks my way. My car is the only vehicle in the lot.

Our eyes meet and I swallow hard. He's nothing like her and yet the air surrounding him proves he's everything like his mother.

Liz's son, Mateo.

I get out of the car, and the boy wanders toward me. He kicks his heel high bringing it to his toe, walking an invisible tight wire.

"We're closed Tuesdays," the boy I think is Mateo Sanchez says in a voice that is too old to be a kid's and not quite ready to crack. He reminds me a little of Holly's son.

"I was looking for a man named Cris Sanchez. Do you know where I can find him?"

"Are you a wine distributor?"

"Would it make a difference if I were?"

"Not really… Only if you're planning to rat me and Corey out for having a grape war."

"Throwing grapes is kid stuff. You are a kid, right?"

"That depends on how much trouble I'm in. Sometimes grown-ups tell ya to cut it out because you're too old to act a certain way. But it doesn't take long for them to flip the script and say you're too young to do something else."

The kid is smart.

"I'm not a distributor, and I won't rat you out. " I wink. "Cris is an old… friend."

He shrugs before he speaks, confirming what I've already surmised. "He's my dad. Come on, I'll show you this office. You gotta name?"

"Jake Ballentine. You?"

"Mateo," he replies, unimpressed. Not that I expected his dad to have mentioned me.

When I've thought of this kid, Mateo's still been an infant, cooing up at Liz.

Inside the barn building, we take a few twists and turns. He guides me past some shiny fermenters and raps on an open door. "Dad, this Jake guy is here to see you."

"Okay, thanks. Tell him I'll be out in a minute." Cris does a double-take when he looks up from the papers he is studying. I'm standing behind Mateo in the threshold. "Well, I'll be goddamned," he mutters, his eyes wide as saucers.

"I'm telling mom you swore." The idle threat Mateo makes accompanies a daring smile.

Cris lifts a finger, his grin as white. "Get back outside and play. Stay out of your mother's way. She's got patients at the clinic today… And keep out of the trellis before you kids do any more damage to this year's crop!" he yells after his son, who is scampering away.

"They pluck the grapes and chuck them at one

another." Cris rises from his seat.

"You don't say?" I tilt my chin.

"You watched them?" He shakes his head back and forth.

I flatten my lips, not giving away a thing.

Unsure of how Cris would receive my visit, I relax when he gives me a bro-hug.

"You look good, man." His greeting ignores that I've driven through four states in less than three days. I slept in my passenger seat after leaving North Carolina. I'm wearing rumpled clothes I bought on the road.

"You look... Different." The port wine birthmark that covered most of Cris's face is gone.

Cris steps back to take an identical gander at me, joking in a fond way. "Were you always this tall?"

I sputter something incomprehensible and we laugh.

"So you're a winemaker now?"

"It's a family business. My father-in-law and I put in a lot of hours getting it up and running. I'm here most of the time, but we've got a decent staff nowadays that takes the pressure off. He's finally settled into retirement and I can pursue other interests."

My lip quirks.

The decision to head west was involuntary. I drove all night after leaving Paisley's. Stopping at Dusty's mountain home in Boone, I used the hidden spare key to let myself in. After crashing on his sofa, the next morning, I wound further into the Appalachian Mountains. By the time I hit the border, and crossed over into Tennessee, I figured what the hell, why not keep going? I'd driven almost five hundred miles already. Nashville was only a few hundred more.

In music city, the sugar-laden gas station candy bars and salty chips I'd sustained myself on had gotten stale. I wandered into a restaurant for lunch. Framed pictures of celebrities adorned every inch of the walls. Wouldn't you know, the booth the waitress sat me at had a black and white of songwriter Cris Sanchez along with the singer of his last hit.

Knew the song from the radio. Never knew they were Cris's lyrics.

Maybe it was that I wasn't starving after a good meal. Or the miles I'd put between me and Brighton. I was already halfway to Texas. So, perhaps I needed to see for myself that the Cris in the picture wasn't the devastated widower who threw the success we'd striven for out the window.

When we got the news of Liz's car accident, Cris was a basket case. Her death upended the band's whole lives, not only his. Now, he's someone else entirely.

So why am I the same pissed-off drummer whose dreams of stardom were crushed in that collision?

An uncomfortable silence passes between us.

"It's been eleven years, and I'm pretty sure the last thing you said to me was 'go fuck yourself'. So, why are you here, Jake?"

"I was hoping you could help me figure that out."

Chapter Twenty-five

Paisley

"I hate to say I told you so, sweetheart."

"Then don't," I retort in a ragged huff and flop onto the sofa. My elbow rests on the arm and my chin catches on my fist. I bend my knee and set my bare foot on the cushion.

My mother is bustling around my living room fluffing pillows. She's not a fan of the new furniture arrangement. I'm not sure she was ever going to be a fan of Jake's.

Not in the mood to argue, I grab the last pillow she fluffed, hugging it to fit the empty spot in my chest.

I was successful at avoiding my mom's calls since Jake disappeared from my life four days ago. But the one thing anyone who endured serious medical problems as a kid will tell you is that there's only so much space a parent used to hovering can stand. Add on that I had a "headache" when I left the gala and that my mother's messages were super-clingy, it left me no choice but to pick up the phone and say my radio silence was because Jake and I had broken things off.

My lips twist and I fight back another wash of tears. How lucky am I that I have someone who calls to pester me? Who would my mother give all of this love to if I weren't here?

"Listen," I call toward the kitchen, where Mom is pouring us cups of herbal tea. "It doesn't make a difference to me whether you approved of my boyfriend or not. I understand why you don't. *Didn't*. It's not like Jake has a stellar reputation. Can we move on to a lighter topic?"

Mom brought a box of chocolate croissants over to cheer me up.

"That's fine." She takes two coasters from the stack on the coffee table and places each of our steamy saucers on top. "I ran into Greer and Karen at Baked Beans. Greer had just told Karen her big news. Karen is thrilled, like an expectant grandmother. Are you excited for her?"

Of course, I'm excited for Greer. How could I not be? Greer and I talked about her concerns over her business partner's reaction.

Previous to opening Mind Your Own Beeswax, Greer and Byron were co-workers at an animal training facility that Karen and her husband own. Finding out Greer and Byron had begun a relationship was hard for Karen. Karen's son died in a tragic accident at eighteen. He and Greer had been close as children and both families had the impression they'd get married someday. With the support of Greer and Karen's husband, Mac, Karen has new strategies to cope with a serious amount of grief she was sure she had a handle on. I'm glad for everyone's sake the gap between the past and the present isn't as deep anymore.

"It's wonderful Karen's going to get to be a part of this baby's life. Byron's going to be a great dad," I say.

"Finding someone like that is so important. You'll see. You'll know when it's right."

"I don't want kids, Mom." I never have, and I've told her this before.

"You say that now." She pats my knee. "Your father was a wonderful father."

My mother is about to sing-song about our family's highlights. The first days of school when my dad walked me to the bus stop, the vacations, and everything in between. We've had this discussion too many times to count. I could repeat the stories verbatim. After all, I was there with adults doting upon me, and I remember almost everything after the age of two.

But today I'm tired and I don't want to hear mom recount her version the same way I don't want her to make me feel like shit by slandering Jake.

"Do you remember how your father took the day off and held your hand—"

"In the waiting room before I had an abortion? Yes, Mom. I do."

Like it was yesterday, actually. He held my hand through the silent parking lot as well. Secure in my choice, the idea that protesters would be there, yelling that I was going to hell, horrified me. I hate to break it to them, but when you're that scared someone intends to hurt you for doing something you have every right to do, you're already in hell.

I was lucky my dad was there for me. He will forever be the best man I'll have ever known that he supported me. That he remained by my side and didn't judge.

"How? When? Your father and I—we didn't have secrets in our marriage. I would have... known..." Her sad voice trails.

"When we went on the three-day weekend the year

I opened the boutique."

I roll my lips between my teeth. Though unintentional, I'm riddled with guilt that I've tarnished my mother's memory of the man she loved. He did so much good in this world.

Dad's own heart condition and the work he did on behalf of his patients were likely the reason he had empathy when I went to him.

I never wanted children. Twenty years ago, cardiac surgeons told my parents it was a risk to my health for me to carry a pregnancy to term. Ten years ago, there was a glimmer of potential. But by then, the vision I had of my life included my store. My hard work fulfilled me. To my dismay, as my goal was coming to fruition, my birth control failed.

I'd been on the pill for years and the man I'd been exclusive with and I stopped using a second method. The marriage discussion hadn't come up. Not that I had any interest. We were the Friday night couple. Committed enough to enjoying our youth that our arrangement worked for us. He was straight out of business school with an MBA. Unable to hire the help I was in desperate need of, I put in insane hours getting the store up and running.

I didn't tell him I was pregnant. Eventually, he moved away to start a new job. Wrapped up in getting my fledgling business off the ground, I missed his presence less and less faster than I thought I would. What we had wasn't true love. It was companionship, pure and simple.

"We would have helped you. I would have helped you!" My mother's voice rises. She wants grandchildren.

"Dad *did* help me."

"He lied about a father-daughter trip so that you could." Flustered, her hands wave in the air.

I grab them, squeezing tight. "So I could live my

life and reach for my dreams."

"Marrying Gavin would have changed your mind about motherhood. Having you was one of the most important moments. I couldn't imagine it if you weren't here. You survived so much more than any child should endure."

I know Mom can't. I don't like thinking about that either because my mom has weathered major health crises with the two people she loves. I'm aware those feelings add to the reasons I find having children unappealing. I don't want to bring a baby into the world who would suffer the way I did. And while I'm intelligent enough to understand it's unavoidable, deep down I don't want to leave anyone else on this earth lonely and longing for me.

"You want me to experience motherhood, but have you considered for a second that isn't what *I* want? I don't need children to feel fulfilled. I left Gavin because I don't want my mind changed. I want him to experience being a parent with someone else. He deserves to be happy and marrying me would've been tragic.

"Having a baby would have made both of us miserable because only one of us pictured our life as incomplete without kids.

"I'm allowed to be as selfish about this, Mom, as anyone who does everything they can to have a child when they're told they can't get pregnant. It's okay not to want the responsibility of giving birth and raising another person. It's okay to not have it in you."

I was assured my father had my best interest at heart. However, when I went to my dad for advice because he was a doctor I trusted, he asked me something I'll never forget.

"Paisley, what if when I was your age someone told me to not become a cardiologist and carry a child instead?"

"No one would have asked you that," I scoffed. *He was a heart doctor. I wanted a simple boutique I'd been planning my entire teenage years.*

"And no one should ask it of you either."

Suddenly, Dad's dreams had the same weight as my own. It wasn't that he was capable of something better than me. It was that I was capable. Period.

"Why didn't he tell me?" My mother wipes her cheeks.

"It wasn't his secret to share."

"You don't like babies?"

"Oh, I love babies. Other people's babies. I plan to spoil Greer's baby rotten." I giggle lighthearted.

Mom gives me a watery smile and a hug. "Is there anything else you need to tell me?"

"I didn't tell Jake about my heart surgeries and that's why we broke up." A straggling tear tumbles onto my lap.

She shakes her head. "That makes no sense."

"Really, mom? He's around tall, perfect women who prance around topless without zero scars between their boobs. Think Jake Ballentine wants to pass a short girl with a cardiac issue off as the epitome of womanhood?"

I hide my scar with pretty clothes. Not because it bothers me that I have a heart condition, but because the inquisitive looks and questions I used to get about it became intrusive. I don't mind discussing it on my terms. But I'm also certain that I didn't want Jake to see it—for him to see me as flawed—and that's why neither of us getting fully naked when we fooled around was a relief.

Not to mention, I don't want kids and Jake definitely held me closer when the subject of having a baby came up on the dance floor.

The only thing we did right was fight... And kiss.

Four days and I miss his kisses.

But Jake and I were so mismatched. My humiliation when he ran out is a taste of my own medicine. As a general rule, I'd say my health wasn't his damn business, but I deserved as much for not disclosing an obvious problem to Jake. I'd begun caring too much about him and what he thought about me.

I even feel like I forced Jake's hand by making him tell me he liked me. He said love—and both he and I know I was fishing for that word—so having our first time together blow up was a pie in my face. It shouldn't come as a shock that Jake lies to get his way.

"I don't know, Paisley. Far be it from me to defend Jake Ballentine, but from what I saw at the gala, you had Jake in a trance."

"I'll get over it." I bat a heavy hand. He was just my hot-as-sin rebound guy. "It's better this way. Plus, Jake admitted he threw the rock and shattered the boutique window."

I wasn't planning on admitting that to my mom.

It's also something I deserve for being naïve enough to fall for a snake.

My mother gasps and hugs me, hard. Mom didn't approve of me dating Jake. Yet she also didn't put any major roadblocks in my way and I made sure if I spoke to her about him, it was in a positive light. It did little to change her ingrained opinion of him, but Mom also understands—even if I'm denying it—that what he and I had was special to me.

We look at one another and the fissures in my heart crack a tiny bit more. She's still upset and crying because she can't fix my life. And it hurts that I can't fix hers and make losing my dad, and finding out he kept things from her, any easier.

My mother uses her thumbs to wipe my tears away. "You look so tired, Paisley. You need a vacation. You work too hard and should have taken a break before the wedding."

"You're right, Mom. I'd like to go away and I'd like it if you came with me." There's something I've been putting off doing for me. It's time I found the strength to do it.

Chapter Twenty-six

Jake

"Country, dude?" I sputter with a hint of sarcasm.

After a quick walking tour of the Kingsbrier ranch, we're in a different office at Cris's house; the Tudor I passed. Instead of blue ribbons from wine competitions, gold records line the walls and there are awards on the shelves.

As part of the cook's tour, Cris showed me the small recording studio in his home. Then we placed my meager belongings in the guest room down the hall that he offered for me to crash in. It's arranged like a mini-apartment with a private bath and conveniences that you'd find in a longer term stay suite. The entire set-up makes me wonder who else Cris has had for company that his wife is okay with the intrusion of some random guy.

There are also toys. Lots of fricken toys. The house isn't a wreck, but it's obvious from the drawings on the fridge that kids live here.

"Country was the space where my head was when the studio approached me. Be as derisive as you want. The heartache I was going through after Liz died, and trying to find my footing with Daveigh, lent itself to the genre. And, not gonna lie, it paid well. Not at first, but the more songs I had to offer in my catalog, the more artists started coming to me. I've co-written a lot of cross-genre stuff, too."

"What's the story behind this one?" I ask, picking up a melted grammy that looks more like someone left a chocolate Easter bunny on the dash of a hot car.

"My wife rescued it from a fire a few years ago." Cris sighs.

I have the creeping sensation that what his new wife actually rescued was him and it makes me think about Paisley.

I place the award back down.

"What about her?"

"Daveigh? She's a veterinarian. The summer before she went to college, she babysat Mateo. Her dad was the one who offered me the original job at the ranch. I made it awkward by writing a few songs about falling in love with her. She married me, anyway." He gives a self-deprecating shrug.

"I meant Liz."

Cris casts his eyes to the floor. "What is it you are looking for me to say, Jake? That you could've loved Liz better?"

"No." I couldn't have. I know that now.

"Don't think for a second that there weren't times when I was so lost without Liz that I hadn't wondered if she'd chosen you instead that the accident wouldn't have happened."

"I never said I was in love with her."

"You never had to. That's why when I couldn't see straight, I asked you to come along to the funeral home and the florist."

"Fucking lilies. She should've had roses. Dozens of them."

"Yep, and if I wasn't a broke-down musician, wondering how I was going to raise a kid on my own, I might have had the money for roses."

My jaw drops. "It doesn't bother you that she didn't get what she deserved."

"It bothers me a helluva lot. Liz deserved to live a long life. She should've been here to watch our son grow up. But if you're asking me if Liz gave two hoots about the flowers on her casket, I don't think she did. I hadn't even considered it until you brought it up the day of the funeral.

"I had everything one minute; the wife, the kid, the chance at stardom. Twenty-four hours later, there was a doctor discussing organ donation with me. While you were picking out flowers, my mind was trying to make sense of how I became a single dad overnight. And if I wasn't worried about all of the ways I was going to fail Mateo, my mind kept going back to the critical care unit, and the moment, for me as her husband, Liz's life ended. Being an organ donor was what Liz wanted. It was the right thing to do. But I've never felt the weight of responsibility like that. In the worst instances, when grief fucked with my head, I felt like I'd condemned her instead of setting her free. That there was something more I could've done than give other patients and their families hope."

"Crap, after all that, getting hung up on the smell of bad flowers sounds dumb."

Cris laughs and claps me on the arm. "We all deal with grief differently. I send her roses now for her birthday, our anniversary, when Mateo reaches a milestone that Liz would've gone nuts about. Sometimes even when a song does well as a thank you for watching over us."

"What happened to her," *Liz's heart.* "her organs?"

"They went to patients in L.A. There's a registry in case any of them want to contact Liz's family. But none have. I'd like to think it's because they're living each day to the fullest."

I release a breath I didn't know I was holding. Illogical or not, the idea of Liz's heart inside Paisley was overwhelming.

"When was the last time you ate? You look like you're about to pass out."

Funny thing about that. The last time I ate anything of substance was when I was in Nashville and decided to travel through two more states to get a handle on my past.

"Too many energy drinks." I excuse my odd behavior.

"We're having leftovers for lunch. Homemade fried chicken. Not as bad as it sounds."

My stomach gurgles. "That actually sounds great."

We head toward the kitchen. There's a woman in her mid-to-late twenties already there. She's pulling out tubs of food from the fridge and a stack of plates from the cabinet. Her long curly brown hair swishes with every graceful movement. She has on medical scrubs and the imprint of wearing a facial mask indents her nose. Trace amounts of makeup are on her face, but what makes her glow is her demeanor.

"How was surgery this morning?" Cris asks.

"Wonderful. Easy. No complications for any patient, which meant I could get back here early and set lunch out." She walks over to shake my hand.

"Mateo dropped by to mention we had company."

"Jake Ballentine."

"The illustrious?" She cocks a questioning chin at her husband.

"One and the same." Cris tucks her to his side. "Jake, this is my wife, Daveigh."

"I gathered. It's nice to meet you."

"You too." Her reply is gracious, as is the spread of food she put out.

We dig into cold fried chicken, warmed biscuits and butter, and sides of corn and coleslaw. The two boys I saw in the vineyard run through the kitchen. Not bothering to sit, they grab drumsticks and beat them in between gnawing the meat away from the bone.

"Jake was the drummer for my band," Cris tells Mateo.

"Cool." The kid drops the bone in the trash and wipes the grease off his face with the back of his wrist. "Later."

The boys dart out the back door. Their energy level is what I remember from summers when I was a kid. And the dismissiveness reminds me of how old I am.

"Don't pay attention." Cris assuages my ego. "I'm hardly worth a second glance, either. Do you still play?"

"Only for myself."

Though still within Brighton's town limits, my own house has enough land surrounding it so that I didn't have to listen to neighbors complain. The drums were my passion. My escape from the pressure of running a strip club I didn't want. Oftentimes, when having a manager enabled me to ignore my responsibilities and fuck off, I'd still practice. Get lost in the beat.

Daveigh stands to clear the plates. "I hope you didn't mind last night's dinner, Jake. Since we fight over who gets the extra fried chicken anyway, we double the recipe the night before surgery day. That way, we can still eat together if our schedules match."

"It's fine. I appreciate the hospitality."

It's obvious why Cris married Daveigh. Their marriage revolves around the other's needs. She is also everything and all at once nothing like Cris's first wife.

"Jake's taking the guest room for a few days." Cris

joins her, filling the dishwasher with the plates she's rinsed. They are the same height. He pecks her on her nose.

"No problem," Daveigh says, as if having extra people in her home is normal. "Everyone is family here, so if you're lost or missing something, don't hesitate to ask. We'll find you a toothbrush."

"I bought one along the way." Not much else than the clothes on my back and the suit that needs laundering. "I may need a dry cleaner and to know where I can purchase a few pairs of jeans."

"We can drive into town later and pick up whatever you need." Cris offers. "How about takeout tonight from The Grill so no one has to cook?"

"Have I mentioned how much I love you?" Daveigh grabs Cris by the collar and pecks the corner of his mouth. "My last patient is at five. I'll get the baby from the sitter and be back as soon as I can."

When Daveigh goes back to her clinic, I take over helping Cris clean. Then we go back outside and Cris suggests driving a utility vehicle to the edge of the property where he needs to inspect some vines. Since my oversized limbs have been tucked into a car, I prefer to stretch my legs and propose walking.

"Do you ever regret giving up your dreams?" I ask him about halfway there.

Cris pauses in his steel toe work boots. "I didn't give up my dreams when my wife died. Sure, I put some on hold. But I wanted to raise my son and have someone to share my life with. I wanted a family. I wanted to write songs."

"You stopped performing."

"My ass I did. Whenever I could get a sitter, I played at the local bar."

He leans against a wood post. I do the same.
"That's not exactly the Hollywood Bowl." Where the night before Liz's accident the record exec's promised

the band was headed once we'd signed the contracts. After her funeral, Cris refused. That's when I told him to go fuck himself.

"Does the venue make a difference?" he asks.

"Hell, yeah."

Cris knows the vibe is different playing for a bigger crowd. Why is he arguing with me?

"Okay, so to you it makes a difference. It isn't like I've forgotten the beat in my chest and the pulsing of a crowd. But I also remember Liz's reaction when she heard us, and the first time I played for Daveigh. For me, it was the intimacy and the connection. Sharing my soul. My heart bleeding out through my voice. Could I have had an amazing run on a big stage along with you and the rest of the band? Hell, yeah. Except, when it comes down to brass tacks, I've still created an amazing life that fulfilled the dreams I had. It's not the same as what any of us envisioned in our twenties. But that's part of the journey, right? Figuring out what drives you to make fulfilling that dream important. I hate to break this to you, Jake, but the person who gave up on music when Liz died was you."

I hate the level of truth my former bandmate is laying on me. At first, our bassist grumbled that his only option was giving guitar lessons while he searched for another band. However, he later opened a vintage guitar shop that enabled him to jam with some of our idols.

Me?

Less than a month after Cris departed for Kingsbrier, I trudged back to Brighton. My father had just brought my mother to her knees. After witnessing two strong couples implode, passion for anything was lost on me. Fidelity, too, as I saw both Cris and Caroline crumbling under the weight of their failed relationships.

Unless I was going to let everything my mother fought for to be for naught, taking over the club seemed like the only option I had left.

Chapter Twenty-seven

Jake

"Jake, I can explain." Paisley yanks the bodice of her gown over her front. I don't want to look at her, but I do.

"I threw the rock." My stomach tumbles and my anxiety heightens.

Don't tell her that! My subconscious screams. *You fool. You'll lose her!*

I try to snap out of it. But filled with repressed memories, my mind isn't finished with what it has to say. *I don't want* her. *I don't love* her *anymore.*

I expect a thousand lashes from the pain in Paisley's eyes. Nothing but her blank stare greets me. It's as if my girlfriend accepted that I'd hurt her and had already put defenses in place. She's not crying when I clearly remember seeing her cry. When I made her cry again. Because I betrayed her trust.

Why isn't Paisley fighting me? Why isn't she asking me what I'm telling her with shrill incredulity? The inflections in her voice, her exclamations of surprise and excitement, make

Paisley… Paisley. I need her to scream for the truth of why I'd be an asshole who pitched a stone through her boutique's window and then cover it up.

But she doesn't because she knows I conned her into our relationship. Finding out I've duped her into believing there was the slightest chance I could be a good guy is the other shoe dropping.

I wake up on all fours as if I'm ready to scramble off the mattress at Paisley's place. I'm in the same position I'd been in right as I was about to snatch my clothes off the floor. All it took for me to turn back into the asshole that I am was seeing her scar from a heart surgery.

I fucking ran out on the runaway bride who ran away from her wedding to a cardiac surgeon. There's some irony.

I lean back on my haunches, patting from my bare chest down, slapping the salutation under my boxers that my dick is giving to the wee morning hours. My fists return to my other head and press into my temples.

Get a grip!

This isn't the first time since landing at Kingsbrier almost a week ago that I've dreamed about that night. Once before, Paisley did cry in my dream. My thumb ached to brush away the tears, but the awful things I've done were paralyzing. I was unworthy when we met and my actions prove I am still.

I tilt forward and fall on my face into a pillow. I've been awake a whole thirty seconds. My neurons are misfiring with the clash between my present and my past.

While we were getting reacquainted, Cris and I talked about organ donation. I know now that no doctor took Liz's heart and put it in Paisley's body. But damn, seeing Paisley's scar made me recognize there's a lot of shit that happened eleven years ago that I haven't worked through.

"You're such an asshole." The pillow muffles the words that to my ears would've sounded like "man-child".

I'd do anything if I could go back in time. When I'm alone, scenarios of me holding Paisley, asking her where she got the scar from, and telling her I'll do anything to keep her healthy plague me.

My hard-on smashed against the mattress is ungodly uncomfortable. I roll, intending on licking my palm and riding my hand—something I've justified doing to images of Pais since the night she came off the good doctor's dick and became mine.

Even if I wasn't sure if I'd pursue pretending we were together, she belonged to me. My reputation was her burden to bear. For many, Paisley having to put up with my immorality was an appropriate punishment for leaving Laughton. I was the only person unaffected by having a relationship with a brilliant, beautiful, fierce businesswoman.

Or was I?

It's hard to come to grips with realizing I'm a reprobate who has spent years with lustful images of my friend's wives on replay. And, no matter how long we were together, I can't lie to myself anymore that Paisley was a woman whose affections I could trifle with. Falling in love with her turned Paisley into the one person who could give me a taste of my own medicine.

Sliding my hand under my pants is now disobedient. It feels unfaithful to her and adds to my list of personal shortcomings. It makes me less deserving of those few minutes when Paisley's body was wrapped around mine.

My phone lights up in the dark room that I'm sleeping in. The bold clock readout indicates that shortly the cleaning crew will descend upon Sweet

Caroline's to get the club in shape for the following night. I pick up my phone to read the incoming message.

Kelsey: I can't keep this up. When are you coming back?

Yesterday I told her tomorrow. That's now today. I've been using the same excuse. I've disappeared and left my manager blowing in the wind. Pais told me months ago to hire Kelsey help. My manager's entitled to be pissed.

Kelsey: Legit coming back Jake. I want an answer or I quit.

Go, Kelsey. That second ping was ballsy.

I don't want to go back to Brighton. There wasn't anything there for me and now that Pais hates me, there's even less.

I pull up my mother's number and let the phone dial.

"You're interrupting my beauty rest."

She makes me laugh. My mom won't ever stop being a night owl. It wouldn't surprise me if she just placed her silk blackout mask over her eyes.

"I need a favor."

"Anything, darling."

"I'm out of town for... for a while, and I need someone to watch the club." I blew it by taking off, acting as if I didn't have responsibilities. "I'd never ask if Kelsey wasn't having difficulty juggling. The dancers are giving her grief and a lot of that is my fault."

The only other people I could even ask, who know how to get the job done right, are Kimber or Holly. I made leaving her role at Sweet Caroline's easier for Holly than I had Kimber, but it's dawning on me that I hadn't shown either of them the respect they were entitled to. I haven't shown a ton of respect for anyone. Asking those women to bail me out, to put my selfish needs above their own, is wrong.

"That might be a fun change of pace for a few days. When are you coming back?" Mom asks me the same question Kelsey posed.

"Can I call you with a tentative date?"

"Jake." My mother draws out the vowel in my name. "What's going on?"

"I broke it off with Paisley and I need a few more days to think is all."

"Oh, Jake." Mom sounds disappointed. Not in me, but for me.

I'm both. I miss Paisley. I doubt she feels the same. Paisley is smart enough to know she is better off without a guy who gets his jollies by making her fight for the things he should give her without hesitation.

"Three days, Jake." Mom lays down an ultimatum. "If you haven't figured out your shit by then, I hate to say you aren't going to."

"I'll come up with a plan, Mom." I don't have a choice anymore. My employees count on me. It's time I stood up and took care of business.

Wide awake, my fingertips tap out the beat of an earworm that's held on since my car ride. If I were home, I'd get up and spend the next few hours exhausting myself behind the drums.

Cris has the guest suite outfitted for musicians. Pictures of his family alongside celebrities who have visited Kingsbrier decorate the shelves in this room. They are similar to the one I found of him in the restaurant. The subtlety is name-dropping at its finest. No wonder the drummer who used to back up his dad over a decade ago wasn't impressive to Mateo.

I reach for a guitar that's sitting in the corner of the room and pick the strings. Keeping the sounds soft so that I don't wake anyone, I get lost in the music and push Paisley out of my mind for a while. Triaging the easier headaches first, I prioritize my damages.

The sun is on the horizon when I have a handle on a few things. Amongst early risers, I throw on jeans and a tee and start for the kitchen. Although my travels have shifted around my sleep patterns, I'm not making any final decisions without a cup of coffee. Hearing noises elsewhere in the house, I dress in the clothes I picked up in town, and wander to the kitchen.

"What's on tap for you boys today?" Daveigh asks over her mug.

Cris is a busy guy. When he's had meetings at the winery, he's set me to work on a simple task. One day it was quality control, inspecting wine bottles as they came off the labeling machine. Another, it was packing cases for distribution with the warehouse crew. I've enjoyed the change of pace while helping around the ranch.

In my downtime, I've actually fed chickens; his son's chore at the barns across the gravel road in the same area as the veterinary clinic. Daveigh, whose specialty is large breed animals, also showed me how to brush and saddle a horse and we took two out for a ride.

I'd later joked with her that if I thought my ass was killing after driving from North Carolina to Texas, it's nothing compared to an afternoon sitting bow-legged.

Daveigh is open and honest. I like her a lot—for Cris. My craptastic behavior in my twenties stopped Liz and I from developing a genuine friendship, but if I stayed here, I can see that happening with Daveigh.

"I have some calls to return." Cris shakes his phone. Scores of messages appear on his screen.

"There are a few I need to make, too." I inhale the steam and sip my coffee.

I must frown when I do.

"Everything okay, Jake?" Daveigh inquires from the table.

"Oh, yeah, no." I stumble for the correct answer. "The coffee is wonderful. I was making a mental to-do list. I put up the capital for a small security company. I'm the principal investor and the owner wants to sell to a larger firm. My approval is the last thing standing in the way."

"My brother-in-law started out as a business analyst for a big security firm in Minnesota. He's the CFO now." Cris is toasting bagels.

"Walsh Security?" I gape.

"That's the one." Daveigh chimes.

"So, have you met Devon Walsh?"

"He's family. Married to another brother-in-law's sister."

"Devon persuaded his sister to buy the firm out and put it under their home security umbrella. The owner, my friend Trig, would still be in charge of the day-to-day. But he's interested in shifting his priorities to his family."

"There isn't anything wrong with that." Bringing two plated bagels to the kitchen table and a bowl of cereal for Mateo, Cris stops to kiss the crown of Daveigh's head.

No, there isn't, is there?

I excuse myself. Outside on the wraparound porch, I breathe in the fresh country air. I'm not ready to have any sort of deep-feelings discussion with Trig about what changed my mind. So I shoot off a one-word message: **Sell.**

He'll understand what I mean. We'll square up later.

After that, I sift through the apps on my phone to find the email account that syncs to Sweet Caroline's. There are a million unopened messages, but the search results hit on the one I'm looking for. And as luck would have it, the contact info has a highlighted link.

I love technology.

I hit the guy's phone number. It rings twice and a groggy man picks up.

"Hey, this is Jake Ballentine. You applied for a job at my club on the East Coast. I know it's early Los Angeles. Is this a good time to talk?"

Chapter Twenty-eight

Jake

The call ends on a sour note. Julian, the prospective manager is originally from Raleigh. He's interested in relocating to be closer to his southern roots and is searching for the right opportunity. The salary I'm offering is on point. The proximity to the state capital makes Sweet Caroline's his top choice… If it weren't for his girlfriend.

She's not keen on Julian working at a *gentlemen's* club.

I can't exactly say to someone who is taking his partner's opinion into consideration that my club has any advantages over your typical titty bar. Although I'm certain that seeing the club, interacting with my staff, and understanding that—even though I've been an asshole—I tried to treat my dancers right when I had an exceptional management team, the girlfriend might change her mind. It took a while for my girlfriend to come around to that conclusion herself.

The thing is, I can't blame Julian. I'm in a funk without Paisley around to fight me for what she wants. Where neither of us has attempted to make contact, I'm halfway across the country nursing a broken heart so that hers can mend. The last person Paisley wants popping up at an inconvenient time is me.

I straggle back into the house Cris and his wife share. Diaper bag in tow, Daveigh waved to me on her way to drop off their baby at the sitter while I was on the phone. I'm surprised to see Cris in the kitchen rinsing the kids' breakfast bowls. He's finished his calls as well.

"Come on." He dries his hands and throws a thumb over his shoulder. "Refill your coffee and we'll go hang out in the studio."

I do as he suggests and follow Cris. I'd gotten the cook's tour when I arrived. The studio's control room is the size of a closet, but the size of the vocal room makes up for that. Hidden in someone's home, the equipment and layout are damn professional.

I'm still awed by it.

"It's not much, but it gets the job done," Cris tells me in a self-deprecating manner. He flips a few switches on the control board and turns the lights on.

We enter the vocal room. Cris moves a microphone and takes a spot on a stool. I spy a video camera near the ceiling that must tie into a studio monitor. The guitar he used when he sang lead vocals for our band stands in the corner. There are more, plus a keyboard, and a baby grand. Opposite the acoustic, electric and classical guitars is a drum kit.

I slide behind it out of habit, push the throne back to accommodate my long legs, and straighten my spine. This is the distance we sat apart from one another in a cramped room like this one over a decade ago.

My fingers itch to pick up the sticks.

"Feel free." Cris nods, acknowledging my longstanding addiction. "Give it what you got."

My foot presses the bass pedal. I have to adjust the set-up that's for a shorter person. Then I twirl the sticks. They fly in tight circles through the air. My wrists loosen. Tighten. Snap. The cymbals crash.

Cris leans, snatching his guitar from the stand.

I soften my *tap-tap-tapping* until I'm able to pick up the chords that Cris is strumming of a familiar song. Broad grins stretch our cheeks. The ease of syncopation after all these years makes us laugh. We don't finish any of the tunes. One song blends into the next. Sometimes Cris belts out the lyrics. By the time we give up, our faces ache from smiling and joking.

"You still got it." Cris compliments me. "Why didn't you start a new band? Go out on the road?"

His question is deflating. I don't know how much got back to Cris about my father going to jail, so I start with a succinct answer. "My mom was in a bind. I took over their club."

"You're the only man I know who'd look downtrodden if he owned a dancing girls club."

"*Dancing girls*. That's a nice euphemism." I sigh and scrub my face. "When I went back to North Carolina, I didn't intend to stay. I'd worked my ass off to get to the point where I could be a successful musician and stay the hell away from Brighton." Running out of reasons not to, I lay the truth on the line. "Your refusal to sign the contract seemed like the worst thing that could go wrong. But then my dad got arrested. His sentence was the fallout from a longstanding feud."

Cary Cass's father, Rex Stanton, frequented Sweet Caroline's before Cary was born. Rex developed a fascination for Caroline. He wanted to marry his soon-to-be wife and keep Caroline on the side. Exotic dancers aren't precisely known for having high morals. Rex expected my mother to be looser with hers. After all, she was a married woman who stripped for a living, so her hesitancy to begin an affair with Stanton wasn't something he could fathom. Caroline refuted his advances and wouldn't leave my dad. They were a team. We were family. So Rex joined in with the rest of Brighton's elite in making her life hell.

My parents weren't seeking acceptance—the sense of legitimacy it would bring—by being members of any country club. But they had the income and understood the connections it would afford them with Sweet Caroline's. The "you rub my back and I'll rub yours", if you will.

It was my mother, not my father, who barred Stanton from the club. A dancer who Rex favored to show him a good time attempting to gain Caroline's attention and make her jealous came in with unexplained bruises. It wasn't that the dancer refused to tell Caroline the truth. It was that past Rex paying her in advance for a private show and then taking her elsewhere, she had no recollection of the night before.

Then the stories from the other girls surfaced. He'd offered them their drug of choice, or slapped them around. Some were raped, but because of their work, and Stanton's overarching public crusade to destroy a business he claimed as sinful, it was their word against his.

An upstanding businessman, Rex Stanton had the ear of the judges. The judges, who were in favor of fulfilling their fantasies by watching young women undress on stage, ignored seeing him sitting at the table across the theater.

I grew up in a household where there was nothing wrong with sex, sexuality, or sexual expression. My mother had a passion for dancing and she did it on her own terms. She raised me in that club and I never recall seeing Caroline so close to the edge of the stage that anyone could touch her. My mother didn't have the same proclivities that I've shown. She didn't entertain random men in the office or behind a curtain. And once Rex wouldn't leave us be, she was careful to never be alone with any man for any reason. Luckily, my father was there to protect her.

You might think I'm stupid. That I saw what I wanted to see to justify my upbringing. I was a kid who found solace from bullying by banding alongside society's predicted losers. The kids who'd be hard-pressed to claw their way out of poverty. I listened to bullies wax on about how superior their lives were, often right before their parents' tumultuous divorce. Yet any time I accidentally walked in on something I shouldn't have, it was my parents in the throes of whatever they were doing. That was the stuff that had me ready to gouge my eyes out.

Stanton acted in his own self-interest, saying my old man threatened him. The police filed a restraining order against my dad. Rex violated it. He tried to come into the club to see my mom, anyway. To force her to choose between her business and becoming his mistress or my dad. Knowing that even though the law should have been on our side, it wasn't likely to help, Caroline kicked Stanton out and increased security, so that any attempt he made to return was in vain.

The changes my dad made to keep Mom and all the other women who worked for them safe are why my employees have escorts to their cars if they want them. Why, while my personal reputation is as a scoundrel, my club has a reputation for caring for its girls. It's also why Carver acts the way he does. Why he selects mill girls… And why Carver lost his shit on Trig when Kimber had bruises.

Rex didn't go quietly. Any time there was a zoning meeting that could affect the club or its entertainment license, he showed up to fight against my parents. Any reason he could find to complain to the town that my parents were doing anything wrong, he took. During the worst years, we had picketers outside our house, tomatoes and eggs thrown at our cars. The good citizens of Brighton allowed that righteousness to prevail because *we* were the evil ones. Their sins are forgivable. Ours? Damned us to hell.

When I moved to California to attend music school, I never wanted to set foot in Brighton again. I wasn't ashamed of my family, but the way others treated us was exhausting. When Cris and I combined our talents, I transformed from the dorky kid into an up-and-coming rockstar. Looking back, the fault line shifting my future is obvious. It happened right around when Liz entered the picture. I'd had a few run-ins where being a good guy didn't matter. Her choosing Cris was a gut punch. The proverbial last straw that took me from sinner to Sinner.

"Right before Liz died, the club's finances were on shaky ground. My dad wasn't ready to throw in the towel. He agreed to accept a shipment of illegal firearms in exchange for a hefty payout that would keep the doors open. But Stanton set him up, counting on my dad keeping it a secret from Caroline. ATF raided the club and found the guns." My dad threw everything away that they'd achieved.

"Man, that's rough." Cris grimaces.

"Nah, you know what the worst part is? My friends have been telling me for years that what my dad did made me cynical. About life. About love. I wasn't willing to believe them. Not being able to let go of the grief I had brought the worst out in me. I've done shit I'm not proud of, including turning into a guy like Stanton, trying to beat the bastard at his own game. The joke was on me, though. The rat bastard died last year. He's pushing up daisies, smelling as fresh as one. Sometimes the bad guys win and there's nothing you can do to help it." I clutch the wooden sticks ."It's... life."

"You know Jake, when you got here, looking like you'd been through the wringer, I thought whatever you were struggling with was about a woman."

"It is." I huff, blowing a deep breath out of my nose. "Her name's Paisley. I've never met anyone who balances putting up with my shit and standing her ground the way she does. She's the kind who will find your weakness and put a band-aid on it." The opposite of me who made a gaping wound bigger. "Her baggage made her stronger. Fierce. Determined. When we met, I was gobsmacked. She'd broken it off her engagement minutes from the church bells ringing and I was more concerned with how stunning Paisley was in her wedding dress than seeing straight away that whatever she does is with compassion. Aside from having this incredible business sense, she gives people no one thinks deserve a second chance the benefit of the doubt. Paisley thrives on seeing others succeed. And I reacted poorly, selfishly, to something that she needed me to be sympathetic to. It's made me realize I never got a handle on everything that went down over those few months between impending stardom and imminent doom."

"In her wedding dress, huh?" Cris raises an eyebrow.

"I thought she'd be easy to manipulate. Instead, she wrapped me around her finger." I tell Cris everything.

When I'm done, my former bandmate fishes a slip of paper out of his pocket and hands it to me. There's a phone number and the name Tom scrawled in blue.

"What's this?"

"Message I got overnight from the rep for a singer-songwriter I've collaborated with who was putting out feelers. They're on the first leg of a summer tour—opening act for another country band. Don't say I didn't warn you. Anyhow, things got rowdy. There was an accident and the drummer is down for the count. Tom is searching for a replacement for the band's drummer for the next six-to-eight weeks."

"Two months is almost the entire tour season."

"Take it from me, you can't go back and make it right with any woman until you've learned if you have what it takes to stay away from her."

Chapter Twenty-nine

Paisley

I'm sipping cold water and using a red, white, and blue funeral fan to cool myself. This Fourth of July is shaping up to be the hottest on record. There's a woman sitting on a blanket a few yards away who is spritzing herself. Jealous, I scoop my hand into the cooler, snag an ice cube, and use the tight keyhole at my collar to pop it down the front of my shirt to cool off.

"Paisley! I saw that." My mother gasps.

"What? I'm hot. My bra is drenched with sweat, anyway. No one will know." I flash a smile at Mom.

"Oh, get me one too. This heat is brutal."

I fish around for a decent sized chunk that hasn't melted into the icy water yet. Mom uses it to wet her arms before slipping it under her top.

"Phew, that's nicer. Now if the sun sets, the breezes might pick up." She moves her low-to-the-ground beach chair closer to mine, slips her sandals off, and leans back. "You're not dehydrated?"

I shake an almost empty water bottle. It's my

second one since we arrived at the park. We'd packed a picnic and come early to stake out a spot at Brighton's fireworks display. Greer, Byron, Karen, and Mac are meeting us here. I just hope I see the light show and am not in search of a vacant porta potty. Rented bathrooms skeeve me out when it's dark. With a crowd this size, it's a crapshoot if the one I get will have TP and hand sanitizer. The thought makes me shiver.

Mom checks if anyone nearby is paying attention to us. "How are you feeling about tomorrow? It's not too late to change your mind." She laces her fingers into mine.

Even on a hot and sticky day like today, it's a comfort.

Tomorrow I'm having my tubes tied. I'm a proponent of safe sex. When I go back to having said sex—not that it'll be soon—I plan on wearing a full body condom to protect all the effort it is taking piece my jagged heart back together.

Sterilization is a choice I wanted to make after my father died and before meeting Gavin because I didn't want to have the added burden of taking birth control beyond my thirties. Unfortunately, I waited, and then I was insecure about having the elective procedure done at a hospital where I was familiar with so many of the doctors. Instead of feeling cared for, I'd gotten it in my head that they'd gossip about me. Yes, I know confidentiality and all that, but once that unsafe feeling crawls over your skin, it's hard to shake off.

Facing that fear was important to me. I'm having my regular gynecologist perform the surgery. Then mom and I are taking a detour. Our mini mother-daughter trip is a staycation at a hotel and spa that's close to Brighton. We can both get pampered, and neither of us has to worry if there are any complications.

"What do you suppose Jake will say if he wants children?"

"Excuse me?" I balk at her flippant remark.

Mom hasn't mentioned his name all summer. I wish she hadn't now. Every time I get Jake off my mind something reminds me of him and I have to start all over again.

"Jake can go make or have babies with whomever he wants, but it's not gonna be me." Annoyed, I chug the remaining water and open the cooler, grabbing a third cold bottle. Pressing it to my lips, I turn my head, pretending to look for Greer and Byron in the crowd.

My mother refutes my brash behavior and addresses my blunt avoidance of the elephant in the room, *er*, park?

"Paisley. Paisley, please. For as disappointing as not having grandchildren is for me, I agree it's your choice. I've put myself in your shoes and I'm not second-guessing your decision. What I'm doing is asking how you intend to handle the conversation later. I don't want you to have any regrets."

"My regret is not doing this sooner." If I had, I could have been honest with Gavin when we started dating that I was only interested in a committed relationship. He would have been free to make his choice when we began dating instead of me feeling pressured to conform to his future plans when we got engaged. "Also, Jake's opinion is worth a hill of beans."

"You're still wearing the anklet he gave you."

I twist my foot. The last flickers of sunlight strike the metal.

"I like the saying. Fierce." I sound insulted that mom believes the jewelry has sentimental value.

It does. But keeping the anklet on has nothing to

do with Jake.

Each time I read those six letters, it made fake dating him easier. Each time he fought me, expecting I'd back down, it gave me strength. Each time I held my head high, and did something I didn't necessarily want to do, being fierce made it worthwhile. And being bold enough to survive when Jake up and left, cutting me with his words, allowed me to take back some of the power I felt he stripped me of. Wearing this anklet is not about Jake. It's about me.

Her voice grows low with concern. "You'll have to take it off for surgery."

The links break when I grab it by the chain and yank. I open mom's palm, placing it in the center to prove my point. Nothing I'll ever do again is about Jake Ballentine.

"There's nothing wrong with mourning a loss." Mom rubs her thumb over the words and arrow, then tucks the anklet into her handbag. "Your emotions are valid."

"Jake's not dead, Mom." That's what makes it harder. He's out there somewhere, carefree. Jake had no misgivings about running out on me. The Norse god had such little remorse over breaking my store window that he lied, leading me to believe the destruction was penance for my actions.

"I was angry when your father's heart began to fail," Mom confesses. "We endured so many doctor's appointments for you. Surgeries. Hospital stays. Our suffering was supposed to have been over. My suffering, watching the agony of someone I loved in pain and being helpless to fix it.

"I hadn't considered myself a martyr when you were born with similar health problems to your fathers. His specialty was cardiology. I was the last woman who wanted a baby who could plead ignorance to congenital defects. I understood the responsibility was mine before we decided to have children. But, before you were born, I wore rose-colored glasses. I only thought about how the stress of a chronic illness may affect an imaginary baby. I didn't have the ability to see how it would overwhelm a real child in real pain, or our marriage. You were so wanted, Paisley. But after asking you to be stronger than any little girl should, your dad and I agreed that we wouldn't try again."

My mother brushes an errant hair behind my ear.

"You're right, Paisley. There are mothers who would do anything to have a baby. We took a chance, and along with it, took away your option to lead the healthy life you were worthy of. My choices were all about me. Yours get to be all about you. I understand why your dad supported the decision you made. And that's why I have no problem with your choice to have your tubes tied."

My vision goes blurry. "I miss him so much." After listening to my mom, my soul can't separate Jake and my father. I wanted to love both of them for so much longer than I got to. The intensity of this hurt is a feeling I've never experienced. "I don't know what to do with my anger," I admit.

"You feel it, sweetie, and then bit by bit you let it go."

"How did you let go of the anger when dad died?"

Mom laughs. "I must have you fooled. I haven't. I am still grieving. Except, the one thing I learned is that I'd taken care of you both for so long that it was time to take care of me. So do that. Care for you. Chase your passion. Build the future you want. But most importantly build the *present* that you want. Life changes on a dime."

Chapter Thirty

Paisley

"I don't think it can get any hotter out there." Holly walks into the boutique with her arms akimbo. She has on a trademark vintage dress with no sleeves, but her posture falls more in line with a scarecrow. "It's eleven o'clock and my mascara is melting."

"You're gorgeous, glowing. The dewy look is in." Kimber tells her, sitting up on the chaise near the dressing room. The unwavering support these women show one another is something I aspire to.

July was hot, but August has been downright relentless. It hasn't rained in weeks, though stepping outside is a lot like swimming in a fish tank. The humidity clings, soaking your clothes to your skin.

Standing behind the register, I offer Holly a polite hello, and mention Greer has new scent cards on her display table. Since my customer base is women, I tend to stock perfume floral lotions, but Mind Your Own Beeswax has a panty-dropping men's line of bergamot and sandalwoods. The beard oil's smell alone is a potent enough elixir to make you want to hump a mountain man. Or at least find a man to slather it on and… Well, you know.

Wow, is that desperation talking? This is the problem with having sex once in the past seven months.

Healed from surgery, I've been in the mindset to make positive changes. I want to confront my failings and I've considered dating again. But I have an inkling that throwing my hat into the dating pool again is something I need to take slower. Normal women don't run from the altar straight into the arms of their rebound guy.

If Jake hasn't ruined my expectations for my next relationship, all the hot and heavy fooling around we did and having sex with him did. I don't think you can compare Jake, or how everything between us evolved, to what it would be like with any other man, but I also know because of the way he crushed me it will be impossible not to. I sympathized with my ex-fiancé before. To say I have empathy for Gavin now is a bold understatement.

In any event, Greer and I brainstormed the cards with masculine scents after yoga about a week ago. The ladies who run my shop on my days off have mentioned they've been a smashing success. They've watched a lot of my customers leave the boutique and go right next door to Greer's. So when Holly picks up the rectangular sample to sniff and wrinkles her nose, it worries me.

Holly doesn't dress in clothes from here. I don't carry anything in her retro style, which has morphed a tiny bit toward classic Jackie O. Except on a mill girls' day out, I've always been able to count on her loading up with various other items. I need Holly to like the products I stock for my business to survive and for her to take my recommendations of other downtown shops to heart for them to stay open. Owning a small business is harder than anyone realizes.

I'd lost a good portion of my spring income because of the rumor mill. I was on the verge of either cutting the store's hours or letting someone go. Some customers returned when my association with Jake ended. It was likely out of pity, but I'll accept the small mercy along with the current oppressive weather. It's worked in my favor. I'm thankful for the sales boon. There's only so much time anyone can twiddle their thumbs at home with the air conditioner on high. People are shopping to stay cool.

My breath stops whenever I remember how crushed I was when Jake left. I have to force myself to inhale. It's for the best that he was the one who let me go instead of it being the other way around. That said, I don't know why I thought the mill girls would swoop in and help me staunch the river of anguish weeping from my bleeding heart. Our newfound friendship—the fleeting feeling that we'd sit at the same table at the hospital gala for years to come—was fragile. I can't blame them for taking Jake's side when my lie of omission was duplicitous. Although I hope Jake didn't say we were in bed when he found out. Mortified that a man would leave my bed immediately after being intimate, I haven't mentioned it to anyone myself.

Holly places the sample back in the cardholder. She surprises me by walking around the counter and wrapping me up in a big hug.

This entire morning has been a shocker, in fact. Beginning when the bell chimed and the mill girls, who had been absent from the store all summer, started filing in.

"How've you been?" Her embrace is too comforting. It brings me too close to the genuine affection between us that might have been without actually letting me touch it. I've had the propensity to let women who could have been part of my support network slip away.

"Fine." My vision goes blurry.

I blink the tears back, noting the corners of her eyes crinkling with concern. Always late to the party, Holly looks as ragged as she had when she was still working nights at Sweet Caroline's and dragged herself out of bed the next day to meet up here with the mill girls as they finished shopping.

"Jake's new at this, Paisley," she whispers.

With every fiber of my being, I want to ask her, "New at what?"

It can't be bad breakups. I'm certain Jake Ballentine has plenty of experience ripping people's hearts out. Tearing their emotions to shreds.

I have enough self-respect not to go searching for Jake. He hasn't bothered to seek me out either, which is fine by me. So, Jake hasn't disappeared without a trace? I figured that we'd meet on the sidewalk and Jake's ego would afford me some half-assed apology that I'd accept just to get it done and over with.

I don't want to look up at Jake and see him looking down on me. I want to move on.

Holly told me at Royce's that Jake didn't give up once he had something in his possession, that he had to have it ripped from him. Nothing could be further from the truth.

Trying to ignore the sinking sensation, I bend for a box. My neck snaps up when Kimber starts talking.

"Nobody knew Jake left Brighton, Paisley."

"He what?" The jolt of curiosity bursts out of me like a balloon.

Kimber continues, "Jake's been gone for more than a month. It wasn't until Trig stopped into Sweet Caroline's on a whim to get Jake's signature on a legal document that he found out. Kelsey said Jake's been missing since the night of the hospital's cardiac benefit."

"Missing?" I don't understand.

"More like not here." The left side of Sloan's face pinches up and concern etches her forehead. There's no love lost between Sloan and Jake. Is she worried about Jake or me?

Sloan approaches where we're huddled. She hangs several tops and a pair of linen pants on a rack, then moves toward the counter. Her posture mirrors Kimber's. Their elbows lean on the glass case and they are resting their chins on opposite fists. "He's kept in touch with the guys. But no one knows where Jake is. He's called and sent enough messages that we didn't have any reason to believe he wasn't doing what he used to do; skipping out on his obligations at Sweet Caroline's."

"Who has been helping Kelsey then?" I stumble back from our huddle and shout with righteous indignation.

"Caroline." Kimber's shoulders pop to her ears. "And on occasion, Morgan or Skye. But those two took Jake ghosting in stride. It was Jake's MO before Holly quit."

"I thought he fired you? Or he forced you out," I fire at Holly, who stays silent.

"Holly was going to quit, anyway. Jake wanted the upper hand." Sloan's recalcitrant answer is as uncooperative as the stories of her run-ins with Jake.

Holly sighs. "Jake didn't want to be left, so he did the leaving."

Doesn't that sound familiar? I keep my mouth shut instead of blurting.

"By getting married, you'd already left him, Holly. Jake wanted the last word," Sloan rebuts.

"Sometimes it's not what people say but how they say it... Jake ditched me on the dance floor at Cary's and my wedding reception and I was sort of dumbfounded. I felt like he..." Holly inspects her shoes, her tooth poised to puncture her lower lip. "Like he loved me. I mean, Jake said he loved me, but I thought he meant as a friend. Not the way he loves you, Paisley." Holly is still speaking about Jake like he is not the monster who abandoned me.

The calculating, vengeful ice god that I know he is.

"Jake doesn't love me," I tell them. Jake says things he doesn't mean all the time. He uses phrases that can be left up to interpretation. "And you yourself said that if Jake loves something, then the big jerk's not going to set it free."

"Don't pretty it up on our account, Paisley. Jake's an asshole." Kimber winks.

"He is *such* an asshole." I agree, offering the abbreviated version of Jake admitting he smashed the boutique's window. I keep Jake running out on me as PG as possible. No matter how many times I recount it, I have a hunch I won't get over feeling like Jake's callousness stripped me bare. I'm not ready to be that vulnerable with anyone after giving my heart to someone who didn't care for it.

Sloan's jaw drops. "Good lord, could he have blown a sensitive situation any worse?" She wraps her hand around my wrist. "It may not help you feel better, but all the guys have had their moments. We're sorry we didn't come by sooner. We wish you would have felt like you could come to us."

"It's okay," I reply with watery eyes.

Since Jake abandoned me, it feels like I'm walking on broken glass. I hadn't wanted them to blame me for the breakup. So I pulled away from the mill girls because I didn't want to be the one to suffer when they moved on.

Doesn't that sound familiar? My subconscious echoes its earlier words.

Until recently, it was a negative pattern I've repeated my entire life. Believing that since I was going to die anyway meant people wouldn't want my friendship made it easier to keep acquaintances rather than friends. Getting to know Greer changed that. And now that I have one close friend, I'd like more. But putting yourself out there, exposing your weaknesses, is scary. When I hadn't received any sincere messages from these three women within days of Jake ditching me, I took their silence as them retracting the unconditional support they'd shown in the ladies' room at Royce's.

As Holly hugs me again, she peers into the box that I set on the counter. It's filled with plush chenille giraffes in a creamy yellow.

"These are adorable." She clutches one to her chest. "And so soft!"

"One is for Greer. I'm planning her baby shower and have been collecting some of the cute finds to do an extra display in the boutique for new moms or anyone who needs that kind of gift. The hardest part is holding onto everything so that she doesn't see what I've gotten for the baby. I want to put it all out beforehand. I was thinking if I added a few items she has been experimenting with, like belly butter that —" I prattle, excited. This is my most recent pet project, taking over the time I used to spend with my jackass boyfriend.

"Greer has belly butter? And can I have one of these?" Holly lifts the tag. She frowns, finding no price on it yet. "How much? I have to bring this home to show Cary."

Kimber spins the jewelry rack, stopping it to inspect a mother's necklace. Like it always does, my eyes catch on the arrow of the anklet that I tore off.

"Holly, is there a little something you want to let us in on?" Kimber wiggles the necklace card.

"Yes, there is." She twists her hips and throws an arm over my shoulder. "I'd like to tell you about this amazing boutique downtown that has the sweetest gifts that you'll go gaga over when you are ready to buy for my baby."

Chapter Thirty-one

Paisley

"I'm sorry I couldn't get here sooner. The clients Walsh puts on the books have to come first." There's no need for Trig to be contrite standing in the front entryway.

He sold his security company to a big corporation. With it comes upheaval during the transition. I'm thankful he could make it. Kimber volunteered his services after I grumbled in a text about my attempts to figure out how to install a doorbell camera. They haven't been as successful as the venture into stocking various pink, blue, and gender-neutral plush toys and some cute booties.

Emboldened by the mill girls' encouragement, that afternoon I set out the giraffes along with Greer's belly butter on consignment and a basket of quippy mom-centric necklaces and bracelets. My customers flocked to the new display. I've already ordered new items to replenish what I've sold, including the giraffe I'd kept aside for Greer when a newly minted grandmother saw it hidden behind the counter.

Who knew that so many babies were born at this time of year? After months of stagnant sales, in all honesty, I appreciate how much everyone is loving it. At least once a day, a customer asks if I'm going to add a clothing line, which makes me wish there was a downtown Brighton storefront where I could send the extra business to. Like I told my mother, I like other people's children a heck of a lot more than the idea of having a baby of my own.

As exciting as things have been at the shop, I'm glad to be home. Today is my scheduled day off. As luck would have it, Trig had a late afternoon opening. He should finish assisting me with my technophobe issues by the time I have to leave for yoga with Greer. Though I'm fearful of what the camera will catch, I can't come home—or stumble over what's been on the doorstep in the mornings—any longer.

"It's no big deal," I tell Trig. "I appreciate your coming at all. It's not like this camera is complicated... for anyone but me." I point to the Walsh Home Security logo on his shirt. "Those new polos are spiffy."

Kimber's husband winks conspiratorially. "I'm drumming up business. But I also like going home and not getting bogged down thinking about anything that's not important."

Trig's devotion to Kimber and their kids is super sweet.

I can't help the *"aw"* that escapes me. I pat his arm. Trig sets down his toolkit to get to work on my silly problem. Trying to stay out of his way while Trig fiddles with the system, I flip open my laptop to track some inventory.

Trig's low whistling fills the comforting silence. It's as if selling his company lifted a burden from his shoulders, too. I can only assume some things Trig did for Jake weren't on the up and up. It's odd to rely on a friend of my ex-boyfriend. I'm coming to terms with the fact that Jake cutting me out of his life doesn't mean cutting the people I've grown fond of out of mine.

I heard what Trig said about commitments. It's easy to fall into a pattern of being a workaholic. That's why I jump at the chance whenever my mother, Greer, or any of the mill girls invite me out. Not in desperation. These are the positive changes I've been trying to make.

I want to be happy by myself in a completely different way than I was happy alone a year ago because what I was doing was making sure that people would be content if I wasn't around at all. And that's no way to live.

"All set." Trig brushes his palms over his shirt.

"Wow! That was faster than I got the box open. Now I feel dumb. What do I owe you?"

"When you've done it a million times, it's nothing... And you don't owe me a thing. First one is on the house. Except, I hoped you'd take a look at something for me?" His bearded smile fades.

"Uh-um, yeah?" I give Trig a befuddled look.

What could I help him out with besides a gift card to the boutique for Kimber? Which she's getting if he's not charging me.

Trig pulls his cell out of his pocket and takes a seat on my couch. "There's something I think that you'll want to see," he says as I sit next to him.

Trig hands over his phone. A video is already playing. There are two men standing on the main street a few paces outside of my shop.

I'd begun to blindly trust Jake when the boutique was vandalized. I was high on falling for him and, after having Gavin's sister throw a fit seeing Jake and me in public, low on believing that I deserved more than anyone's contempt for moving on so fast. I blame our chemistry for addling my brain. So when Jake had Dusty fix the window, I relied on his dirty, rotten word that looking for the perpetrator was under control.

It shouldn't have come as a surprise when Jake pulled the curtain back and admitted that he was responsible for the damage to my store.

And now what I'm watching in black and white on the small screen is none other than Jake. The nighttime footage is grainy, but he seems to be wearing what he had on at Royce's. His left hand is in his pocket, and his sport coat hangs against his thigh. He's having a discussion with another man. I recognize the back of the second man's head because we'd spend the majority of our relationship moving in opposite directions. It's Gavin.

Wide-eyed, I snap my face to Trig's. "Is there any audio?"

"I wish there were. That would help the rest of it make sense." His lips press to a flat line.

I shake my head, not understanding what Trig means, and go back to watching the surveillance footage.

I can only make out portions of Gavin's dejected face when he turns toward the camera. Both men have similar hunched shoulders, giving me the impression that two of the most put-together people I've met are slumped and rumpled. Their chins dip to the ground while listening to the other, though they give the other an occasional glare. Each time their stances change, I wonder what one has said that the other reacts like they've been stabbed in the heart.

Gavin and Jake dance around one another, pacing to-and-fro, though neither especially leaving the individual squares of sidewalk they started out in. When Gavin gets too close to Jake, I keep waiting for a physical fight to break out. For Gavin's anger to become visible since there's no sound to help me comprehend what I'm seeing. I'm on pins and needles waiting for Jake to rear back and throw the first punch. I imagine him hitting Gavin in a way that makes my chest flutter.

Those palpitations aren't in a good way either because I can't interpret if Jake is defending me after Gavin's sister's tirade… Or even if I want the callous man who abandoned me coming to my defense.

Except, it doesn't seem as if either is goading the other, and where Jake fought me on everything, none of this tense discussion makes sense.

The feed continues playing, making me nauseous. The less confrontation there is, the more confused I become. I'd hit fast forward if I weren't in rubberneck mode, trying to glimpse the scene of an accident. I'm afraid I'll miss a key detail. Something that soothes the sting of what I'd done to Gavin, and how Jake's treatment of me was equally unfair.

From the uncomfortable taps of Jake's loafers on the pavement to the way Gavin uses one hand to ward off the night chill by tucking his zippered sweatshirt closer to him, I'm lost as to what's going on. I can't figure out why Trig thought this was important for me to see.

Eventually, Gavin puts a large, solid object he was holding in his other hand down by the side of the road. He turns and leaves. Jake stands there pondering what I know is the rock because I'm the one that found it inside the shop after the alarm went off.

I see Jake pick up the rock. He measures its weight in his palm. His lips move in a scathing swear, creating a peculiar warmth to the trail of prickles up my spine. The split-second hangs in suspended animation. His next action is all too obvious before Jake pitches the stone through the plate glass. All of a sudden, shards fall into view, dropping and shattering into smaller pieces on the sidewalk.

My gut anticipates Jake running. He ran from my scar, so why wouldn't he bolt from the scene of a crime? Instead, his forehead falls into his open palms as if he can't believe what he's done. Jake crouches on his haunches. He scrubs his face, peering between his fingers at the damage he's caused.

The security strobe light from inside my store is spinning to alert passersby. Yet there's no one on the desolate street besides Jake. Shadows fall left and right, casting his silhouette on the ground in tonal lights and darks.

He falls on his ass, still staring when the screen goes blank.

Bewildered, I look at Trig again. "I don't know how I'm supposed to respond to this."

"I don't want you to say anything. Not to me. Hell, I don't even care if you speak to Jake again. He's my friend, but my automatic reaction when Kimber told me everything he did to you was that Jake's not ready for a commitment. I feel awful. Jake dragged you into his fucked up scheme to get us off his back about settling down and finding a wife. All we wanted was for him to stop faking happy, you know? The mixed-up thing is that it hadn't taken too long before we all had the impression that you were it for him, Paisley."

"So why would he damage my business when he already knew my reputation was on the line dating him?"

"For the same reason Jake destroys anything. It's part of his charm." Trig presses the fingers of his hand together in prayer. They move, making a slithering, snakelike motion. The corner of his mouth curls up and I roll my eyes. "He's had a few things rougher than you'd think. Powerful people don't much enjoy being powerless."

"Jake likes to be in control."

Trig hums in agreement. "I have to be forthright with you, Paisley. I've had this tape from the get-go and you've always had the right to see it. The trouble is, nobody got anywhere by telling an obstinate horse like Jake Ballentine what to do... 'cept maybe you." He nudges my shoulder. "I can't explain why he couldn't admit it was him and covered his tracks. However, beyond everything that rumor has it Jake does in his spare time, he had a vested interest in my company. Jake stopped putting up a fuss about me selling out to Walsh around the same time he skipped town. I think whatever happened between you two had a lot to do with his decision. So, I'm showing it to you as my way of saying thanks."

"You could rake Jake over the coals with this."

"So could you. He's my friend, but I won't stop you even though I don't think pursuing it would make Jake have any significant change of heart. I'm pretty sure if Jake didn't regret what he did then, he does now."

The tender achy part of me searching for any way to soothe the pain wants to string Jake up by his toes. The problem is, turning this evidence over to the police also incriminates Trig.

So I guess the video adds to my unanswered questions. As does what Trig's just said.

If Jake feels any remorse for hurting me, then where is he?

Jake

The guitar intro booms over the speakers. Cymbals crash and a symphony of strobe lights explode like lightning. I stand at the side of the stage as the crowd roars. Their anticipatory smiles morph into whoops. The noise and chaos build. Their energy thumps in my chest. A sly grin tips the corner of my mouth. My toe taps like I'm still striking the bass pedal on the drum set the roadies hauled away to set up for the next performer, and I clap along with the beat.

I hear this beautiful noise when I'm up on stage and we strike the first chords to the current number one single on the country charts. By the time the singer I've backed up this summer starts into the refrain, the chorus of voices in the audience has built. It drives my actions forward until I'm spent and sweaty.

But here, on the sidelines? I experience the complexity from the fan's point of view.

I have been to concerts. I have played in concerts.

But I've never had the chance to play night after

night after night in concerts. It's enabled me to witness so many varied perspectives. From behind my kit to sneaking into the crowd, they've become innate.

But I have to admit, I prefer this one—hiding behind the long black curtain—over the rest.

And it's as big a jolt to me as it is to anyone else.

It makes me wonder if the familiarity has to do with all my years at Sweet Carolines. As a kid, I'd hidden offstage, too. The last thing my parents needed was a child being seen during operating hours and someone reporting them for endangerment, or whatever cockamamie reason social services used to vilify my upbringing around strippers. Mothers, actually. I had a lot of good women looking out for my well-being. However, those aren't the mothers anyone in charge takes seriously. Everyone presumes they're cut from the same cloth as Carver's... And, wouldn't you know, it was my mom who took Carver in when he needed a place to stay.

So yeah, fuck anyone who thinks only virtuous people do good and only sinful people do bad. And if no one is willing to take my word on it, they can ask Cary Cass what his upstanding father did to him. I wish I'd cut my need for revenge against Rex Stanton out like the cancer it was sooner.

Hours on a tour bus have left me with a ton of time on my hands to reflect on how much shit I've gotten wrong. Starting with my jealousy toward Cris and my unwillingness to forgive him for mourning his wife the way a devastated husband needed to. I've been lost the past few months without Paisley, but at least I know she's alive.

I've thought about sending her tickets and backstage passes. I've wondered how she'd react to finding out I disappeared to go see an old friend. I don't think I believed what I saw in that picture in the restaurant in Nashville until I saw Cris for myself. My original intent wasn't a sentimental journey, though I expected we'd commiserate over our mutual losses. Except Cris was right. The only person who'd made the choice to give up my dreams and live in misery was me.

Someday I'd like the opportunity to introduce Paisley to Daveigh. My old pal's new wife gives Cris hell for staying away from her; his advice to me when it came to mending fences with Pais. However, it is exactly what I've been doing since Cris floated my audition tape in the right direction, and I set out on the road to replace the band's drummer.

The first few nights on stage, I felt like an imposter. A no-talent, washed-up musician who'd usurped some young guy's big break. Or girl's. The headliner's backup band includes a kick-ass female with a guitar of her own. It was her talent that lit up the audience before a single note was sung, and she's playing her heart out right now.

But the reality is in any situation it's not what you know, it's who you know. If I hadn't been able to cut it, the tour's management would have cut their losses as fast as they'd offered me the fill-in spot.

There's a firm pat on my back, and I turn. Tom, the guy who reached out to Cris, shakes my hand. I thank him for taking a chance on me. Tom says another high-energy country band has dates booked in Raleigh. They've been out a drummer this season, too. Instead of hiring a fill-in like me, they've been scoping local talent to play those dates. He offers to give their manager my name so they can look me up when they are in town. Tom can't make guarantees, but the one thing I'm hard-core realizing is that there is a difference between saying life doesn't come with a guarantee and accepting that it doesn't. You have to keep plugging away at success and define it on your own terms.

Once we've said goodbye, I head toward the tour bus to grab my bag. I have a flight home in three hours that I don't want to miss. The whole way to the airport, I'm mulling over what I thought I lost out on in my twenties when the lead vocalist quit the up-and-coming band I was in. It is a far cry from what I want today.

And what I want more than anything is for the woman who I've stayed away from to give me a chance to explain. Paisley's sweet sass and fierceness broke down the walls surrounding my heart. I plan to wipe away her tears... But I haven't yet finished chasing down my dreams so that I'm able to listen when Paisley tells me what kind of leg up she needs me to give to her to chase hers.

I've felt the proverbial heat since arriving back in town. Yet it is the scorching temperatures I escape, unlocking and entering Sweet Caroline's. The theater is dark and cool. I take a minute to enjoy the reprieve.

Along with the rest of the south, the heat in Brighton is insufferable this August. I've been able to stand it from the comfort of an air-conditioned tour bus where I've slept off the meet and greets with fans, the late parties when everyone is gone from a venue, and even later nights on the road to the next stop.

Along with a lot of other things, my sleep schedule is about to change. At least in the interim. And wanting to start the morning off on the right foot, this is the second time in two days that the first thing I've done when I've stepped outside was take an early drive over to old man Johnston's. His garden is where I found the not-quite-coral roses when I needed to apologize to Paisley for not listening this spring.

Seems I made a habit of that, huh?

Today Mr. Johnston cut me four petite roses from his garden, warning that he only has so many corals in bloom. When I paid Mr. Johnston for the roses informed me the remaining coral buds he's tending won't be ready to open until later this week. Tomorrow, I'll have to get my roses from the nursery he sold to Holly. My choices are limited to red and white.

I can already see how much effort Holly has put into transforming the place. Paisley's favorite is the coral, but I doubt someone as gracious as she is will fuss about what color roses I lay on her doorstep since supporting small businesses falls along the lines of something Paisley would do. She's all about whatever benefits the little guy.

"Look who is up with the crows." Arms extended, my mother saunters toward me from the hallway.

"Did you even go to bed last night?"

"What a silly question. Of course, I didn't. I'm too excited to see my boy. You've been gone all summer. And there is a reason God invented cucumbers."

She makes me chuckle. "For the bags under your eyes?"

My mother shoots me a coy wink.

Whatever Mom's secrets are, her habits have cracked the code to the fountain of youth. Caroline is ageless and appears as impeccable as she had on stage thirty years ago.

I pull Mom into a hug. I drove over to her house the moment I got back, but today I'm feeling nostalgic, and I'm sure she is, too.

"Are you ready for this?" I ask. We're expecting other people here soon.

My mother's brow raises. "Are you having second thoughts? Come sit." She beckons me to the same table I sat at on Valentine's Day when my entire life felt out of balance.

"I don't remember a time before Sweet Caroline's," I admit.

"That's because there wasn't one for you, sweetheart. The two things I wanted more than anything were born right here: my career and my family."

"When I came back to Brighton after Dad went to jail, all I wanted was to fix the damage he caused."

"I know you did. I know you were struggling with your own losses. I needed you here. But I also thought that you'd leave again."

"You did?" Mom hadn't said any of this when I got off the plane.

"Jake, your dad and I were a team. We had the same goals. When your band broke up, I was mourning what could have been. Processing everything the same way you were. I don't respect what your father did. To this day, I still don't understand why he did it. But I'm within my rights to cherish the moments before he got involved with the wrong sort of people.

"Love isn't a light switch. It's a lighted path. It's been my experience that vibrant lights flick on the path while falling in love. And at some point, the love is sprinkled like fireflies, guiding you along a longer one clouded by shadows, until the sun comes back out and it brightens again. But how long the dimness lasts, and when it happens, is different for everyone." Her shoulders squeeze together. "There's no such thing as timing it perfectly. There's no such thing as the perfect match. But if you are lucky, you meet the *almost* perfect person. You accept that their flaws make them human and they find a way of doing the same for you.

"The love your dad and I had was once in a lifetime. He cared about my hopes. He kept my dream of owning this club and the people here safe for so, so long. Your father never stepped out on me. He never betrayed our marriage vows in a scenario where I was the one who was taking off my clothes for other men. Our newer female employees often threw themselves at him, thinking it would help them keep their jobs. Do you have any idea how difficult the constant strain on fidelity was for either of us? We were conscious and conscientious of one another's feelings. I'm not ashamed to say we had angry sex, or sex to take the edge off. I've been your mother long enough that I'm not ashamed to tell you that your dad and I had *constant* sex. It was a huge part of our relationship and it helped keep our marriage healthy."

"Can we move past the sex part now?" I cringe like a teenager.

"My point is that sadness, regret, remorse, and fear, shattered souls and broken dreams are as important to this life we live as holding onto hope, accepting apologies for the kind of hurt your heart won't ever stop weeping over, and picking your knickers up off the floor and trying again.

"I'm proud of you for trying again this summer. I'd wished, even if you never joined another band, that you'd see past your sorrow and make the choice you are making today. I retired and gave you Sweet Caroline's so that you had the option of doing whatever you wanted with it."

"You wanted me to close the club?"

"No, I wanted you to *use* the club. You could have sold this place to finance your goals. Moved back to California… as long as you had a guest room for me." She squeezes my knee.

I blanch and lean into the chair, reacting to this news. My mother could've said this as her time on stage faded.

She places her hand on my knee. "Everyone makes mistakes. Everyone has a unique interpretation of how someone else's actions affect them. Sometimes we fall so far that we lose the grace to hear what's truly in someone's heart, only to respond out of fear and loneliness. Don't hold our pasts against us. I loved your dad through the toughest years of our lives. And I will always love you, no matter what choices you make."

My mother has put up with a lot. The reputation I garnered, trying to defend her against a bully by becoming one, led me to commit more crimes than my father committed. Yet, she's not judging me the same way she withheld judgment for my dad's actions.

Instead of flying off the handle and making false accusations that my mother should have been forthright, I find an ounce of humility. I finally understand that I've spent a decade hearing what I want to hear. It added to my heart's deepest and darkest narrative that the only way to get what I desire is to get back at the people who stand in my way.

I couldn't have been more wrong.

Paisley

Sloan is browsing the shop. We're waiting for my sales clerk to come back from her lunch break before we meet Kimber at Baked Beans. Kimber and Sloan are throwing Holly's baby shower. I'm hooking them up with favors at cost and have a stack of promo catalogs and websites for them to peruse.

By the time I held Greer's shower, I'd found so many cute things it was hard to choose. Not only for what gift to give but also the plethora of gender neutral decorations—Greer wanted the baby's sex to be a surprise. Also, as someone in a situation where whimsical baby bottles filled with jelly beans aren't ever going to be useful once the candy is eaten, I had a yearning for something more advantageous for guests to bring home. When it comes to parenting advice and shower gifts, people are generous by nature. I wanted to meet that kindness with appreciation.

Greer's baby was born this fall. I've nicknamed her pink bundle of joy "Fancy Nancy" because every time

I see the gorgeous little girl, she's wearing the cutest tights with ruffles on the bum to keep her teeny-tiny toes warm.

Holly, who knows she's having a girl, is enamored with these darling stockings. I swear her daughter is going to have the same sort of stellar wardrobe as her mother. I love that Greer had someone to be pregnant alongside. Everyone's excitement makes having a second party right around the corner twice as much fun.

"Goodness, it's cold out there!" An amiable young woman, who I haven't seen before, stands in the doorway. She rubs her hands together and blows on them. "Why on earth is it this cold here?"

"My friend, Cece, says the same thing every winter," Sloan replies. "But this winter is as cold as last summer was hot. If we're lucky, maybe the weather will even out and next year will be milder?"

"Here's hoping." She tugs off her beanie and smooths flyaway strands of hair.

"What can I help you with?" I ask. "I'm Paisley, by the way."

"Layla, and also, I don't know. Everything?" She touches a cashmere sweater on the nearest hanger, and I know she's already made her mind up to get it. "I got a recommendation to come in here from Kelsey. She works with my boyfriend, and she was so nice about it that I figured I'd pop in. What else is a girl supposed to do when she's just moved and out of a job but spend?" Layla lets out a tinkling laugh, though her falling expression says she's having second thoughts the last comment made the wrong impression.

"What do you do?"

"A little of this and a little of that. We'd planned on moving east sooner, so I quit what I was doing and started waitressing at the club my boyfriend ran on the Strip."

Her answer gives me pause. "Where are you from?"

"West Hollywood. Don't get too impressed. It's hellishly expensive if you're only making tips."

"And your boyfriend was a club manager there?"

"Yep." Layla brings the sweater and a matching scarf over for me to ring her up. "Julian is managing Sweet Caroline's when it reopens."

My mouth forms an "O" and I dart a quick look across the store at Sloan.

I'll go out blocks of my way rather than drive past Sweet Caroline's. The marquees are empty. The neon pink sign hasn't been lit in months and the parking lot is dark.

A lot of the customers, who hadn't been into the store since the rumor mill went crazy outing Jake's and my "affair", returned. They spoke boldfaced lies about Caroline without any shame. In these four walls, they circulated gossip about why Jake closed the club. The expectation that I'd shoot off my mouth and give them the real scoop was wildly unfair. I was a good person before I met Jake and none paid any heed that his dealings might be a sensitive subject for me.

I like that the mill girls don't poke around. They meant it when they said everyone is entitled to their secrets.

The doorbell cam Trig installed confirmed Jake is in Brighton, but I haven't seen him. Not in person, anyway. And frankly, his sneakiness isn't winning me over enough that I care to ask what the hell he's up to.

Sloan refuses to meet my gaze, pretending to rearrange a few items on display.

I roll my lips between my teeth and snatch the sweater from Layla. "I am so sorry!" I say when I realize what I've done. I use the garment to cover my red face. "I thought it was about to fall!" I make an excuse.

Layla accepts my apology. I add her contact information to the computer and offer to email her receipt. She thanks me and, after telling her to stop in again, I mention that Mind Your Own Beeswax has a soothing lotion for chapped hands.

Sloan stays quiet. The back of my neck gets sweaty and my pulse hasn't returned to normal when we pick up our drinks from the order line at Baked Beans.

I know I'm the one who has to break the stifling silence, and I pull the top paper out of the folder I've kept Greer's shower details in.

"The lease on the adjacent storefront is up for renewal and the shop owners have decided they're moving to a larger location. What would you think if I took over the space?" I slide a draft logo of my boutique's paisley symbol in a yin and yan formation toward Sloan.

"I like the pinks and blues. The hue matches the boutique's coral. They're a little spermy looking separated like that. Maybe move them closer, so they touch? They sort of resemble amoebas in a Petri dish like this. Wait!... Is this a baby boutique?" Sloan blinks.

"I don't have a catchy name for it yet. It's just an idea." I bite the inside of my cheek.

"A brilliant one. So many friends are having babies. You should totally go for it." While Sloan's words are encouraging, she inspects the lid on her coffee.

"Are you sure?" What I'm desperate to shout is, "Jake's moved on, why can't I?"

Because I'm trying. I really am.

I'm still supporting as many local businesses as I can. My mom and I keep an open dialogue about my dad's choice to keep my abortion from her and how it affects her perception of their marriage after the fact because she assumed they told one another everything. Her support after my surgery has strengthened our bond, and we've gotten closer.

During a normal week, I'm not just going out to yoga with Greer, we're often invited to the mill girls' events. I've made new friends. But even if I go to bed at night completely fulfilled, I wake up the next morning to Jake cutting down all that progress when I stumble over the stupid bouquets he's left on my doorstep for months.

After what he continues to put me through, I wouldn't accept Jake's apology anymore if I met him on the street. I don't want to see Jake and that's why I don't confront him face to face. Even now, it feels like Jake is taking advantage and I can't be as happy for Kelsey as I should be. I'm not normally the sort who seeks credit. However, the big jerk, *the pompous ass*, hired Julian when finding help for Kelsey was my idea.

I wish he'd crawl back under whatever rock he was hiding beneath.

It's obvious I'm still a pawn in his game. I'm trying to face the day he decides to use what I can do for him again with courage. I'll also never confess my weakness to a soul. With each rose, he's put a chink in my armor. If Jake intends to continue hurting me, he's doing a bang-up job of it.

Coral has become my least favorite color, and it's everywhere from my signs to the window clings—that I'm loath to admit I ripped clean off. The behavior was juvenile. But I was tired of the reminder that Jake tried to destroy my business and then swooped in to save the day. Seriously, who does that?

My pulse beats as furiously as it did whenever we argued. I swear it is a good thing my blood pressure hasn't kicked up a notch to what it was like waiting for Jake to kiss me to put his hands on my body. Except my cardiologist has mentioned if I don't start controlling my stress level, and stop taking my anger out on *his* doorstep, that man will drive me into an early grave.

"You could ask Layla if she'd want a job."

"Huh? Who?" Sloan knocks me out of my internal ranting. "Oh, yeah. I've also thought maybe my mom might like a position. Something part-time. That way, whatever extra hours I have to put in, we won't miss out on..."

I miss him.

"Out on?"

"Sorry.' I bat the air. "Brain cramp... on spending that time with one another."

"It's cute that your shop is your baby. I've always liked that about you. How proud you are of it."

"Thank you. I've always liked that you like my shop. Your recommendations are a boon to my business, and that means a lot."

"What else is a girl supposed to do when she's got a platinum limit and nothing to do but spend?" Sloan twists Layla's words.

We share a laugh, but Sloan seems sad.

I slip the new logo idea under the bottom of my pile of papers and stack my laptop over it so it's out of sight, fidgeting in my seat. "You know, I just remembered I have something pressing that I need to take care of. I'm going to text Kimber. Let's do this another day."

"Paisley, stop." Sloan puts her hand over mine. "You're not the first friend who has tried to make me feel better about the fact that I don't have children of my own."

"I'm not—"

"Don't worry about it, okay? It's my choice. It's

deliberate and, even when it's painful, I have my reasons."

"That's understandable." I give Sloan the respect she deserves.

"Maybe I'll work in your new store... with Layla, and your mom." She adds with grace.

"New store? What did I miss?" Kimber's purse lands on the table and she slides into the chair next to her best friend.

"I will tell you all about it later. Let's get down to business!"

Amidst chatting and poring over ideas, we have to stop to refill our drinks and to get croissants. I have mine poised at my lips, inhaling the spicy scent when the wail of sirens breaks the normal bustling noises downtown. Pedestrians outside on the sidewalk pause, watching the fire trucks zoom by. An ambulance is hot on its heels. I've all but put the interruption out of my mind and am ready to lick my fingers when a police car speeds in the same direction.

Sloan glances at her pinging phone and clicks the screen off. When the reminder sounds a minute later, she turns the entire thing over.

As a general rule, I adore anyone who puts what they are doing above the draw of technology, but I have a sneaking suspicion that she doesn't want me to see the message.

It doesn't take long before her cell begins vibrating incessantly. Sloan flips it back over. She looks between the device and me. "I hope you don't mind, I have to take this," she apologizes.

Lifting from her seat, she answers the call asking, "What's going on?"

And then Sloan freezes.

In an instant, it is obvious something is wrong. I hate that I have the acute awareness of Jake's smooth voice on the other end of the line.

The color drains from Sloan's face. "I've got to go," she croaks.

Kimber grabs her by the elbow. "I'm coming with you."

I don't hesitate, snatching everything off the table. "Me too."

I've avoided Jake at all costs, but the last thing my animosity towards him is going to cost me is friendship.

Chapter Thirty-four

Jake

"Jaaake!" I hear Kelsey yell for me.

"In here, I holler back."

She appears in the doorway a moment later with a puzzled, but cheerful expression and hands me a work order to scrawl my signature on. "Sorry. It's still weird that you're where you say you're going to be. I'm not over chasing you to get shit done."

"Never chase a man, Kelsey. You'll wind up with someone like me." I have glue on my hand and the pen sticks to my fingers. I make a funny up and down gesture and it drops to the clipboard.

"Nobody wants that," she replies in jest before getting serious. "The beer and wine distributor rescheduled for late tomorrow afternoon, so I may duck out and bring those boxes over to Caroline. The new barstools are on backorder for another month. The carpenter called and wanted to know which stain you prefer on the bar top."

"Same as they're using on the floor once it's laid. What else?" I return the paperwork to her.

"Nothing I can't handle, and the rest of the messages are promoters and band managers looking to book up-and-coming acts. Not my circus. Not my monkey. But I think we're scheduling into the fall."

"Excellent." I knew keeping Kelsey on the payroll would pay off. "Go home after you're done at Caroline's," I call after her.

Shortly after my mom and I had our heart-to-heart, the Sweet Caroline's employees descended on the club. While I never enjoyed being here, it was strange to have missed the familiar faces. And even more weird to let them know I'd appreciated all their hard work over the years, and that I'd miss them when the club closed. So as not to pull the rug out from anyone, performances continued until the end of the month, which wasn't that far away.

Mom's dream shut down quietly… We switched off the neon pink light in the parking lot together, retiring it with little fanfare. The important thing to us was that our family's business survived decades of negativity. No matter what rumors the gossips spread, nobody forced us out of Brighton, and that's something to be proud of.

Afterward, I took my mother dancing in Raleigh. We stayed out until the wee hours. It seemed appropriate. We've lived most of our lives at night.

Each staff member got a letter of recommendation and an extra paycheck. A lot of the dancers scattered. There isn't much work for them in Brighton unless they are going to switch careers.

Despite the help I sent her way, Kelsey was ready to spit rocks at me the day of the announcement. Mom had taken the burden off of her so that she could focus on managing the club and not the girls. Morgan and Skye filled in when she was short-staffed and on her regular days off.

When everyone had cleared out, I called Kelsey

aside and told her she still had a job if she could still stand me as a boss. She'd remained loyal to me when everything was going to shit and deserved my appreciation. She teared up and called me an asshole. But then she hugged me and we made a deal that she's allowed to call me out on my bullshit.

Kelsey has the option of rehiring any of the employees she worked best with when we reopen. That's how Kimber and Holly got by. They trusted one another. They trusted the people they suggested get hired. And they trusted me to keep my fucking nose out of it.

Everything I know about success is because of something a woman taught me. It would be stupid of me to discount that now.

The next phase of the plan was having Kelsey call to interview Julian. She let him know that the job description was updated, and he agreed to the offer. Julian and his girlfriend, Layla, moved to town a few weeks ago.

Julian is in his element handling the acts eager to perform, except like the rest of us, he's done more heavy lifting than managing. With opening night a ways off, that's unlikely to change anytime soon.

Being on the road was an experience I won't forget. Cris was right. No matter the venue, it's the connection between the artist and the music. By converting the club into a concert hall, I'm able to feed my soul and start the journey for some pimply band geek with stars in their eyes on amateur night. The connections I made through Cris and Tom are paying off, though. A good number of country acts want to promote next season's tours in more intimate venues before hitting the road for the summer. We're booking big names for one night only. The amount of calls we field when they add Sweet Caroline's to their website's tour updates feels like we're cashing in before tickets go on sale.

Aside from the stage, not much of the original Sweet Caroline's remains. Dusty took the building down to the studs. The new walls are up in my office and backstage in the dressing rooms. The bigger restrooms with extra stalls—that the mill girls told me I had to budget for—are framed, as is the theater. Walsh is doing the security at the same time as the sound system goes in. All of it will tie into a central control room for crowd control.

It's good to have friends. *Period.*

Not friends you can con into doing shit for you, but the kind who'll show up and support you no matter how big an ass you've made of yourself.

I rub my neck, forgetting my palm has flaky bits of paste stuck to it. They crumble down the back of my shirt. Whatever, I'm a filthy mess. A little glue isn't changing that. Although I slap my palms over my grubby jeans to brush off the rest.

I'm not sure what I thought I was getting myself into when I volunteered Carver and me to hang wallpaper in the dressing room. Owning a strip club is easier than manual labor. However, since the first sledgehammer made a hole in the dusty wall, I've been enjoying getting my hands dirty, building something special instead of being hateful.

"I've been thinking about doing something nice for Sloan," I announce.

Carver moves aside the delicate wallpaper that's flopped over his head. He turns, flashing a quizzical expression. "Who are you, and what have you done with Jake Ballentine?"

A throaty chuckle escapes me. "I'm serious."

There's a baby boom in town and Sloan sees Paisley often. On occasion, Sloan feeds me bits and pieces of how Paisley is doing.

I couldn't stop loving Paisley if I tried. Every

morning I still drop roses on her doorstep. Almost as often, I find a bag of withered petals on mine. I keep them. Some are so dried and brittle that the best description of their beauty is haunting. Sort of like the woman I'm keeping my distance from so that someday I may not have to anymore.

The connection is still there. Paisley wouldn't fight back if it weren't.

I grab a mallet, flip it and catch the handle.

"There is nothing you can get Sloan that she doesn't already have." Carver flatly denies my request.

"*Ah,* but does she?" I jab a finger in his direction. "Tell me, what's the one thing your wife wants more than anything?"

"You're not going to give her that, moron." Carver finishes wrestling with the sheet he's pressing to the wall.

The intricate pattern matches the last one he hung exactly. He's pretty dang good at this.

"So, she still wants kids."

Carver wipes his hand on a cloth and gives me the side-eye, waiting for me to make an inappropriate remark. He puts the towel down and I lower the mallet. It hovers over Carver's left hand.

"What would happen?" I ask, "If you had an accident."

"I'd be out of commission." His voice is gruff.

"Why does that bug you so much when you want to be done? You've said it yourself that you've made enough money. That you're tired of being tied to this outfit. Sick of the snobbery from collectors who've searched you out. The only reason you go back when they beckon is your gut questioning if they'd do the things we've done."

"That *you've* done, Jake. I just didn't stop you from blackmailing anyone."

Pa-ta-toe, Pa-tat-o. Carver's as complicit as Trig.

His next thought is sentimental. I can see how the outcome of what I'm putting forth fills him with uncertainty. Carver has a picture in his head. If anyone gets how hard that is to shake, it's me. But dreams are fluid. The precise point of their hazy ambiguity is that they're supposed to change to fit the actual goals you have in life.

Now that I've set a new course, I wish I'd gotten my shit together sooner. Trig is the happiest I've seen him. Why can't it be that way for Carver?

I also wish I had more misgivings about doing what I'm asking Carver to contemplate. But we both know I'm the only one who'll do it without an ounce of regret.

"You give up the real kid entirely for the fantasy kid? Is your imagination that unwavering?" I ask in a brazen way only a brother would.

"You think I don't question that all the time, Jake? Whatever I choose, it can still blow our world up; Mine and Sloan's.

"Chen got out."

"Felix got old. Senile." I hear my old excuses in Carver's righteous, indignant huff.

I lift the mallet, but Carver doesn't move his hand.

He looks me dead in the eyes. Defeat stares back at me. The same longing and hopelessness I saw from Cris when Liz died and she took his dreams along with her.

"Right now. Make a choice right now. Sloan or the money. The dream or the kid," I dare.

Carver's hand curls into a ball. He closes his eyes and gives me an almost imperceptible nod. His lungs fill, and before he releases the breath, I bring the sledgehammer down. The force it takes to crush the bones from his wrist to his fingertips isn't gentle. But the decision to do it is likely the most considerate one I've made.

Like me, there are threads of his past that Carver has held onto. Lies we've told ourselves that money is enough to buy happiness. To absorb our pain and set us free.

I wasn't worthy of Liz. I didn't go after Kimber fast enough. I held myself back from Holly because I couldn't settle for not having all of her. The one-sided feelings weren't as big as me not making amends with my ghosts. I didn't know how until Paisley came along. And I still had to shutter her out to move forward.

Sloan is the best thing that ever happened to Carver. He needs her like the air he breathes. And although he's committed to her, he hasn't allowed himself the final step. As a kid, what he saw of a family was out of reach for someone raised by an addict. He can't break down the last barrier to get what he wants now.

Not without my help. And what I've given my best friend is the ability to strip away his past and set the stage for the rest of his life. Ironic that it is in the same building where our mothers stripped off their clothes.

"God-fucking-dammit-all-to-hell-you-goddamned-asshole." Carver's blood-curdling bellow echo surrounds us.

He crouches, holding his painful shattered limb close, and I call for an ambulance.

Chapter Thirty-five

Paisley

Kimber parked her car the closest. The three of us jump inside. A tense Sloan takes the front seat and tells Kimber where to go. Our words that everything will be fine don't assuage her.

I'm worried, too. Aside from giving us directions, the only other thing we know is that Carver is hurt. Sloan fights back tears on the short drive.

We arrive at Sweet Caroline's. Emergency vehicles dot the lot. In the daylight, the fire truck's flashing lights replace the pink neon glow I'd become accustomed to. A paramedic with a red bag slung over his shoulder leaves the ambulance's back doors swinging.

The scene is chaotic. Self-preservation had me avoiding this stretch of road, so I hadn't known the building was undergoing renovation. Chain link construction fencing protects the materials workers are storing to use inside. We dash by two-by-fours and drywall scattered near the entrance.

I haven't allowed myself to worry about Jake. Yet,

now I can't help the way my stomach churns.

Is anyone else is injured? And how badly?

Inside, the police officer on the scene allows Sloan to pass when Jake waves her over. Jake's eyes meet mine for the briefest moment. Seeing him safe sucks the breath out of me. A flare of awareness flashes across his face, making me weak in the knees. But as fast as both happen, Jake turns, ushering Sloan down the hall. The officer stationed at the door stops Kimber and me from going further into the theater than the entryway.

"We need this area clear for the medics to wheel him out. They're taking him to the hospital," the cop says with authority. They won't answer any more of our questions.

Frazzled and clutching one another's hands, I look around while Kimber dials Trig. Ear pressed to her phone, she tells her husband to meet them at the emergency room as soon as he can.

Their conversation peters out, and other noises come to the forefront. The building is busy and at the same time work has come to a standstill. Voices echo through the massive space. Open plumbing is visible where the bar used to be. The reserved booths are missing. It's a blank wall now. At least there is a wall there. In darker corners, some areas appear skeletal with no drywall. My toes twitch, seeking to spread out and sink into the carpet. Except under my shoes is cold gray concrete. The heavy red velvet curtains surrounding the stage are gone. The stage itself is the only recognizable feature. Upon it sits a large sanding machine. Below it? A pile of sawdust from stripping the wide wooden floorboards.

I'm astonished. Gutted, Sweet Carolines looks nothing like the strip club I ran into on Valentine's Day.

Around the same time I'm able to pick my jaw up,

the EMTs roll Carver out on a stretcher. The red bag the paramedic carried rests by his feet. Carver has his arm, splinted and bandaged from the tip of his hand to his elbow, crossed over his chest. Pain radiates from Carver's tight features and the stillness of his body.

Sloan is walking beside him, guided by Jake, who has a gentle hand on her back. Her fingertips play at her parched lips and her face is tear-stained.

Both pause at the exit so that the stretcher is free to cross the threshold.

"I can't believe you broke his hand." Sloan turns to hug Jake.

"You're welcome," he says, holding her tight.

Sloan pushes at his chest. "I didn't say 'thank you'."

He looks down at her with a goofy smile. "You will."

She wipes her eyes and wraps her arms around his neck.

"Now go." Jake's voice booms in an all too familiar Jake manner.

"You're such an ass," Kimber remarks, shaking her head, and following Sloan out to the parking lot.

The door closes. I'm stuck in place, confused by what I've just witnessed.

"It's nice to see you, Paisley. I didn't think I was going to be, but I'm glad you're here."

"What did you do, Jake?" I want answers.

"Dusty agreed to teach me how to use a hammer."

"Not very well, apparently." My palms rest on my hips.

"I think we have better things to argue over."

"That's where you are wrong. We have nothing to discuss, since there is nothing between us." I make a wild gesture back and forth.

The theater is empty and I have no desire to be

alone with this man. I spin on my heel to leave.

"Hey, *Corazon?*"

"What?" I yell. Jake using the pet name he'd given me sets me ablaze. How dare he?

"How mad does a person have to be that they'll return a dozen roses to the doorstep of the person who sent them?"

"Not angry, Jake. Unwilling to let you hurt them." By returning the flowers, I maintained the upper hand.

"Funny thing about those roses. I started sending them the day I didn't have to. It was a coincidence that our six months were up."

I pause before leaning into the release bar and speak into the metal door. "I'm thrilled you found humor in toying with me."

"*Nah*, it's funny because you becoming my girlfriend stopped being make-believe before we'd pulled the wool over on my friends... Come over tonight?"

"No!" I whine in shock.

Who does this man think he is? And why is my heart clinging to his words?

Jake's front meets my back. He laces his fingers into mine and turns me around.

I'll sink into that warm spot where I felt so safe if I look up or stop defending myself.

"I won't kiss you." He cups my cheek.

Jake's once pristine fingernails are riddled with hangnails and cracked at the cuticle. The callouses on his hand are more pronounced.

"Well, that's for certain," I balk, still not meeting his gaze.

He laughs. It's soft, like the smile playing on his lips.

"I'm not kissing you because I'm done using it to my advantage."

"Cocky bastard, you're so sure a single kiss is going to change everything." I'm ready to blow my top.

"It did once. One completely unexpected kiss flipped the script on our lives."

"It won't now."

Without warning, he lifts me to sit on a wooden storage box. "That's better. Now we can see eye to eye." Jake's head bobs from side to side, measuring my anger.

Unwilling to meet his blue gaze, I glance over his shoulder at a blank wall. I need to calm my nerves, but I'm so agitated with Jake this close to me that my senses aren't picking up any solid forms but his. My normal calming techniques are useless.

"Paisley, I don't want to lead with something physical. What I want is for you to tell me everything I did wrong. All the ways I abused your trust. Everything I've fucking missed out on in your life. And, if you're able, I'd like to know how you got that scar."

"I don't owe you any explanations, Jake. Not after what you did."

"You're right. But I was giving you the chance to go first."

I growl when his palms land on my knees. He has me caged in again the way Jake did when he forced me to be here when the club was open.

"Being on the same level doesn't work if you won't look at me."

"Fine." I snap my head in Jake's direction, focusing on the hole I'd like to smash in his forehead.

Jake's quiet and patient with me. My line of sight drops. His eyes are warm with flecks of gray and lavender.

"I've spent the past few months trying to find the right words to tell you I'm sorry for the things I've done. From the get-go, I had a total disregard for your feelings, until I started having feelings for you. Even then, my kindness was arrogant. I used affection as a way of keeping you. I'd seen enduring love betray people I loved. It soured me on making any commitments to anyone that wouldn't leave me coming out on top."

I cackle because I can't let Jake see me break down.

"Leaving you the way I did turned me inside out. Faced with the reality of losing another thing I was desperate to have, proved how big a coward I was. My instant reaction to the fear was to self-sabotage. I did it the night I took you to Royce's, too. It's the only excuse I have for throwing the rock, Pais, and it's a sorry one at that."

"My reputation was already on the line, Jake. I may have been the one to put it there when I ran out on Gavin, but you kept nudging it forward. How could you to to harm my livelihood? Why did you stop Gavin and then ruin it, anyway?"

What led up to them facing off on the street in the middle of the night?

Jake scrubs a hand over his head when I admit Trig showed me the footage.

"I'd been on edge about our official first date at Royce's. You'd been the perfect girlfriend. I wanted to show you I was ready to be what you needed. But then the girls ganged up on you in the restroom and Laughton's sister turned the night into a spectacle. When I dropped you off, I was angry. I wasn't the man you needed by any stretch. You were one more dream out of my reach. It was better to let you out of the deal.

"I took a walk to clear my head and wound up in front of the store. Laughton had wandered there, too. He was embarrassed by what his sister had done. He loved you and whenever he thought he'd be able to get over the sting of betrayal, my name would get tossed into the mix. Brighton hadn't stuck to gossiping about you, Paisley. Gavin's name was on every tongue.

"He started talking about how amazing you were *before* me. How brave and bold you were. That I'd changed you for the worse... But I hadn't. Laughton didn't know that you came to me exactly the person who you were. I hated that he'd had you and didn't see that. I hated that he wanted to hurt you by breaking the window and I talked him out of it. Except I did it in a way you'd never be proud of me for. Laughton walked away, and I realized I'd defended you because I'd fallen in love with you."

"You screamed, and then you pitched the rock." And then he fell on his ass.

"I told you, I'm a master of self-sabotage." Jake tells me about how his best friend's wife died the exact day their band was to sign a recording contract and he lost his big break in the music business. Not long after, his dad got arrested and Jake took over the club. "Whenever something went wrong, I was picking up pieces. It was safer for me to forsake what I loved than wait for the betrayal. That way, I didn't get my hopes dashed. Except it's pretty clear now that everyone else held onto their hope. I was the only one who gave up."

I shimmy and slide off the box. Jake gives me a wide berth while I stroll the empty space.

"Is that what this is all about, Jake? Finally getting what you want?"

"Only part of it, because I get now there will always be something that is a hair's breadth out of reach. Before you, I skipped out on Sweet Caroline's because in my heart of hearts, I didn't want *that* club to succeed. I wanted to see my own successes come to fruition. And to do that, I had to cast away any doubts I had that I'd given up on my goals. So that's where I've been, Pais, figuring my shit out."

I scratch my temple. "I'm not sure if you understand this, but people with their shit together don't break their best friend's hands."

"The pleasure was all mine. He'll thank me. Sloan already did… In her own way." Jake shrugs his broad shoulders. His muscles stretch his shirt.

"You are insane. What do you want from me?… *Why am I still here?*" I say to the wall, soft enough that Jake doesn't pick up on my muttering.

"For you to come over tonight. I promise I won't make excuses for lying. My reactions were immature. I'm sorry for everything I put you through." He apologizes.

"There's no selfish reason?" I lift a brow.

"Of course there is. I miss you like hell, *Corazón*. I want to hear what you've been up to and listen to the amusing way your voice trails when you talk to yourself the way you just did. I like the weird talking with your hands thing that you do."

The cleft in Jake's chin becomes pronounced when his cheeks bunch, catching me wringing my hands. I hate how handsome his confidence makes him look.

"Don't be self-conscious. I picked up the habit and do it now, too." He strolls over to the stage where I'm standing. "I also like how your voice gets louder when you get riled up, forcing me to pay attention to you—like you haven't been the only thing I've seen since you barged through those doors." He points.

Jake has overshadowed everyone else for me as well. I want the moments back when we kiss and stopping, breaking apart from one another, doesn't seem right. But I don't know if I'm ready for this version of Jake Ballentine.

His fingers tickle behind my ear, lower against my neck, sending chills up my spine. "There's no one else like you, Paisley. No one else I've loved, nobody

I've failed so completely, and no other person I've wanted to make changes in my life for so that I might be deserving of them. I won't blame you if you run away from me now. But not running after you if you walk out that door doesn't mean I'll ever let go of making what I did wrong up to you."

Jake

I scoop eight overstuffed grocery sacks out of my trunk. The weight of the handles pinch as I carry them to the front door. I fumble with my keys, stepping over the roses Paisley must've thrown on the doorstep this morning.

It is normal for Paisley to return my tokens of affection. There have been quite a few instances that she's collected several days' worth, throwing the roses at the door and scattering them on the porch.

I wait before returning to the entryway to retrieve them, not staggering back the way I normally do, feeling like I've done something wrong by reminding Paisley she still exists in my world. This is the first time her rejection isn't matched by my pride that she won't put up with my shit.

After sticking perishables into the fridge, I grab the bag I use to gather the long stems scattered on the porch. It's full to the brim with petals and so is my hope that tonight will go well.

Paisley is still leery about my intentions, but she

agreed to come over. Like every other time I've put one foot in front of the other lately, it's a step in the right direction.

I turn on some tunes and belt out the lyrics while searching the spice rack for the savory herbs and the spicier ones. Then I grab a cutting board and start chopping vegetables to the beat of the song.

I'm making pan-seared salmon, and I was smart enough to ask if she ate fish. Unlike the coffee versus tea thing, I didn't want to plop down a plate of something for Paisley to eat that she didn't enjoy the taste of. Cooking is something I'd prefer doing with Paisley, but if I have any intention of getting my girlfriend back, then I'm pulling out all the stops.

I pat myself on the back for finding a low-carb substitution for Paisley's Asian food habit. If I'd taken any time to see the forest for the trees, then we'd have gotten takeout less and eaten healthier more. Although, I was more of the noodle and fried wonton guy and she chose the vegetables.

I'm rinsing the spinach in the colander for the bed of greens when the doorbell rings.

Paisley gives me a brusque hug. It's similar to the awkward goodbye we shared on the sidewalk when I walked her back to the boutique this afternoon. As if we haven't spent the entire summer and fall separated by my stupidity, my head dips and her chin lifts. My stubble brushes her soft cheek. Both of us pull away before we kiss.

Kissing isn't a bad thing. We're exceptional at reading the other's desire. I want to kiss Paisley. But our chemistry has overridden our sensibility a time or two.

I stuff the dishtowel I dried off with into my pocket. With too much exuberance, I pull her into the living room to continue our earlier conversation. A tug pulls my shoulder out of the socket. Paisley's stopped dead in her tracks.

"Why do you have those?" Bewildered, she points to the brimming sacks of withered roses.

I have them for the same reason Paisley threw the long stems at my door. And the same reason I now know I kept the napkin. We've been connected by an indescribable force since the moment we met. It will take more than distance for either of us to fall out of love with the other. I'm willing to bet that it'll take more than my appalling past.

After rising to the challenge to make better choices for my future, I want Paisley there. I don't want to be Carver and give my girlfriend the finest of everything. What I want is to give her the best of me. Paisley needs to be certain I'm worthy of her.

Unspeaking, I beam at her because I never understood sentimentality until I saw the woman I love mystified that I'd save her garbage.

I twirl her on her heel, dancing towards the couch. She laughs at the dizzy spin. I'm about to ask her to sit with me when she shakes her head, becoming standoffish.

"I don't want this to go too far before we clear the air." Her body language doesn't bode well for me.

Restoring harmony is why, when she showed up with the mill girls at the club today, I took the chance on inviting her over tonight. Staying away from Paisley was becoming too difficult. So much is happening with the new club. The only person I want to share it with is her.

"I can't have children, Jake," she admits.

It's not what I expected Paisley to say. I flub for the right words. Because how the hell do I say to the firecracker standing here, unsure if she wants to give me a second chance, that I'm all in for a long-term commitment—say, fifty years—without scaring her off?

I sit on the edge of the couch, holding her hand and looking up at her. "That's not a problem. If you want, we'll find—"

"No, I can't have them, and I don't *want* them."

Something about Paisley's remark makes her braver and stronger.

"I'm uh, I'm a little—"

There is a hint of cynicism in her voice. "Confused?"

I hesitate responding. "Relieved?" My lips pinch.

"Are you really, Jake? Men say a lot of things. You said you loved me." She expects me to flinch.

I knew the night of the benefit if Paisley requested, I'd go above and beyond being her sperm donor. But for as much fun as hanging out with Cris's son, Mateo, was at Kingsbrier, I've never had the desire to be a father.

"That was your secret." I press my forehead to the back of her hand.

I used her over something so small, yet so significant.

"If I had it, I lost the right to pry. But right now, it seems like you are using the choice you made to leave Laughton to push me away before we've even discussed how badly I hurt you. Give me the benefit of the doubt that I can do better this time, please."

Paisley touches my hair. I draw her into my lap. My shoulders hunch. Her tiny body fits cocooned against my chest. It always has. It always will.

I rest my cheek on her head, inhaling the rose scent that surrounds her.

She sighs, sinking in. "I was born with the same congenital heart defect that my dad suffered from. I was lucky enough that doctors could do more to fix it. That meant multiple surgeries when I was a kid. I should have been honest, but flawless women were always parading around you. I felt like you wouldn't see me as sexy if you knew about the scar."

Paisley doesn't know how wrong she is. "There's not a part of you that's not gorgeous. At every turn, you stood up to me. You'd proven your strength, your dignity, and your determination not to let go of anything that was meaningful to you. Those traits attracted me to you in the first place. Not being able to touch you whenever I wanted, however I wanted, made you sexier."

Fiddling with the collar of my shirt, Paisley peeks up. A wary smile at my compliment graces her face.

"It's true," I say.

"I've been pregnant, Jake," Paisley replies.

I tighten my arms around her, listening to Paisley recount the long hours she worked when her boutique was brand new. She knew what decision she was making before the doctor started talking about the health risks. Hardly eight weeks along, she had high blood pressure and her body was showing signs of stress. The threat of a later-term miscarriage was a wait and see situation. The hours she'd put into the boutique were rough as it was.

"Having a child would have broken my spirit. My boutique is my baby. It's everything to me that I succeeded at building a place women recommend their friends shop at. I want to give back and be that person for other small business owners, too. Despite what everyone assumes, I'm not unfulfilled. I made my dreams come true and bit by bit I reach toward another goal." She mentions the space available soon next to hers and the possibility of expansion.

I kiss the crown of her head. "*Corazón*, nothing could break your spirit, not even me. Not even how rough it had to have been making the best choice for you."

"I was lucky my dad was there for me. When his heart began failing, I started pushing people away. I thought giving them space was the best way to care for them. After my father died, my heart specialist, a former colleague of his, introduced me to Gavin. Gavin performed the surgeries on his pediatric patients similar to the ones I had as a kid. I thought that marrying Gavin gave my mom a sense of security if she lost me the way she lost my dad. Gavin would understand better than anyone else. He and I already spoke the same language, filled with medical jargon and statistics. I didn't have to explain my scar or my medications. I didn't have to justify the way I ate, insisting he wash his hands, or get a flu shot. We were in tune."

"Except for one note."

"I sang off-key about kids." She huffs. "Gavin wanted to look into other alternatives; adoption, surrogacy. We should have talked about how he wanted to be a father in the beginning. It wasn't until our relationship got serious that I saw his dream of parenting slipping away. Gavin was amazing with kids and it made him even more amazing at this job. Withholding that from him would've been unfair, but I didn't know how to end our engagement. Everyone kept saying I'd change my mind. It made me feel guiltier that I knew I wouldn't. That everyone shouldn't have wasted their energy on getting excited for us—especially my mom and Gavin." Paisley finishes sounding as if she doesn't expect me to understand.

When she ran out on Laughton, she was leaving behind a life she couldn't bear to lead any longer. I won't judge Paisley. I'm determined to make changes after not only making the mistake of lying, but leaving her as well. I'm glad she can confide in me when I've proven untrustworthy in the past.

"Jake, I'm scared to be in love with you. One thing I learned about myself is that I put myself on the sidelines. It's not like I have an expiration date on my forehead, but my dad did everything right and died early."

"And you're worried the same thing will happen to you."

"I have every right to be afraid."

"I'm not disagreeing. Only trying to understand."

"I didn't want anyone to miss me."

"If the past few months are any indication, there isn't anything you can do to stop that. I'm going to miss you, Pais. Every damn day I'm without you I feel your absence."

I understand a little more why Caroline says what she and my father had was once in a lifetime. I won't make Paisley promises I can't keep. I can't force my help on her mother any more than Paisley could've convinced herself marrying Gavin was the right choice. But if Mrs. Cooper needs anything, I'll be there to help her.

"When you left, I didn't reach out to anyone to help me through it. I didn't have many friends left until we began pretending in front of your friends. And all of a sudden, you—the person I'd spent the most time with—were gone. I was so lonely.

"I listened when you told me why you stayed away. I'm excited for you and the remodel at Sweet Caroline's. It still hurts, though, Jake. And what happens when I'm not interesting to you anymore? You don't have a secret to hold over my head now."

Of all, her last confession stabs at me. It isn't that I haven't worried about the same thing.

"I'm finally doing what's right for me. But I need you, *Corazón*. I should have told you that using the secret you were keeping against you was less important than being with you. I was afraid that if you knew, you'd have no reason to stay. I've been surviving these past few months, taking chances on something new, with the promise of you on the horizon. I'm hoping tonight we can start fresh."

I hold my hand out for Paisley to shake. "Hi, I'm Jake Ballentine. I own a club downtown. And, until recently, I've been hopeless."

She gives me an odd glare, but the corners of her lips turn up.

"Paisley Cooper. I, too, am a business owner in Brighton. Recently, I've…" She stops short of shaking my hand "You know what? Pretending we don't have a history isn't going to work for me, Jake. Do you think we could—

"Just go with it?" I finish her sentence. "Do you remember what happened when you said that to me?" Because I have to admit, kissing Paisley Cooper is the most amazing thing that's ever happened to me. I wouldn't have attempted to make any changes if she hadn't run into my bar.

Paisley flushes. She shifts to straddle my lap. I cup the base of her neck, bringing our foreheads to rest together.

"You're everything I ever dreamed of," I whisper. "Please, let me back in, *Corazón*." I nip, tugging her plump lower lip into my mouth.

Paisley opens for me so I can dive in deeper. Her velvety tongue strokes against mine. It's as if the last time we did this was yesterday, and dinner can wait a little while longer.

Chapter Thirty-seven

Paisley

I scurry into Brighton General Hospital with three minutes to spare. Grateful the elevator is open and empty, I punch the button for the third floor. As the metal doors shut, I check my fuzzy reflection, smoothing my skirt, and fluffing my hair over my shoulders.

My molars clench. Stowing myself, I push the air out of my lungs, let my shoulders fall, and try to relax. I should've known that finding a parking spot may be difficult and had to use the parking garage across the street.

"Layla has it under control." I let the affirmation slip out, speaking to no one in particular. I'm the only person in the elevator.

Of all things to come down with, one of my favorite employees has been sick with Chickenpox! I lamented over it when she'd first called in sick. That day, I'd brought Jake lunch from a new deli and we were picnicking, using a cardboard box as a makeshift table. Layla stopped in at Sweet Caroline's to see

Julian and she offered to help me out of the bind, needing a distraction from her own job search. Having run a register before, she's proven to be a quick study.

I don't have a permanent position to offer Layla, or if she'd even want to stay on at the boutique, but her willingness to cover shifts has been a godsend. Not having to worry about missing out on what little time Jake and I have for one another is a relief.

Sweet Caroline's grand reopening is approaching. The renovations at the club seem like they require Jake's twenty-four/seven attention. Meanwhile, I'm sorting through the boutique's yearly receipts, studying my savings account, and hoping that I can find a small business loan with good terms.

Both my mother and Jake offered to put up the money. I appreciate their support, but like everything else, I need to reach my goals on my own. Plus, when I questioned Sloan about Jake breaking Carver's wrist —and she told me that allowing Jake to hurt him allowed Carver to move on from where he was in his life, the way Tom's offer for Jake to go on the road gave Jake closure—she cautioned me against mixing any of Jake's earnings from Sweet Caroline's with Paisley's Boutique.

It was a hard pill to swallow, knowing Jake has done a lot of unscrupulous things in his past. It brought up my own negative feelings about Jake's disappearance and if he's not showing me who he really is. For someone who I can't get enough of, finding a level of trust with Jake is complicated. He says he's committed to keeping shady deals out of the concert hall. However, there are certain commitments he made, that there is always the possibility he could wind up behind bars for, that Jake can't back out of.

Kimber and Sloan are on the periphery of those situations as well. My curiosity got the best of me, and both mill girls sat me down and said if Jake was unwilling to confide certain details, it was for my safety. It's frustrating for my friends when Trig and Carver keep secrets, though they understand that, in all likelihood, knowing what's going on would implicate them. I appreciate having the reassurance to talk my concerns through with Kimber and Sloan.

I've come to recognize the reason they don't judge is because they live in the same glasshouse that I do. Navigating loving someone who made conscious choices to engage in criminal activities that can cause problems in the future is hard. There are so many more shades of gray in the world than I thought existed before I heard about what my friends have endured and how those experiences shaped them. I may have a broken heart, but their journeys are heartbreaking.

Jake and I have been taking things slowly. I find it funny that a man who claims he doesn't have a lot of patience has never been anything but with me.

We started dating after he made me dinner. We go on proper dates to the movies and out to eat. Although, Jake prefers holding my hand in the grocery aisles and bringing what we've bought home to cook.

He even attended Holly's baby shower. Cary, an amazing stepdad to Holly's son, was thrilled they were adding to their family, and Sloan and Kimber decided the party would be better as a Jack and Jill. Jake and I had fun celebrating with everyone… And then Jake booked us a couple's massage at a swanky hotel and we rejoiced in our lack of responsibility.

There's been kissing. I mean, how could there not be? Getting a lip-lock on my boyfriend is a perk of being in a relationship with Jake Ballentine.

We fooled around that night at the hotel, driving one another crazy the way we had in the spring whenever things between us got hot and heavy. Except, we haven't taken it further. I'm not ready and Jake respects that, given how badly our first time together ended. If we waited when we were fake dating, then delaying that bit of gratification the second time around doesn't feel like a compromise.

The first time I let Jake unbutton my shirt, he was so apologetic, so sweet and sensitive to how I'd react to his touch that I couldn't help wondering if I was upfront about my scar in the beginning if the shock would still have chased him off.

But had I done that, would Jake have finally chased down his dream or found that his passion lies in opening a music venue of his own?

See? Shades of gray. What happened happened and I can only hope that we're building from it instead of letting the past drag us back down.

The elevator is quick, and I step into the conference room with a minute to spare. Three members of the board of directors for the charity gala sit at the far end of the mahogany table. One at the head and two close to the bank of windows. The men have their suit coats unbuttoned and their elbows on the table. The woman leans back in her seat with her legs crossed. She has a pen poised for writing and a yellow legal pad in front of her, though each of them has a leather folio or something to take notes on, too. I think she's merely prepared. Opposite those board members is Gavin, wearing a white coat and a pleasant smile. They all turn. The only person surprised to see my ex here is me.

I'd received a message from the chairman, telling me that they had something to discuss regarding the benefit and asking me if I'd join them today.

The board members stand and shake my hand, inquiring about how I've been. One hugs me. He and my father were close. Gavin keeps his distance, but motions for me to take the chair beside him.

"We're delighted you could join us, Paisley," the chairman begins. "I'm sure you received the letter Deborah penned after the gala this spring that each of our contributors received in the mail. The generosity of contributions was astounding. It was a record year for the hospital. A great deal of the credit goes to you."

"Me?" I press a hand to my chest.

"Many of our benefactors made specific mention of you when we've delved into their reasons for giving." Deborah, the other woman, speaks up. "You're an integral part of the community, and it makes them feel you have a stake in the hospital's success."

"Of course, I have a stake in it. My dad's name is on the invitation. I've had heart surgeries at Brighton General."

"I didn't know you were a patient," Deborah says with thoughtful concern. "Why didn't I know that?"

"It was when I was a child," I reply.

I've spoken little about my health for the better part of a decade—around the time I stopped wearing tops that showed my scar so that I wasn't discussing my medical prognosis with curious strangers.

"We'd like you to entertain the idea of giving the keynote at next year's gala." The chairman suggests I speak about my dad's legacy. "And we'd like you to consider taking an upcoming vacancy on the board."

"I, um, I'm flattered." Of course, I'll accept! I want to yell. This is an incredible opportunity. "But what's Dr. Laughton's opinion?"

I look at Gavin, who nods in agreement with the chairman's offer. When the meeting concludes, we all shake hands and I'm told how much they're looking forward to the spring. The board members file out, leaving Gavin and me alone.

Without an audience. I hope he's comfortable

enough to give me an inkling of his true feelings. Unlike other doctors who cruise through their department's fundraisers, making appearances and not much more, it's a cause Gavin is fully behind. Cardiology is his life's work. He didn't stumble, refusing to support a charity that bears my family name. He puts in a good deal of time for the benefit in the weeks leading up to the event.

"I'm humbled, but are you sure you are okay with this?" I ask.

"Yes. The board came to me first. They expressed open apprehension about our personal situation."

"They did? I can withdraw my name. No one will be the wiser—"

"You should take this, Paisley." Gavin interrupts. "I have feelers out to other hospitals."

"I don't want you to have to leave on my account."

"I'm exploring my options. Nothing is set in stone. This year has been difficult." He huffs. The crooked smile on his face fades. A telltale sign he must have a lead on a new job, but he's hesitant to put his faith in it coming to fruition. "I heard you are back together with Jake Ballentine."

Oh, that lovely rumor mill.

"Yes, we're seeing one another again." I won't lie. The secret trapped between us, that I didn't leave the perfect wedding to the faultless groom for the corrupt strip club owner I was having an affair with, is bad enough. "Gavin, I'm so sorry. I didn't set out to hurt you. I was living someone else's life. The life of the woman who you are supposed to marry someday. Afterward, I didn't realize that anyone in Brighton was tormenting you. I hate to sound conceited, but I thought the rumors were all about me, or at least that your reputation was above reproach, and that it would blow over faster for you than it did for me. I left because you deserved better."

"For as embarrassing the situation has been, I see that now... And it's not about Jake, in particular, Paisley. I want someone who wants me. I'd like the chance to start over and be happy... The way you are with Jake... I don't know if I stay in Brighton that my sister will get over her animosity towards you. And I'm unwilling to let that bring me down to the place I was at the night she made the scene at Royce's and upset me." Gavin toes the carpet. "I won't risk destroying my career over another near-disaster. After what the two women I was closest to put me through, twice is ample embarrassment."

"I saw the surveillance video of you and Jake outside the boutique. It didn't have any sound. Can I ask what you discussed?" Gavin doesn't owe me an explanation, but I've always wondered how Jake talked him into putting the rock down.

"We talked about loving you, Paisley. And how hard you were to walk away from." Gavin leaves it at that and exits the room.

It strikes me that Gavin punched the door and walked away from Sweet Caroline's. He skirted me in his anger when I arrived home and his groomsmen were carrying boxes out to his car. And this afternoon, Gavin has informed me he's prepared to leave Brighton. His actions are justified. Except this is the third time he has walked away.

We were close friends once. Although, I'm curious if me becoming Gavin's wife was never an unwavering draw for him... The same way Gavin becoming my husband wasn't a constant pull for me.

Jake ran, and as he boomeranged back, he worked on becoming the man I needed him to be.

Chapter Thirty-eight

Paisley

I flipped the open sign in the window to closed twenty minutes ago but didn't lock the door. The boutique bell jingles, alerting me to the person who's stepped inside after hours.

"I'll be right there!" I sing an octave too loud. Nervous energy has gotten the best of me.

I'm in the back, tidying up so that everything is in the proper place for tomorrow before getting ready to leave.

Exhaustion slides over me, worrying about the last-minute things that Jake had to tick off his list. When we finally get to bed, I plan on sleeping in. My sales girls wrote "DO NOT DISTURB" in bright red marker on the calendar. They even tried to cajole me into taking today off. But I knew pacing the apartment or getting underfoot at Sweet Caroline's wasn't for me. My excitement about tonight has been building for weeks.

I grab my purse and the black garment bag with my outfit and shoes in it. Coming out from the storage room, I stop in my tracks. "Well, look who it is!"

"Good evening, Miss Paisley." Carver lifts his hand with the brace on it, touching his thumb to his lower lip the way I've noticed he does when he gets conscientious of his injury.

He's making progress with physical therapy, but his dexterity and range of motion won't ever be the same. Sloan says the reality only seems to bother him when Carver forgets agreeing to Jake breaking his hand means his dreams aren't what they used to be.

"Why so formal, Mr. Galloway?" I tease to ease Carver away from his insecurity.

"It's a big night. You're the lady of the hour."

"Ha-ha!" I laugh and point. "I'm pretty sure Caroline is still the lady of the hour." I love how Jake honored his mom by the naming the concert hall after his mom. Say what you will, the original Sweet Caroline's was a Brighton institution.

"How do you feel about it all?" I ask.

Carver's mother danced on that stage. The club holds a lot of history for him.

"The end of an era speeches are getting trite, but seeing as the club is where we spent our youth, I'm not sure we'll ever stop reminiscing. I'm glad Jake's brought the old girl into the future. It was past time to build on what he was too stupid to understand he already knew about running venue. I'm happy he's finally settled, too."

I snort at Jake's oldest friend's forthright description of how much Jake's outlook changed after touring.

"Speak of the devil. Where is my boyfriend?" Jake planned to pick me up like always.

Each evening that I'm free, he strolls the main road to come get me. Jake's eagerness to bring me back to the club to show off the amazing progress that's been made is contagious. Though we jaunt through downtown Brighton at a slower pace, sometimes we fetching dinner along the way or stopping in at another store to browse.

"Kelsey is hung up with delivery delays and the main act arrived earlier than Julian expected them. Jake's got a mild case of opening night jitters." Carver pinches his thumb and forefinger together. "Although I wouldn't get overly concerned. He's in his element, glad-handing and acting like the Jake who couldn't get enough of throwing big events. Since it's dark out, he asked me if I wouldn't mind walking you to the club."

"So, I don't get to ride in your posh car?" I act insulted.

I'm not.

Carver holds his key fob out for me. "I thought you might want to make it to the church on time so I brought the car. I'll let you drive. If you don't tell my wife."

"Are you flirting with me?" I punch him in the shoulder.

He's got biceps like Jake's and Carver laughs when I shake out my hand, sputtering a tiny "ow". We've both endured bigger hurts.

He tosses me his keys. Behind the wheel, adrenaline pumps through my veins by the time we pass the newly lit Sweet Caroline's Music Hall sign. I park out back in a reserved spot. I thank Carver for coming to get me. He suggests we walk around the building to the front entrance to get the full effect. Security lets us pass.

Inside, it is breathtaking. The polished bar is massive, wrapping around where the rounded booths used to be. It matches the rich wood floors that are as yet unscuffed by shoes. Some walls have exposed brick, like the mill. Others are papered in a rich brocade pattern with shimmery strands woven in.

They sparkle and reflect the lighting when the strobes flash. New seating set twelve feet in front of the bar so that anyone ordering drinks can see the show includes booths with low backs and smaller tables. And the dancing isn't just on stage anymore. There's ample space to move about in front of the stage the way you'd expect to do at any concert.

Kelsey scuttles toward the far end of the bar, greeting me as she goes. I wave, offering a cheery hello back. Jake is by the stage with Julian, speaking to someone I haven't met yet.

Jake is as different as he is the same, and he's worked so hard to reopen Sweet Caroline's. I don't want to interrupt anything important, so I try to bypass him. But our eyes meet and he reaches a hand out for me. The pull to his side is magnetic. I grin like a fool when he beckons me over for an introduction with the main act's lead vocalist.

"I'll only be a minute, *Corazón*. Can you heat up the shower for me?" He requests when I excuse myself to go get ready, kissing the crown of my head.

The years of old flyers papering the wall in Jake's office are gone. Along with the mirrors behind them. The walls are rich and warm, smelling of fresh paint. The furniture we picked out together once the drywall was up is blemishless. Even the adjoining private restroom had a complete makeover.

I duck in and unzip my garment bag. I pull out a pair of high heels and slip them on in place of the flats I stick to at the shop. Then I turn the gleaming shower faucet on to steam the room, letting the dress I've chosen for the night breathe to rid it of any latent wrinkles.

The door to the office opens and snicks shut.

"I would have been quicker." Jake apologizes. "I brought us a drink."

I hear a single glass thunk on a flat surface.

"You didn't get one for yourself?" I kid from around the corner.

I look at my reflection, plumping my breasts in the lace bralette I'm wearing. I adjust the straps and pucker my lips.

Yup, that'll do.

Jake is moving around outside the bathroom. He flings the shirt he was wearing onto a chair.

"Is everything all set?" I ask, turning off the shower and closing the door to trap the heat.

"As set as it's going to get. Fuck me if I ever open another location. This was a hell of a lot more work than I expected."

"I'd be glad to." I want to say, but I go with, "Wait and see. It'll be worth it."

The headliner is well known. A coup for a new venue. Tickets sold out almost before they went on sale. Jake expects the club will be at capacity before showtime. I have the utmost confidence in him and that the band will bring down the house tonight.

"How was your day?" He asks me this every single day with genuine interest.

"Actually, I wanted to show you what the boutique got in." I lean against the door frame crossing one leg over the other.

Jake has his back to me. He's working his belt undone. "We gotta make it fast. Cris and Daveigh will be here soon." He turns, lets his pants fall, and bites his fist as I saunter toward him. "I thought you'd be dressed already."

His fingertips slide over the high-cut fabric covering my hip, up my side, then under the lace of my bralette.

While I err on the side of modesty at work, one of the things I realized after Jake knew about my scar was that any little bit of me that's covered drives him wild. A short skirt and a top with a high neckline and he's got his hand skimming my panties. Long sleeve t-shirt with cold shoulders and his lips are on my bare skin. Backless dress? He's reaching inside and cupping my tits.

I agonized over what the former dancers were showing when what revved Jake's engine was the opposite.

"Those are cute." His Adam's apple bobs when he swallows.

My eyes are drawn to his broad shoulders. Unable to resist touching him, I graze my hands over his pecs.

We sleep at one another's houses but still haven't had sex. However, a girl's restraint can only take her so far before it snaps... Or he acts like a gentleman, not wanting to push her into things he thinks she's not ready for, and she's the one who gets underhanded.

I've concocted a plan to seduce my sexy-as-sin-not-so-rebound-guy on the biggest night of his life.

"Aren't they adorable panties, though? Know what I like best about them?" I stroll over to the couch, turning my back to Jake as I rest my knees on the cushions.

"It's a thong."

"Mmm hmm," I hum. "I'm not sure. Do you think they'll sell?"

I place my palms on the sofa back and kitten-stretch. My boyfriend crowds me and my ass meets Jake's groin.

His warm left hand encases my bottom. I look over my shoulder. With his right hand, Jake's shoved down his boxers and is palming his already hard cock.

"They may need product testing." His voice is a low rumble.

"Vigorous product testing," I agree.

I feel his knuckle at the cleft of my ass. He slips a finger underneath the elastic. Tugging it to the side with more force than necessary, I hear a tear.

"Sorry to say, I don't think they're going to hold up."

"Whatever will we do?" I ask, coyly.

"Don't tease, Pais. Tell me what you want."

"You inside of me."

"Like this?" His cock nudges my entrance. The mushroom head is slick with my juices. I whimper at the invasion. Jake slides out just to do it again.

Sometimes we fight this way. Taunting one another to get what we want. When what we really want is to see how far we can push the other to see what they'll do to get their way.

"Beg," he grits out, his fingers tight, clutching my hip.

Incoherent expletives tumble from my lips.

His hand moves to my clit, and I seize speaking, instead relying on unladylike sounds. I want Jake's cock in me, filling me.

"Beg and once the show starts, I will bring you back here and eat your sweet pussy."

He retracts again. The ultimatum is clear. How am I supposed to argue with a man whose tongue is that clever?

"Please, please, fuck me, Jake," I whisper in agony because his huge dick is breaching me again.

"Louder. I want to hear you shout."

I suck in a deep breath. The first syllable slips out of my mouth, and I gasp. Jake drives into me, setting my body ablaze. I lose sensation in my toes and my fingertips, gripping the back of the couch. My nipples tingle. My thighs are drenched. My cunt is sore, making room for him. Yet, the more Jake thrusts, the more I chase the intense feeling that builds. My walls grip him. Leaving me satiated in a way no other man has ever made me feel.

Chapter Thirty-nine

Jake

I kiss Paisley. It starts sweet and slow and turns dirty as fuck—similar to the way she made me take her, ass tipped up and back bowed, bent over the new couch in my office.

Resisting Paisley lately has been difficult. We've waited as long to have sex as we did when we were fake dating. Some nights I've wanted to plow into her for stress relief. So I gotta say, I did not see this coming.

Thank heaven for this woman. Paisley planned her intervention well, and I was definitely more relaxed than I was trying to pull off that I was when I walked in with the cocktail.

She knows me. She anticipates my needs. I've figured out I'm patient with her because she was what I needed all along... Her and the swift ass kicking she brought along with her the night she jumped into my arms.

I suck her bottom lip. It pops when I let go and she dives back in. I have to lift her up. Our size difference makes holding her perfect, but kissing her less than ideal if I have to lean down for too long. That's okay, though. It gives me a chance to grip her ass, and show her what act two will entail.

Breaking our kiss, I lower Paisley to the floor. She scampers out of my reach when I swat at her lush bottom. I catch her by the elbow. She graces me with a few quick pecks and a crowing giggle.

I grab the back of her neck. "Wear your hair down." I insist.

Her lips twist as she thinks about telling me no. But her thumb grazes my nipple and the spark in her eyes tells me she won't fight.

It's as likely later this evening her mouth will surround my dick as my tongue will lap at her core. Not that I haven't missed having her wrapped around me, but we found out a lot about what the other likes by avoiding sex the past few months.

I fasten my pants and sit back on the couch, admiring her in the bathroom. I love watching her dress. The way she points her dainty toes, gliding those stockings over her silky legs. My dick twitches when she slides her feet into new black Jimmy Choos and wriggles the bra she wore at the boutique over her head and searches for her black dress.

Lost in my thoughts and admiration of Paisley's body, the knock on the door startles me. I slip a tee on before answering. Music floats in from the hall.

It's Kelsey.

"Everything good?" I ask.

"You wanted me to tell you when Cris Sanchez got here. They seemed acquainted, so I sat him in the VIP section with Tom."

"That's great." I'm amped for Paisley and Daveigh to meet. "Damn, I haven't showered yet. Can you get them drinks on the house? Don't let Cris start a tab."

"Already done."

"Julian?" I question.

The opposite door swings open, giving me a glimpse of the kid who broke the top ten on the charts this week and his band doing their pre-performance rituals in the dressing room. Julian exits, raising his palm for high-five. Kelsey slaps his hand.

"We've got it covered."

Julian agrees and heads to check on the guys in the security and sound booth.

"Thanks, Kelsey. And thanks for sticking by. I wasn't the best boss in the beginning."

"Know what, Jake? I couldn't have done this without Julian. But now that he's here, you can disappear, and we'll be fine."

"I'll keep that in mind. And Kelsey, if the two of you are confident in handling it, remind me I promised you both a raise."

Paisley's been supportive during the hectic end of the renovations. Being there for her, showing I'm as excited about her attaining her goals as she is about me reaching mine is important to me. If I can take the time off to be with my girlfriend, I'm going to do it.

A bar back hollers for Kelsey. "Gotta go, but a raise isn't something I'm forgetting." She walks away backward.

Pais is brushing mascara over her eyelashes when I bring the trousers and button down to the bathroom that I'm wearing of the opening. We switch places and she goes into the office to give me space and a few quiet minutes.

In the shower, I let the hot water run over me, loosening any lasting tension, and appreciating what I've accomplished so far. Whatever this Jake Ballentine's skin that I'm wearing is, it fits me.

Outside the office door, my future awaits. VIPs

who are eager for a glimpse at the venue before the house lights go down will arrive soon. There's a ton of crap to finish before the doors open. I let it slide because Kelsey and Julian make a great team.

I pull on the clothes Paisley picked out for me to wear. She has exquisite taste. Paisley is my future, too. She's also my here and now. My everything I didn't know I was missing.

On the couch cushion, I notice her torn panties and offer them up on a finger.

"I didn't bring more." Her shrug is playful.

"I don't recall saying you needed another pair," I quip.

She shoots me an arched brow, taking them from me and dropping them into the trash.

"Zip me up. You're going to be late to your own party."

I do as I'm told. Then wrap my arms around her. She laughs again when I say, "They all know to wait. My girlfriend is a bad influence on me."

Pais turns, adjusts my collar, and plays with the button on my shirt over my breastbone.

"I love you," she says. "No matter how any night after tonight goes, I'm proud of you. I'm..." She pauses, stowing herself. "Don't do it again, but I'm glad you ran to figure out you."

I cup her cheek. "I'm glad you ran, too, so I could figure me out... Don't you do it again, either." I press a gentle kiss to the crown of her head. Then I chase after Paisley when she drags me toward the door. We have a whole road ahead of us and I don't want to miss a moment of it.

Bonus Chapter

Jake

"You guys can play on without me," I say, reaching into the hole to pull out my ball.

"Are you kidding?" Cary spears the flag into the ground. "We have another nine rounds."

"And you're winning," Carver adds, shaking me by the neck.

"Like that means anything. I can't remember the last time Jake lost a round of golf when it wasn't intentional." A scoff precedes Trig's chortle.

I bend, blocking his mock punch to my middle.

"I'm quitting while I'm ahead." My tone is apologetic, but I'm not the least bit sorry.

Cary raises a hand to his mouth and in a loud whisper says to Carver, "He's whipped."

"*Eh*, give him a chance to figure it out. This is all new to Jake," Carver responds.

"Sage advice." Trig knocks Carver's knuckles. "But our wives are still asleep and we get the golf cart to ride back in. You can walk your sorry ass back to the hotel."

I sling my clubs over my shoulder and stride over the green. My friends make juvenile kissy noises behind my back, but I couldn't care less.

"You could have left your bag. We would have brought it back," Cary yells.

I wave my middle finger over my head.

"We're buying the beers this afternoon," Trig bellows.

I'd hope so, given how much money I've spent on alcohol.

Despite a brief stop at the concierge desk, I'm hot by the time I'm standing at the entrance to the pool. It's the kind of deceiving morning that if you aren't careful, you'll wind up fried to a crisp. A temperate breeze blows, cooling my warm skin as I enjoy the view.

Paisley is wearing the same white bikini she's had on most of the weekend. The strings gather the scant fabric of the top into a large teardrop, leaving her ample cleavage on full display. She sips her water and checks her phone. Then she takes a deep breath and wiggles, getting comfortable in the lounger. Her sunglasses block the harsh rays of the sun she's basking in.

Unfortunately, Paisley looks so relaxed that she doesn't care how hot it's getting. But that's why we're here—so that I can care for her.

The boutique expansion has kept Paisley busy over the past few months. The new store stocks not only baby items but clothes for kids up to ten. I didn't know anyone could get so excited that matching Easter outfits for moms and daughters would be a hit this spring, as were coordinating looks for little boys, but Paisley did. I helped her slip flyers into the bags that asked customers to use a cute hop-along hashtag and tag the boutique in pictures of them at their family celebrations wearing the new clothes. Both boutiques' social accounts got an influx of new followers. The stores' employees chose their faves, and Paisley gave away prizes.

Once I saw her success, I suggested Julian and Kelsey do something similar for Sweet Caroline's Music Hall. It's funny how we're using social media to our advantage when the same fickle platforms brought Paisley's Boutique close to closing its doors.

When we left Brighton on vacation, the construction company had hung plastic sheets and was about to knock down a portion of the wall to join both stores and increase foot traffic between the shops. Seeing it in person fills Pais with nervous excitement. She's been keeping up with the project via text.

Likewise, the new Sweet Caroline's has kept me on my toes. Kelsey and Julian make an amazing team. I knew they would and I trust them implicitly, which is fantastic. I had an inkling that I'd spend about as much time at the new Sweet Caroline's as the old one. Although the reasons are different.

I enjoyed that summer on the road too much. Whenever the opportunity presents itself, I'm back on stage. It's not often—a random tour date that needs a fill-in drummer, or at the request of bands that Tom put me in touch with when they play surrounding cities—but often enough to fill my well and keep my passion for Sweet Caroline's Music Hall and supporting up-and-coming talent alive.

Pais and Daveigh hit it off the night the club reopened. The four of us met in Nashville for a country festival where Cris suggested he and I try co-writing an occasional song. A famous artist picked one up for their latest album. It hasn't gone number one. Paisley likes to remind me it isn't a number one *yet*.

She tells me all the time she's not sure what's more impressive, my confidence in having a song on the charts that half the country knows the words to, or my determination to keep reaching for what I want.

What I still want is her. And most of the goals I set are to prove to me I'm worthy of her forgiveness.

The truth is, when we got back together, Pais wasn't sure my trip to Kingsbrier, summer on tour, and decision to turn Sweet Caroline's into a concert hall were changes that would make an actual difference. I was a man who made a decade's worth of questionable choices. In her Jimmy Choos, I wouldn't have believed me either.

It took us a while to get used to the changes one another went through during our dating hiatus. Conning Paisley into posing as my girlfriend made her jaded, and I left a lot of hurt feelings in my wake when I took off.

However, the underlying chemistry was still there, so there's that.

Nowadays we're as likely to be seen strolling from the boutique at lunchtime into Baked Beans holding hands as we are leaving the club in the dead of night after a concert. Everything about us feels right, not only the kissing parts. But I'll never turn down a kiss from Paisley, if that's my first choice.

"Your room is ready, Mr. Ballentine. Would you like me to store your clubs?" a kid from guest relations asks.

He's already got ahold of the strap, so I pull a bill out of my wallet and tip him for the initiative before lazily strolling over to where Paisley lies.

Her lips quirk when my shadow falls over her, but beneath her glasses, her eyes are still closed. I nudge her knees over on the deck lounger and lean forward. My fingertips skirt her collarbone, finding her fierce pendant that's now attached to a chain around her neck. I bring it forward, placing the arrow in the direction of her cleavage, and press my lips to the teardrop hollow that her bathing suit top doesn't cover.

She stifles a moan, threading her hand into my hair.

"I better not find out you forgot to put sunscreen on, *Corazón.*"

"Or what?" she sasses.

I reach for the sunscreen and snap the lid open.

"Or this." I squeeze the bottle. A glop lands on her belly and I finger paint rays of sunshine around her navel.

"You are going to rub that in, right?" The corner of her lips curve up.

"*Hmm...* I thought you'd never ask." I take my time smoothing the lotion on her stomach and run my hands up her rib cage, sliding them under her bikini top. "I have to make sure you're fully covered," I tease. Squirting more lotion in my palm, I tug at Paisley's bottoms, rubbing it from above the crease of her hip, down over her knee, and massaging it over the bridge of her foot. "Almost done. The front, anyway."

"It's a good thing this is an adults-only resort." She indulges me by sitting up and twisting to place her feet on the concrete decking while I coat her shoulders and neck.

"Have I mentioned how sexy you are in this bikini, Mrs. Ballentine?"

"Yes, when I wore it to our wedding yesterday."

I proposed to Paisley spur of the moment, and we were engaged long enough for everyone to pack their suitcases. We got married on the beach, surrounded by friends, who—go figure—were thrilled at the proposition of a vacation away from their children.

It's strange to admit, but deep down I've always known that marrying Pais was in the cards. We had too many things in common. Our paths were bound to cross, and it's a wonder they hadn't until Paisley made her own whopper of a bad decision. Fate, fortune, or dumb luck, her not calling it off with Laughton sooner set the wheels in motion for our paths to cross.

"This is my absolute favorite formal wear that you've ever recycled. Any chance you'll wear it while cooking dinner at home?"

"That depends. Am I cooking alone?" She drops her dark glasses over the bridge of her nose and winks.

"Only if I get to watch."

A waiter drops by two mimosas the concierge offered to send. We have a huge party staying at the resort and, big request or small, the service has been top-notch.

Paisley and I clink the glasses and recline, soaking up the sun while holding hands between the chairs.

"I need a shower and I have a feeling once the guys are back from the golf course we won't have a chance to be alone for the rest of the day," I tell Pais when we've finished our drinks.

She agrees to join me and clean up before brunch.

I toss her things into a beach bag, pull Paisley up to standing, and help her slip on a floor-length transparent coral beach cover-up. The dress hides nothing. I'm not sure what the point of wearing it is other than to turn me on.

Paisley nuzzles into my chest, and I wrap my arms around her waist and let my hand roam lower to palm her ass.

I carry the bag in one hand on the way back to our suite with my opposite arm slung over Paisley, holding her close. My wife tells me the text she got was from our mothers. They've booked an entire day at the hotel's spa, but will be on time for our dinner reservations. It confirms I'm right. We need to be prepared to entertain our guests, so now is the best time to sneak away.

Opening the door, I usher Paisley into the sitting room that blocks the bedroom from view. I drop her bag on the nearest table and lift the hem of my golf shirt over my head. "Warm the water up?" I request.

Pais pauses to run a manicured fingernail over my pec. I let her put her hands on me so that I can get mine on her again. I catch sight of her sparkling rings, and she slides her finger under the waistband of my shorts. I cup my left hand over hers, bringing them to my sternum.

Forsaking all others, she's mine. So long as I live because I understand at my very core, I'm never going to get over it if I lose the woman that is my heart.

I kiss the crown of Paisley's head. She looks up with devilish intent before twirling toward the bedroom to start the shower. My wife's agreeability this morning has far more to do with Paisley having her way with me on our honeymoon than becoming docile. Little does she know...

"Jake, what have you done!" she squeals.

A throaty chuckle escapes me and I walk to where my wife is staring at the rose petal covered bed.

It's cheesy as fuck, but I'm now the guy who does shit like that because of seeing how she responds to my gooey sentiment. And you know what they say about a happy wife? It's true.

"They're all coral," she says in wonderment.

"As close as I could get." Some are lighter.

"What if we squish them and make a mess?"

Her innocence makes me laugh. "That's sort of the point, isn't it?"

From behind, I untie the strings keeping her bikini top on. I push the straps of the sheer cover off her shoulders and both garments puddle at her feet. Then I brush Paisley's chestnut hair to the side and suckle the sweet spot between her neck and her ear while cupping her tits.

She leans back, making a soft mewl sound that has my hard cock punching at my fly. I lift her so that she's kneeling on the bed facing me. A pouty smile plays on her lips as I strip off my shorts. She eyes my jutting erection and her tongue darts out of her mouth.

"I could *just go with it,* or you could tell me what you want?" I step forward on instinct, loosening the tie at her hip and skimming under the silky fabric. Pais took a trip to the spa herself and she's bare down there. My mouth nudges her plump lower lip. Meanwhile, my fingers glide through her dampness. Her hips buck forward and I kiss her hard.

"Stretch me," she pleads, pushing my palms close to her core.

I plunge one finger inside of her. Then two, scissoring them and thrumming my thumb over her clit. It's a good thing she's kneeling on the bed. Paisley's whole body is shaking when I'm finished. She rests her head on my breastbone because the weight of her legs can't hold her up. The color from the petals under her has already bled onto the duvet.

I push her so that she falls backward onto the mattress. The feminine giggle when I grab her by the ankle and pull her to the edge drives me wild. My wife knows what's coming. There's no preamble of her pretending to scramble away so that I'll give chase.

Instead, she demands, "fuck me."

I smooth her hair from her face and caress down the center of her chest. Skimming my hand to her hip, I tent her leg and grip her thigh, sliding inside of her heat. Paisley's walls grip me as I thrust. I listen to every little whimper, every dirty whisper. I hold myself off until her gasps subside. And then I grunt my release with her nails digging into my ass.

If there's any damn good reason to be late for brunch, this was it. Not to mention the follow-up when I pin Paisley up against the tile in the shower and we let the water run cold.

Finally dressed, we walk with our hands intertwined to the hotel's restaurant.

"There they are!" Cris points a fork in our direction as we enter.

A cacophony of cheers, whoops, and clapping comes from the long table our friends occupy. I bow. However, what we were doing that made us so late has Pais blushing and turning her head. I capture her in my arms as she tries to escape the joyful harassment we knew we were in for on the walk here.

"Nope. You're officially mine and you promised not to run," I tease her.

"My heart wouldn't let me go further than you could catch me, anyway. I love you too much," she says, looking up at me.

"I love you too, *Corazón*. I never want you out of my reach."

The mill girls have gotten smart about seating arrangements. They've stuck all the husbands and boyfriends at one end of the table and took the other side for themselves. I pull out the chair they left open for Paisley. She's opposite Daveigh and next to Greer. I'm to my wife's left. Next to Byron and opposite Cris.

It's interesting how our friends make room for everyone. How accepting they are. Though it may be we all have a level of misfit and tragedy in our pasts that knit us together. These are the people we will grow old with. Whose kids Pais and I are happiest playing doting aunt and uncle to. *This is our family.*

I blink and rub my nose, hoping my sentimentality has gone unaware.

"You okay, Jake?" my bride asks.

"I'm perfect. Everything is perfect."

Thank you for reading Bleeding Heart! I hope you loved Jake and Paisley's sexy banter as much as I loved writing it.

Please enjoy the following preview from Kingsbrier Legacy's **Love Thy Neighbor**, featuring Mateo (all grown up!) in his own Small Town Fake Relationship Romance...

LOVE THY NEIGHBOR

Mateo

I set my teeth square, locking my jaw with a diabolical upturn of my cheeks. Opening the glass door to my mother's veterinary clinic as slowly as possible, the faint brush of the black bristles catching the outside step are only audible to my ears. Making sure the sound of the door closing is as muted, I pinch my fat hand in the process.

Not good since I make a living with my hands. I stifle the guttural instinct to grunt and shake off the pain.

There's a woman waiting in the reception area with her back to me. Her dark hair curls down her back, ending above the waist of her blue jeans. To the untrained eye, she's one of two people. And given where we are, if anyone ventured to guess they'd probably mistake my cousin for the poised and sophisticated Daveigh Sanchez, DVM.

But I know better.

Gracyn is shorter, and she packs a whole lotta attitude into those fewer inches than my mother has.

I haven't seen my cousin in weeks and happened to

spy her as I reached for the handle. Along with Corey, our other cousin, we are the eldest among the generation of grandkids here at Kingsbrier. I came along first. Gracyn's a year younger than Corey, but that didn't stop her from becoming our ringleader.

Our parents are siblings. Quintuplets, if you can imagine that. I suppose my grandparents were so used to having five kids terrorizing the ranch the trouble the three of us got into wasn't intimidating in the least.

Now, we're all fucking grown up. But hell, if it's any fun to act it.

I stalk low, keeping my shadow from sight. The squeak of my worn work boot gives me away at the last second.

Gracyn turns her head.

I lunge, grabbing her at the middle, and pinning her hands at her sides. I've wrestled with this girl enough times to know not to leave myself vulnerable. She kicks her feet forward and I stumble back with adequate time to stop the soles of her feet from hitting the reception desk. She'd use the leverage to land me on my ass.

My cousin fights dirty. Mainly, because I taught her to. Guys were all over Gracyn in high school, and Corey and I weren't going to be around to defend her forever. I'm sure in a match of wits, Gracyn would prevail. But guys are assholes and high school boys after a pretty girl are even bigger shitheads.

Gracyn may not have inherited the refined elegance my grandmother passed onto my mother, but they are dead ringers. I don't think I could have lived with my conscience if anyone hurt Gracyn. I look at her and I see my mom. I'd probably see my little sister, too. If I had one. However, my mom got saddled with three boys. So, lucky Gracyn got the focus of my brotherly love.

"You suck, Mateo!" she shrieks.

She proceeds to call me every name under the sun, a few of which she translates into Spanish; a skill I taught her. It was important to my dad that I was bilingual. Not sure he saw it as something that would come back to bite him. The volume of her scolding lowers a notch as she runs out of cuss words. Both of us know we're not too grown up that my mom won't chew us up and spit us out for misbehaving in a place of business.

"Put me down," Gracyn seethes.

The waiting room is empty other than a stack of cat crates. Each has one or two feisty felines inside, meowing their displeasure at being cooped up and that my cousin and I get to have all the fun.

"Nope." I drag her toward the door. "I told you I'd get you in my chair somehow—"

"No needles!" She panics, squirming against my tight grip.

I've got a decent impression of a serial killer's maniacal laugh going on until my shoulder hits the door. Then I drop my cousin like a sack of potatoes.

She lands in a lump on the commercial carpeting. "Ow! My butt." She rubs her tailbone.

I kick my leg over her head and offer Gracyn a hand up.

"Are you this rough with your clients, or have you gotten so used to spending your time with masochists and forget there are normal people who don't find pleasure in your brand of pain?" Gracyn gives me the stink eye.

I shrug and my lips twist. I'm a tattoo artist and some of my clients bliss out at the hum of the needle and the sensation of it etching their skin.

There were any number of jobs waiting here at the ranch when I got out of art school. I had the pick of the litter if I'd wanted one. Mom runs a clinic specializing in large breed animals, and Dad is co-owner of Kingsbrier Vineyards, which he and Grandad started twenty-plus years ago. I already had ink of my own when my trypanophobic cousin persuaded me to apprentice tattooing.

Gracyn's an anomaly and I've learned what parts of her personality to take seriously. She'll caterwaul about me teasing her about her pristine canvas and, by the same token, has drummed up business and handed out my card more often than she'll admit.

Cousin. Best friend. Little Sister. I love the girl. But man, my condolences to the poor sap who she sinks her claws into.

I tap my finger on her forehead. "The next time you're passed out drunk and I'm inking 'Daddy's Girl' right here. And it's going to be daddy's with a Z."

She smacks my hand away and laughs because there's no sense denying it's true. "You will do no such thing."

Gracyn hugs me and playtime is over.

"It's injection day I see." I toss a chin at the tower of barn cats waiting their turn in line to see the vet.

They're a feral bunch, but each fall Mom insists, where she has the ability to keep them healthy, we round them up and do exactly that.

"Yep. I drew the short straw. They're all accounted for, and this is the last of them. Bonus, the girls and I are headed to The Grille for dinner afterward. Aunt Daveigh is treating. What are you doing here?"

I take a key out of my pocket and twirl the ring around my index finger. "Dropping off." I sigh.

"Pepper's moving in! That's so nice of you." Gracyn snags the key, teasing, "Momma's boy. With a capital Z."

She's not far off.

Although my parents weren't married until I was

in elementary school, Daveigh is the only mother I've ever known. When I was five, I blew out my birthday candles, wishing she was my mom. I thought if she were, maybe it meant she loved me enough that she wouldn't go back to college. Hell, I didn't even care if my dad was too old for his then boss's daughter. I just wanted a family like everyone else had.

My wish was granted a few years later. Since then I've pretty much done whatever my mother wants. This includes letting her strong-arm me into renting the other side of the duplex I own to the vet clinic's office manager. It's been unoccupied since I moved in. I'd been using the living room as a studio and one of those bedrooms to stockpile empty pizza boxes. I'd been too lazy to toss them and decided they'd make a great sculpture. The smell proved me wrong.

It's taken me a week to air out the space and to store my art supplies on the side I live in. Mostly, I dragged my feet because I didn't want a neighbor. My house is closer to town. I intend on opening my own shop once I have the experience and a decent book of clients. Even though that's not in the near term, derailing the plan makes me edgy.

"What's she like?" Never having met the woman, it's not the only thing making me cautious. "Did she really burn down her apartment building?"

"A grease fire can happen to anyone." Gracyn blows off my concern, using the you're-so-stupid tone.

"It can happen to anyone, but don't forget, I've lost all my shit in a fire once. I don't want it to happen again because somebody made an oopsie."

I've made sure every smoke detector has new batteries and installed a few extra in both units. Better safe than sorry. My entire portfolio is in that house. It's my life's work so far, and a few years' worth of images of my sketches transferred onto other people's skin, showing the progression of what

I've learned in my chosen trade. All of these things are what I aim to build a career on. And no, photographs stored on a cloud server aren't the same as seeing a piece of art in real life. The last thing I want is anyone who is accident-prone taking what I'm working toward away from me.

"Drama llama. Your mom trusts Pepper. So should you… And Aunt D raised you better than to be mean to anyone just because you didn't get your spoiled way."

"That's rich coming from a Kingsbrier princess," I mutter.

Gracyn smacks the back of my head.

"Ow!"

"You need an attitude adjustment… or to get laid. Whatever happened to the girl you met last month through work?"

"Didn't go anywhere." I don't confess to my cousin the blonde in question came back to show her assets off to all of the other artists who'd look.

I may be a tit guy, but it doesn't get me hot anymore when a woman pulls her breasts out of her shirt to be inked. And I've witnessed the aftermath of enough clit piercings—where the lady has jumped up and spread her legs just to leave the studio sobbing and walking like she's spent two days riding bareback on a horse—that the whole thing has lost its appeal. It isn't sexy anymore. It's work. The only guys in the shop sporting wood are new on the job.

Thank fuck I'm not a gynecologist. If I'm this cynical about women's bodies before my thirtieth birthday, then I'm not holding out hope that a decent relationship is in the cards.

The swinging door leading to the exam rooms flies open and all hell breaks loose. A petite woman is wrestling with a surly tortoiseshell barn cat. At some point, the cat was wrapped in a blanket, but it managed to wiggle and claw its way out of a swaddle-hold. Its front paw pushes against her conservative button-down and the fabric bunches to the side, revealing a camisole underneath. The cat's got no affection for either layer. The more it attempts to get the woman to release her grasp, the further down the fabric gets pushed. Its claws get stuck in the lace underneath her top and, all of a sudden, I'm on the receiving end of an eyeful of boob.

They're nice boobs. Or rather, the boob I saw was nice for the pair. Lush and firm. I decide they're definitely not fake. But still, not the bird's-eye view I want in my mom's veterinary hospital when I'm avoiding it at my workplace.

"Are you okay, Pepper?" Gracyn rushes up, grabbing the cat from behind. "Let me help!"

There's a flurry of fur as the blanket drops to the floor. Plain Jane in her office wear starts sneezing. The cat's got all four limbs going in four different directions along with its head and neck in a fifth as it tries to bite my cousin.

There are plenty of times I'm involved in whatever is happening at the ranch. Family comes first but, "I do not miss this." I stand back, taking in the scene.

Between sneezing, picking cat fur off her tongue, and grabbing the blanket which has landed at her feet, the tenpenny lady and Gracyn exchange information about the cat. It's been vaccinated and has a clean bill of health. Gracyn slams her hip into the glass and tosses the unamused kitty out the front entrance with a "shoo."

I also pick up on my cousin using the woman's name again and stifle a second groan.

This uncoordinated mess is the pyro moving in next door.

First impressions are lasting. Dr. Sanchez has pictures of her sons scattered on the bookcases in her office. Some old. Some new. They aren't from cheesy staged portrait sessions. In all of the photographs, the family is bright-eyed, smiling, and having fun. The candids set the tone for my interview at the vet center, and Daveigh's warm, welcoming demeanor set me at ease.

The Sanchez family is gorgeous. Cris and Daveigh's three sons have dark hair like their mom and dad. The younger boys, Cruz and Alex, wander in and out of the clinic after school. I've noticed one has hazel eyes and the other the same green that tends to be on-trend at Kingsbrier. The only person who is a more frequent visitor during a workweek is the elder Mr. Cavanaugh, Daveigh's father. He has those friendly green eyes, so the genes must be passed down from there, along with kindness since Mr. Cavanaugh is all about lending a helping hand whenever possible.

The veterinary center seems like a revolving door of Dr. Sanchez's nieces and nephews as well. They come in for whatever reason, or no reason at all.

I especially like Gracyn. She graduated from college and came home to learn the ropes of the family wine-making business. Cris Sanchez is her boss, and Gracyn works beyond the clinic's parking lot and past the field at Kingsbrier's vineyard.

It didn't take me long to catch on that Gracyn often uses bringing a message Mr. Sanchez was capable of texting his wife as an excuse to come hang out. We're closing the clinic early today and her aunt is taking everyone to dinner as a thank you. I think Gracyn volunteered today to round up the barn cats at the winery and in the stable as a change from tackling her usual responsibilities. But don't quote me on that. And also, I don't necessarily see it as anything Gracyn is doing wrong.

A vet tech calls Gracyn back into one of the exam rooms with the last of the barn cats in tow. By Mateo's forlorn expression when his cousin leaves, he's ready to renege on our pity arrangement.

The town safety marshal condemned my apartment after my kitchen caught fire. Trying to find a new place for my water-logged belongings as fast as possible wasn't going well. Daveigh offered to ask Mateo to rent me the empty other half of his duplex. I cautiously agreed. I hope she didn't use her mom voice to strong-arm him into doing anything he hadn't wanted to.

For as long as I've worked for Dr. Sanchez, I've never met Mateo in person. He's significantly older than his brothers, and he doesn't live across the street in the to-die-for Victorian his parents reside in.

What I do know about Mateo is from Gracyn, who talks about her cousins nonstop, and the few things I've gleaned managing the office and having access to Dr. Sanchez's calendar.

My boss is a little more private about her oldest. I figure it has to do with the fact that he's an adult. She's not shuffling him to music lessons like Cruz or begging him to turn in his homework on time like Alex. When Daveigh does bring him up her face lights up the way it does when she's venting to me that she's scolded her youngest. Imagine that, being upset at your child, but not acting like you love them any less?

Although, I'm pretty sure I am an embarrassment. So my own experiences make perfect sense.

However, I did try to put my best foot forward with my new neighbor. Instead of tossing on scrubs this morning, I've dressed professionally. The chocolate-colored pants I'm wearing are now covered in cat hair. No wonder I'm a snotty mess from sneezing. To boot, the pink silky button-down layered over the cream-colored satin chemise isn't as discreet as I bargained for. It didn't hide a damn thing when the cat's paw slipped over my boob and got caught in the lace of my bra. So now I've also flashed my boss's son.

Great first impression.

And did I mention, like every other member of his family, Mateo is gorgeous?

His dark hair is clipped short. He has a square jawline. Broad shoulders stretch the limits of his t-shirt. Tattoos—though not as many as I'd thought he'd have—peek out from under his shirt sleeves. I can't help wondering where they are on his chest. His dark jeans fit him like a glove.

I've seen my fair share of cowboys since moving to Texas, but damn. You can tell off the bat this man has hauled plenty of hay bales in his lifetime. He's probably had plenty of rolls in the hay, too.

Mateo clears his throat and I realize I'm staring below his belt.

Way to make it awkward, Pepper.

I pinch the bridge of my nose and shut my eyes, counting back from ten. The mental reset likely won't do much for anyone else, but it's what I've learned to do to regain my confidence.

Cat dander covers my sweaty hands and I achoo again.

"Uh, bless you?"

"Thanks." The "th" sound comes out akin to a D. I grimace and reach for a tissue, turning my back on Mateo to blow my nose.

For all that's good and holy, please do not make there be any snot on my cheek when I face this man again. I search out the nearest reflective surface in case. All good.

"Let me get this right; You work for a vet and you're allergic to cats?" Mateo chuckles.

"Uh-huh." I bobble-head. "Not dogs or ferrets, horses—which is really fortunate given your mom's specialty—sheep, snakes..."

"You like snakes?"

"They're nothing to sneeze at."

My comment makes him laugh, and not at my expense, which is a huge relief.

"I'd think sneezing would startle them. You might get bitten."

I agree. "Good thing it's cat dander and not snake skins."

"Venom?" he taunts.

"Everyone reacts to poisonous snake bites. Except possums. They have a protein in their blood since snakes are part of their diet."

"My mom mention that? She's rescued a few."

I fidget with my top again, letting Mateo believe it's true.

I love animals. I've always had a soft spot for them, especially the ones whose place in the ecosystem are misunderstood. People think opossums are ugly with their hairless rat-like tails, but they are mistaken. Their little pink noses are adorable and the way they care for their babies, carrying them around in pouches and then on their back, is endearing.

He holds out a shiny object with a tag. "Here's your key."

"I can't tell you how much I appreciate this. It won't be for long. I'll bring over what I owe you once my insurance finally pays the claim."

Mateo hasn't mentioned how much the rent will be

each month. I'm a little behind. Not much, but boy does it help having someone willing to cut you a little slack.

I'm hoping a hefty security deposit will make this situation seem a lot less like he has a squatter. It would settle my mind too and invoke a sense of trustworthiness after I accidentally set fire to my last place.

"I'm in no hurry. Besides, I know where you work."

It's a joke, but for me it has an overbearing feeling. Though I was the sole resident facing eviction, a lot of my previous neighbors are still pissed because of the water damage to their apartments when the sprinkler system went off.

All I can do is shrug and answer with a breathless, "Yeah."

My insides cringe. Did that sound suggestive? My hand slaps my forehead and a dust cloud of cat hair surrounds me.

"Whenever you have a check it is fine." Mateo remarks after my second sneezing fit subsides.

"You don't know how much this means. I've had a ton of bills—" I almost start rambling about the motel I've been living in, and storage fees, eating fast food—which makes dining out tonight and letting his mother pick up the tab seem irresponsible.

"I get it." He cuts me off. "If you need anything, text. My number is on the key tag."

"I will." I grin like a goof.

I have his number. Totally normal since he's my landlord/neighbor, but Mateo's also hot. Attractive men aren't exactly beating my door down to give me their contact information. Score one for Pepper, finally. I mean, I won't use it in some creepy, stalker way. However, there are probably a lot of women who want Mateo's number and I have it to give to someone who wants it. Not that I'd willy-nilly give out anyone's private information. But yeah, there's a point to my internal babbling.

Men make me stupid. And stupid's easy to disregard.

I figure that out all over again when I realize I'm standing alone in the lobby and see Mateo's truck pull out of the parking space. Between the clumsiness of starting a grease fire, staring at Mateo's crotch like a perv, and getting just as wrapped up in my head, it doesn't take much to recognize why I'm unattached.

"Did Mateo scoot?" Gracyn sidles up from behind.

"Yes." I catch myself before my dreamy sigh is audible.

"Bummer. Aunt D wanted to see him. She'd probably have offered him dinner. But, oh well, his loss." Gracyn links her arm through mine. "Come on. We'll meet the rest of the staff at The Grille after they set the rest of the kitties free. Do you mind driving?"

"No, but I should…" I point to my office and the pile of paperwork.

"You can cut out already. Everyone knows we're picking up Gran."

"They do? We are?" My stomach flips.

In her eighties, Mrs. Cavanaugh is ridiculously beautiful. My mother would be jealous. Heck, I am. I've never met anyone so gracious and I'm always conscientious to not embarrass Dr. Sanchez whenever Mrs. Cavanaugh is present.

Gracyn gives me enough time to gather my purse and keys before we head up the county road to the expansive Tudor home her grandparents live in.

"Hello, Miss Corbin." Mrs. Cavanaugh greets me when she gets into the passenger seat that Gracyn has given up for her grandmother. "You look lovely today. Pink is a very nice shade on you. It compliments your dark hair and your complexion."

"Thank you, Mrs. Cavanaugh."

"Miss Rose or Gran will do fine." She pats my knee.

I choose the former, since it's more professional and what I hear my contemporaries use. Although I've come to recognize a lot of the younger ranch employees, the ones in my generation, refer to Mr. and Mrs. Cavanaugh the same way their grandchildren do. It must be the familiarity of being raised alongside them in this small town. It's sweet and lightens my mood, making me curious if I could ever be as bold as switching to Gran.

"How'd Aunt D rope you into coming to dinner with us?" Gracyn asks from the backseat.

Miss Rose turns to admire her granddaughter, winking. "No, ropin', Sugar. Colette and Devon are staying at Newgate with Rodger and Lily Anne. Grandaddy is off fishing with the men, so it provides me the ability to have all the ladies on my list in one spot at the same time. I simply added a few guests to the reservation."

"So you commandeered Dr. Sanchez's idea?" My cheeks widen and I blush at my forthrightness.

"Would I ever do that?" Miss Rose flips her gaze to the backseat again, asking Gracyn to answer for her.

"Never, Gran. You don't have a mischievous bone in your body." Gracyn hides her snort.

I roll my teeth between my lips. I've heard stories townsfolk tell about Miss Rose in her youth, and sometimes well beyond, but there's no way those rumors could be correct.

She leans a shoulder toward mine. "Of course I do, Pepper. Do you really believe my children—and their children—could come up with such magnificent ideas if mischief wasn't in their genes? Now all that strait-laced stuff? They get that from my husband. You have to find a good man, or a woman, capable of loving you when your schemes go awry. Remember that," she instructs while Gracyn's doubling over behind us.

"I will," I reply to her advice at the same time Gracyn says, "Love you, Gran," as if Miss Rose has spoken one of life's most important truths.

Ready to read more?
Love Thy Neighbor is available now!
www.jodykaye.com/lovethyneighbor

The same way from the outset I knew Gracyn existed in the Kingbrier Quintuplets series, Jake and Cris were always linked. If anyone was smart enough to flow the breadcrumbs, I'd made it obvious by using Jake's name in Forever In My Heart, a love letter from Cris to Liz that's been available to Newsletter Subscribers for several years.

What took me by surprise was Jake's decision to close and reopen Sweet Caroline's, changing it from a swank strip club to a nightclub and concert venue. The Jake I've known for years is the same broody ass that many of you met in Sliver of Truth. A guy out for himself, who couldn't do something nice for anyone if he tried.

I love this about Jake because writing flawed characters, and exploring how one experience that they've had snowballs affecting their future, is my cup of tea.

For Jake, closing the club seemed a logical choice to make on the path to reaching his goals and winning Paisley's affection back. For me? Even though I knew his origin story, I wanted to push back. I worried it sent readers the wrong message. That someone would interpret it as me writing Jake as atoning for a sinful situation. And that's not it by a long shot. It wasn't until Jake got to Kingsbrier, and Cris handed him the slip of paper, that I got the nudge he'd get a second chance on stage. Having a venue to build upon what he lost when their band broke up was kismet.

While we're on the subject of the people who live

in my head making their own choices… Many of you have been anxiously expecting Shattered Soul. I set that book aside to write Bleeding Heart because Carver, Sloan, and I were in disagreement. The harder I tried to tie them to what was supposed to happen, the harder it became to get any words out. That's what made it easier to go along with Jake's choices. I'm happy he got his happily ever after sooner than I'd planned.

When I first started thinking about this series five years ago, I matched Jake with a friend of Hailey's. (Yes, I know Hailey hasn't been around as much in more recent books.) By last year, it felt like an age gap romance with a younger heroine wouldn't work. There were too many significant experiences Paisley needed to have had. Cramming them into a shorter amount of time seemed immature. Jake also needed a foil who countered his arrogance with kind confidence.

Paisley is a good person. And good people end pregnancies. *Period.* This detail was a part of her background from the onset. In an early version, she did not tell Jake. Not because she was ashamed. But because a woman's decision to have an abortion is <u>no one else's business but her own</u>. In the end, I think by telling Jake it proved her convictions; that Paisley understood the right choices for her, and that she'd stand up for herself. As someone who has raised three kids of my own, I have a lot of respect for any woman who remains childless by choice.

(BLUNTLY: This book's plot was drafted before, not in response to the SCOTUS ruling.)

Know what I was really worried you'd hate Paisley for? Admitting so soon that she liked the *kiss*. I mean, isn't it silly that I thought you'd find a way to forgive Jake for throwing a rock, but you'd judge Paisley on her inner monologue? Obviously Jake liked the kiss, too, or he wouldn't have conned her into posing as his girlfriend!

On my final re-read how much Jake and Paisley had in common surprised me. There were even points I laughed at how often they made similar remarks.

Bleeding Heart was a joy to write. It's been too long since I've been able to say that, which is sad since this is my 20th book. But it also makes me happy—Sort of once you've jumped a hurdle jumping the next one isn't as daunting. So, whether Bleeding Heart is the first book of mine that you've read or you've been a fan from the beginning, thank you for allowing me to entertain you!

Kate, we've shared twenty-plus years with our families simultaneously collecting significant memories, so dedicating a milestone book to you feels appropriate. There are very few who've seen me —helped me—through my best and my most heart-wrenching moments. I'm grateful that you've been one of those friends.

Jill, thanks once again for your advice. I'm not sure this is what *she* envisioned of our relationship. But I can't help thinking that *she'd* be proud of the bonds we've made without *her* here.

MJA, what can I say after twenty books that is as meaningful as the million little moments when you've encouraged me along this path? The greatest gift you've given me is the understanding that you love me *more*.

Also by Jody Kaye

Shattered Hearts of Carolina
Splinter of Hope
Shred of Decency
Sliver of Truth
Holding Onto Hope
Home Wrecker
Deep Gap
Bleeding Heart
Shattered Soul

The Kingsbrier Legacy
Love Thy Neighbor
Gray Sin
Going Down

The Kingsbrier Quintuplets
Eric
Brier
Daveigh
Miss Cavanaugh
Cavanaugh
Adam
Colette
Colton

The Canvas Duet
Canvas
Imprint

To view more great titles,
sign up for Jody Kaye's newsletter,
or find her on social media
go to www.jodykaye.com or

Scan Now!

About the Author

Jody's husband asked what she'd been doing all day. After five years she finally confessed, "When no one is around, I write."

Okay, it was more like a bunch of stammering and trying to get out of saying a thing. Jody's a writer. You want it pretty. Let's compromise.

"Just finish one," he said, challenging her to complete a story and share it. Little did he know that those words of encouragement meant they'd return from a family vacation with a wild and defiant set of quintuplets stumbling their way into adulthood. Wasn't raising their three sons enough?

A native of nowhere, Jody settled in New England for 17 years before agreeing to uproot her brood of boys and move to North Carolina. She's a part-time graphic designer and marketeer with over twenty years' experience, and full-time writer. If Jody ever gets lost, you'll find her reading, all the while hoping that her ravenous children haven't eaten all the ingredients before she's cooked dinner.

Add your voice and help readers discover
this love story by writing a review!